BRIDE OF THE WIND

JUDY HIGGINS

GOSSART
PUBLICATIONS

Books by Judy Higgins

The Lady

Unringing the Bell

Bride of the Wind

Call me Mara, the Story of Ruth and Naomi

Available November 2018

To receive publication notifications,

Sign up at http://www.judyhigginsbooks.com

First Gossart Publication Edition, March 2018
Copyright © by Judy Higgins, 2017

Published in The United States in 2018
Published by
Gossart Publications
900 Brown Street
Washington D.C.

Photo Credits
Cover: Nat Jones
Author Photo: Studio Walz

First Gossart paperback edition March 2018
First Gossart e-book edition March 2018

Printed in the United States of America

Judy Higgins
Bride of the Wind: a novel/Judy Higgins

Summary: "Detective Laskey explores the past to discover the secret of the missing daughter of Goose Bend's token Jewish family." --- Provided by publisher

ISBN 978-0-692-06548-8

DEDICATION

Dedicated to my A-team cheering squad:
Kyle, Jon, and Karina,

Thursday

October 18

Vienna, Austria

"When one man plays another for a fool, then doesn't the one taken for a fool have the right to strike back?" There was no one else in the room to hear the man's question.. He'd sent his assistant . . . What was it the others called her? His secretary? His nurse? His jailer? No matter, he'd sent her on a useless errand. He wanted to be alone when the call came.

He pressed his face to the window of his fifth floor suite and gazed across the rooftops in the direction where he and the one who played him for a fool had lived. He smiled. He was about to have the pleasure of taking from his adversary the treasures that should have belonged to him from the start.

The handkerchief in his breast pocket had been carefully folded into a triangle, a work of some minutes by his housekeeper, but a job undone by him in two seconds. He shook out the folds, wiped away the cloud of mist his breath had formed on the window, and then crammed the handkerchief back in his pocket. His only regret was that he hadn't retaliated years ago. Had his son been willing to help, he would have known about the girl earlier. Instead, he'd had to wait for the knowledge of her existence to come floating up like a feather bobbing in the wind. How apropos, he thought: a gift from the wind.

He hobbled over, sank into his desk chair, and pulled the phone from the drawer where he'd hidden it beneath a stack of mail. A map appeared when he clicked on the app, and a tiny green circle showed the girl about to walk into the trap. Before the end of next week, he'd have the stolen objects back, and as for the girl: she was the interest owed him.

Friday

October 19

Chapter One

GOOSE BEND, PENNSYLVANIA

Detective William Laskey, caught in the act of tying his tie, tensed when the phone rang. Disappointment shot through him as he wondered if he was going to have to scuttle his plans for the evening. On the third ring, he realized it was his landline, not his work phone and breathed a sigh of relief. He'd been looking forward to breaking the vow he'd made thirty-five years ago never to have anything to do with another woman and, nervous as he was, he wanted to carry through. He didn't want to have to go out and solve a murder, kidnapping, or any of the other crimes the Criminal Investigation Bureau assigned him.

After seven rings, the phone stopped. "Bloody tele-marketers," he grumbled and finished doing the tie into a proper knot — evened sided and smoothed out. He hadn't paid this much attention to how he dressed since his days in the FBI. Thankfully, no one from the Pennsylvania Criminal Investigation Section expected him to conform to a dress code. Or maybe they did, but in his case, turned their heads. Catching a whiff of cut grass, he wondered if he'd applied too much aftershave. But it was too late to worry about that. He slicked his hair back — at least what was left of it. The barber had gotten carried away, haranguing about what was going on down in Washington, or rather what was *not* going on, snipping at his hair without paying attention to how much he snipped. Regrettably, neither had Laskey who had been leafing through the latest issue of *Time* and only half listening. The good news was that half the gray was gone; the bad: half of his rapidly diminishing dark was gone, too, fallen in heaps at the base of the barber's chair.

The phone rang again. Giving in, he answered.

"Laskey?"

"Fritz. Good to hear from you, old friend," he said, recognizing the soft, slightly accented voice of Fritz Herschmann. "You don't have my cell phone number?"

"Somewhere, but not with me."

"What's up?"

"Sorry to bother you, but . . . . I'm in Lansdale. I was supposed to pick up Rebekah from the train station yesterday, but she wasn't there. She does that now, takes the train into Lansdale when she flies in from Jordan. After my . . . Well, she's decided it's too much stress for me to drive into Philadelphia. And she doesn't want her mother having to navigate the traffic along the Schuylkill. We know how Leah drives." Fritz made an attempt at a chuckle, but it fell flat. "I assumed we'd written down the wrong date, so I came back to the station today. But she isn't here."

"I'm sure she's fine, Fritz. You've tried calling her?"

"Only a few hundred times. Nothing happens on her end when I try. The phone doesn't even go to voice mail. We share an ICloud account. It was easier for her that way — us taking care of her phone service — so usually we know exactly where she is by using the *Find my iphone* button. When she's at a field hospital, there's no signal, but she wasn't at a field hospital this week. She was in Amman. Her last call was on Wednesday evening when she rang up a colleague, Annemarie Leitner." He sighed. "I called AT&T but they were no help."

"Maybe her battery died?"

"I can see when her battery is running down on my phone, but there's nothing where the signal should be. The phone company suggested she might have taken the SIM card out. I assured them she wouldn't do that. I know there's some logical explanation for what's happened, and you're the one who can make me believe it."

"Of course there's a logical explanation," Laskey said. "People miss planes; they get bumped; they mix up which day they're flying. Happened to me once. It sounds like there could be some sort of malfunction with her phone."

"It's been more than twenty-four hours. She would have found a way to call."

"She might have given you the wrong date and hasn't realized it. Don't worry. Nothing's happened to Rebekah."

"I guess I just needed to hear you say that. Leah is here with me and says to tell you 'hello, and to stop by anytime.' You know how she starts baking when she gets nervous? We have enough dessert right now to feed everybody on the block. You need to come help us eat it."

"I was about to head out to Goose Bend for an early dinner at The Tavern by the River. Maybe I'll drop by later this evening?"

"I wish you would."

Laskey hung up. It wasn't like Rebekah to mix up a plane flight or to not inform her parents that something had changed. Quiet, studious, responsible, Rebekah had always been, as far as he knew, the ideal child. Even as a teenager, she skipped the rebellious period that drove parents to insanity. She'd gotten a full-ride to Dartmouth, graduated from the University of Pennsylvania Medical School, done a residency at Johns Hopkins, and then gone to work for Doctors Without Borders in Jordan.

Fusty old bachelor that he was, he didn't have a child, but he'd spent enough hours worrying about his godson, Jacob Gillis, to understand how parents agonized. Unlike Rebekah, Jacob, blonde and blue-eyed as an angel, had been anything but an angel. But in the end he'd turned out fine; just fine. And Rebekah, wherever she was, was fine, too. It was just a mix-up of some sort.

He grabbed his sports jacket and strode for the door. Outside, he took one last look around his old Sequoia to make sure it wasn't littered with things it shouldn't be littered with, then climbed in and headed for Goose Bend and Dr. Zuela Hay – *Dr* as in PhD, not

M.D. It had been more years than he wanted to count since he'd invited a little female softness into his life, although he wasn't sure *softness* was what Zuela – pronounced *zueeeeeeeela* – exuded. Never mind, he liked sass in a woman.

FRITZ KNEW Leah was having trouble concentrating on her crossword puzzle as she sat inside the Saab while he waited outside the car. From her knitted brow and tightly drawn lips, he could see she was as distressed as he was, but at least she was making an effort to pass the time patiently which he couldn't say for himself. He fidgeted and rolled his shoulders in an effort to untense, but kept his eyes glued to the train tracks in the direction from which the five o'clock train would appear.

Fifty minutes ago, the four-o'clock from Philadelphia had pulled in and disgorged about a dozen passengers. Most had gone directly to their cars in the parking lot; a few had jumped into cars driven by someone else; and two or three had gone inside the station which was a small, dreary building with a ticket window, four benches, a large clock mounted on the wall, restrooms, and a musty smell. When the last of the passengers had disembarked, he'd gone in, too. Just in case he'd missed her. She could have rushed in to use the bathroom. He'd knocked on the ladies room door and then waited for someone to answer while the ticket master stared at him.

"My daughter said she'd be on the four o'clock," he'd explained. "I'm just checking to make sure she's not stuck in there. Maybe she's on the next train." He'd shrugged at the ticket master as though to say whichever train she arrived on was a matter of indifference, and that he had all day. Then he went back out to the car to wait for the next train.

He leaned against a front fender and crossed his arms. Laskey was right; there was a logical reason why Rebekah wasn't here. Tomorrow, maybe even tonight, they'd laugh about an email that had disappeared into the great wilderness in the sky, or a text message that flitted off to Neverland.

His heart thumped – the steady, but loud, beat of a bass drum. Inhaling slowly, he willed his heart to beat *piano* instead of *forte*. The doctor said he was fine, but to take it easy. Relax. Not work so hard. *Not worry about Rebekah.* He gave a snort of a laugh. Not worry about your only child?

His nostrils burned as he breathed the fumes of exhaust pipes from cars thumping across the railroad tracks at the intersection. He shivered. It wasn't cold; the temperature hovered around seventy, yet he shivered. He drew his jacket closer. Except for the dusty, gritty smell of exhaust, the day was gorgeous, still sunny even in the latter half of the afternoon. It had rained for the past three days, but now the sky was blue with only a few wisps of clouds.

The only thing lacking to make it a perfect autumn day was Rebekah's arrival. They hadn't seen her for six months. She usually came twice a year. April and October. "My colleagues are glad I'm Jewish," she told him and Leah once. "That means one of them can go home for Christmas while I stay and work; then I get to go home for my favorite seasons."

Fritz had mixed feelings about that. Her *work*, not that she was Jewish, although that concerned him, too. A Jewish girl in the Middle East? But it was the contagious diseases she treated that he worried about. He couldn't even remember all the bugs and viruses she described crawling, floating, and swimming about the refuge camps, and now that the Syrians had crowded in, the ailments had notched up. Hepatitis A. Salmonella. Shigella. Tuberculosis. Cholera. Scabies. Middle East Respiratory Syndrome. Rabies. And those were the ones he could pronounce. They'd also begun to worry about dengue fever. So when people told him not to worry about Rebekah, he suffered their words with a wan smile and tried to hide his uneasiness. Over tired, under staffed, stretched beyond what he would have thought were the limits of human capacity, how could the doctors and nurses in those camps work in the midst of all those microbial trespassers and not get sick themselves? Not worry? Worry ate at him like worms devouring carrion.

The tracks began to vibrate and he heard a distant *chuff-chuff-chuff*. A few seconds later, the rumble of the train sounded from down the tracks, and the lights at the intersection began flashing. He took a couple steps forward and watched the engine roar into the station like a belching, snorting beast. His hands went up to cover his ears against the screeching of brakes as the train shuddered to a stop. The doors swung open, and two men wearing suits and clasping brief cases disembarked followed by a young woman dressed in jeans and stilettos. An older woman emerged, checking her balance on each step before descending to the next. When she finally set both feet safely on the estrade, a stream of commuters poured out.

The last of the passengers trickled away, and once again he went inside the station to see if he'd missed her, although he didn't see how he possibly could have. A few minutes later, he climbed back in his Saab, a foreboding weighing him. What had happened to Rebekah?

Chapter Two

Laskey and Zuela sat on the restaurant's terrace enjoying a last glass of wine and probably one of the last warm breezes of the year. He'd suggested they move their chairs side by side so they could both face the Pumqua River even though the tumbling waters were fast disappearing into the darkness. It was here, at its widest point, that the Pumqua took an abrupt turn in its journey toward the Delaware. Thanks to the unseasonal rains at the beginning of the week, the current ran faster and the water crept higher up the banks than normal. The rushing water, the soothing breeze, and the hum of conversation had lulled them into tranquility. Or maybe the tranquility had more to do with the bottle of Mountain Vineyard's *Pride* they'd consumed, Laskey decided. He smiled. It wasn't that many years ago, it seemed, when all he could afford to offer a date was a bottle of *Boone's Farm*.

Zuela arched her eyebrows at his random smile. "Something funny?" Her eyebrows were a couple shades darker than her short white hair. She was tall, slim, and a bit stiff-postured. He guessed she'd never been much of an athlete.

"Just thinking how awful *Boone's Farm* tasted, and how we hardly knew the difference back then." He drained his glass and then gestured toward the river. "Jacob and I used to fish a little way up from here."

Zuela propped her elbows on the table. "Have you been fishing together since Jacob got back from Africa?"

"No. We've both been too busy. Jacob's new job has him hopping." Laskey's godson had returned to the States after a five-year stint in Africa working on international environmental treaties.

"You should take a day off and wet your lines."

"As a matter of fact, we're going tomorrow. Up to the Susquehanna."

He could barely see the river now, just the glint of lights on its surface, wavering and twinkling. He and Jacob had enjoyed many fishing outings on the Pumqua and the Susquehanna, and other rivers as well, sometimes with luck, other times without.

"It's odd that our paths hardly ever crossed," he said, turning to Zuela. "The only time we ran into each other was when I picked up Jacob for an outing or dropped him off and you happened to be visiting." He knew Zuela and Jacob's mother had continued to be best friends even after Jacob's mother had moved to Carlyle to teach in the college.

"Our paths might have crossed more often if you didn't persist in living with the high and mighty over in Doylestown." Her voice had taken on a bantering tone. "Why *do* you live there? I'd think after all the excitement of solving murders, arsons, and grand theft you'd want to live in a quiet, boring town like Goose Bend."

"I'm a slave to the job, I guess. Doylestown is the midpoint in the county, and that makes it a whole lot easier when I have to work the lower part. Besides, they can't do without me on the old fart's baseball team. I also have three cats and a beehive. The cats don't want to move."

"You asked them?"

"I did." He frowned down at the tablecloth. "You know Rebekah Herschmann, don't you?"

"Everybody in town knows Rebekah because of the 'Bekah Bars and because of who her father is. Unless they're living in a cave. Although, I suspect a few might be. But even the cave-dwellers must have seen her picture a few thousand times on the candy bars. Why do you ask?"

"She was supposed to come home yesterday. She didn't show up."

"That doesn't sound like the Rebekah I've heard about."

"It's just a mix-up in communications, I'm sure."

Zuela ran her forefinger and thumb up and down the stem of her wine glass. "Our token Jewish family. Did you know Fritz's father?"

"I did." Laskey had pleasant recollections of the round-faced man with a mustache, shiny bald head, and a mischievous twinkle in his eyes. "You know the story of Joseph Herschmann II, don't you? How he escaped from Vienna a few days after the Anschluss and arrived in this country with nothing much other than the clothes on his back?"

Zuela nodded. "I heard that he escaped the Nazis barely in the knick of time. Was Fritz's father a candy manufacturer in Austria?""

"No. He was a chemist and a partner in a pharmaceutical firm." Laskey had been sitting with his arm draped over the back of his chair. Straightening, he faced Zuela. "They're worried about Rebekah not showing up. Any chance you'd like to drop by for dessert? I understand Leah handles stress by baking, and she's been doing that all day. I'd like to remind them of all the glitches that can happen when you travel."

THEY LEFT The Tavern by the River, located three miles east of Goose Bend, and drove along Rutherford Road which eventually became Main Street. Zuela's chatter required only the occasional *Uh-huh* or *Really?* or *That's interesting*, leaving Laskey free to consider what to say to Fritz and Leah.

The first few blocks of the town consisted of the same mish-mash as most towns with a population of less than six thousand – older houses, a service station, the high school sitting a few hundred feet back from the road and the football stadium beside it, a large Baptist church with a sign saying *'Coming ready or not!' – Jesus*. There was a corner grocery store with a black and red striped awning. So far, no McDonalds or Burger Kings had invaded the village-scape. The Lutheran church, constructed of red brick with steeple towers anchoring both corners of the façade, stood at the beginning of the commercial section.

Laskey fell silent, as he always did, when passing through the two blocks which fire had consumed twenty years earlier. The business section had consisted then, and still consisted, of nothing more than four blocks of commercial buildings. His godson, at the age of twelve, along with a friend, had accidentally set off a fire behind the hardware store. Between the wind and the old buildings, the blaze quickly spread down the block, and then leapt over the intersection to consume the next block. The destroyed Victorian structures had been replaced with cheap, functional edifices which the locals referred to as *New Town*. The two blocks untouched by the fire were dubbed *Old Town*. Correctly named, he thought, since the buildings were nearing decrepitude or, in some cases, already there.

A half mile beyond the Pennston Hotel, which anchored the west end of the four block business section, Laskey turned left, and after two more turns, pulled up in front of the Herschmann's modern glass and concrete house, conspicuous among the traditional two-story Colonials lining the street. But it was what they had *inside* the house that struck him with awe.

"Have you been in before?" he asked Zuela.

"Several times. And I'm amazed every time."

He got out and stood on the sidewalk, waiting for her to come around from the other side. When he told Zuela that Joseph Herschmann, Fritz's father, had arrived in the country with not much more than the clothes on his back, he hadn't been entirely correct. Joseph had persuaded an American contact based in Vienna to help him smuggle out a few pieces of valuable Viennese art which the Herschmann family owned. Over the years, Fritz and Leah had added to the collection. Paintings, pastels, drawings, and etchings filled the walls of every room in the house, including the bathrooms. "All that," Laskey had chided Fritz, ". . . and you don't even have an alarm system."

"COME IN. COME IN." Fritz waved them through the door. A tall, spare man, his eyes appeared to be brown from a distance, but turned out to be green on closer inspection. His hair was a tweed: brown and silver woven together in loose curls. "Leah, . . ." he called over his shoulder. "We have company."

"Make yourself at home," came the answer from the kitchn. "I'm putting coffee on." The smell of cinnamon, chocolate, and baked apples drifted from that direction, accompanied by the clink of dishes being set on the counter.

"You had a nice dinner?" Fritz asked as he motioned for them to go ahead of him into the living room.

"We had a great dinner," Zuela replied and described their meal as she walked into the living room with Fritz.

Laskey moved more slowly, taking in the surroundings even though he'd been there dozens of times before. Like the rest of the house, the walls of the foyer were painted an off-white and were alive with paintings emblazoned in every color of the artist's palette. An Afghani Tribal Rug in rich reds stretched over the travertine flooring. To the left of the foyer, an archway led into the living room, and to the right, an identical arch led to the dining room. At the rear of the foyer was a flight of stairs and beyond the stairs a hall that led to the kitchen on the right and Fritz's den on the left.

"Have a seat." Fritz said, when Laskey joined them. "Leah will be along in a minute." As always, he was dressed immaculately in a pin-striped dress shirt and tailored trousers.

There were two sofas: one in front of the panel of windows that looked out over the street and the other against the wall facing the arch. Zuela sat down on the one in front of the street windows. "If you haven't tried their fish tacos . . .," she said to Fritz, " I highly recommend them."

Laskey sat beside her, happy she'd taken control of the conversation. Frivolous chatter on the subject of fish tacos and Mountain Vineyard's *Pride* would probably distract his friend from worrying more than anything Laskey could say. He settled back, listening to their chatter, but admiring the room as he had so often before. The upholstered pieces were the same off-white as the walls. The color in the room was contained in the paintings, making them seem to jump out at you.

The only non-modern furniture in the room was a burled chestnut antique grandfather clock. The middle portion was shaped liked the bottom half of a violin and contained a dinner-plate-sized pendulum bob. Rebekah had named the piece simply, *Grandfather Clock*. "Grandfather Clock rules Dad's life, but not Mom's," she told Laskey once. The remark had made him smile. He knew Leah was habitually late, much to Fritz's chagrin.

"Well, hello." Leah appeared in the door, wiping her hands on her apron. She was twenty pounds past slim, on the short side, and had a curly mass of thick, auburn hair. "I'm so glad to see you two. I've been worried to death about Rebekah, but having you here gives me a break from obsessing."

Laskey rose and extended his hand. "Thanks for letting us drop by. I'm sure Rebekah's fine; it's just a mix-up in communications."

Leah shook his hand and then looked past him to Zuela. "What a nice surprise that you came, too, Zuela. I knew Laskey was coming, but Fritz didn't tell me the pleasure was going to be double. When did I see you last?"

Laskey noted that Leah's normally deep husky voice had risen in pitch, and that she was wringing her hands.

"Was it that bridge tournament down at the Lutheran Church back during the summer?" Zuela asked.

"Oh, that." Leah touched her hand to her forehead and blew out a little huff. "Never again will I participate in something run by that awful Molly Spangler. Good lord, I don't think she could organize a walk in the park if her life depended on it."

With Zuela and Leah launched into conversation, Fritz picked up a cigar from the chair-side table and raised his eyebrows as he held the cigar toward Laskey. Laskey nodded. They rose and walked across the hall to the dining room, and then into the kitchen where a Sachertorte and an Apfelkuchen sat on the counter next to the oven. A built-in desk stood to the left of the door. Fritz took a second cigar from a box in the cabinet above the desk, handed it to Laskey, and then led the way to the French doors that made up one wall of the kitchen.

They stepped out onto a patio overlooking the side yard and moved to the far edge of the flagstone surface, away from the kitchen lights. A twelve-foot high hedge of arborvitae blocked the glow from the neighbor's downstairs windows. The sky was clear; the stars bright. The moon hadn't appeared yet, although Laskey knew it would be visible from the other side of the house. A gust of wind rattled leaves across the patio stones.

Fritz's candy factory was two short blocks behind the house on a street that ran along the river. It was there they'd created the 'Bekah Bars that had made the company famous. The shiny blue wrappers featured Rebekah's photo as a six-year old with reddish-blonde pigtails. Fritz had objected to using her picture, but his father had been determined. Herschmann Chocolates produced products on a par with Godiva's and Vosge — *Chocolate-Caramel Confectionaires, Pomediddles, Orange Liqueurettes* — but it was the 'Bekah Bars that had first propelled the company to the forefront.

"Thanks for the cigar," Laskey said, nipping off the end.

Fritz nodded and held out a lighter.

One thing he'd always liked about Fritz, Laskey mused as they stood puffing in the dark, was that Fritz didn't feel the need to fill every moment with talk. When he was ready, they'd discuss Rebekah. To ease Fritz's mind, he'd offer to check the airline manifest.

Laskey stole a glance at his friend. In the dark, where only the gods and Laskey could see him, Fritz let his mouth droop and the furrows in his forehead deepen. He'd met Fritz years ago at a wine tasting. They had in common an interest in good wine, chess, a predilection for heated political discussions, and music. Many a time, Laskey had dropped by in the late afternoon to find Fritz lounging in his favorite chair with his feet propped on an ottoman as he listened to a symphony or a string quartet while reading *The Economist* or *The Atlantic Monthly*. Sometimes Fritz didn't read, but just listened. He could pretty much name every symphony and major string quartet as well as tell you which orchestra was playing. Compared to his friend, Laskey's musical knowledge ranked down in elementary school. Fritz also built model boats. Sailing ships, dinghys, trawlers, even a middle eastern dhow, lined the shelves of his den. Laskey had tried to get Fritz interested in baseball, beer, and fishing, but with zero success. It didn't matter, though. He loved the man because he was one of the kindest, gentlest men he'd ever known.

"I'm worried," Fritz said.

"I know." Laskey blew out a puff of smoke. "She's fine, but it's in the nature of fathers to worry." A leaf fluttered from a maple and landed on his shoulder. He brushed it away. Only the middle of October, yet the air already smelled of dry leaves and, because of the rain earlier in the week, the beginnings of leaf rot.

"She's a Jewish woman living and working in a Muslim country. I know, I know . . .," he held up his hand to stop Laskey from speaking, ". . . Jordan is a stable country, and she shouldn't have a problem. Yet. . . . Well, who knows who those refugee camps might be harboring? Especially since so many poured in from Syria before Jordan closed her borders."

Laskey studied his friend. Fritz had had a heart attack ten months ago. Supposedly, he was fine now, but stress did bad things. Like bringing on a second heart attack.

"Remember, a couple years ago, she missed her plane and couldn't get hold of you because your phone was on mute and Leah had misplaced hers?" Laskey asked. "And the time she had to delay her vacation because something happened to one of the other doctors? I'm sure you're going to hear a similar story when she gets here."

"There's the bit about the pharmaceutical companies, too." Fritz shuffled his feet. "Did I tell you she's been involved in some protests?"

Laskey shook his head.

"I know it's ridiculous to think a pharmaceutical company would pay attention to a few protestors, but right now my imagination is working overtime." He shrugged and tried to grin. "I guess

I'm as silly as the women in there when they get going on Molly Spangler. It's ludicrous to imagine that Pfizer would try to silence my daughter to keep her from protesting the cost of their pneumonia vaccines, or whatever medication she's protesting this week or next month." He took a long puff on his cigar.

"You're right; it's ludicrous."

Laskey had watched Rebekah grow up since the age of ten. She called him *Uncle Bill*. An active, brilliant girl, her interests roamed freely and broadly. One spring she spent crossbreeding day lilies, but when the first hot days of summer came, she switched her attention to studying the leaping mechanisms of frogs. At various times she focused on the science of winning at black-jack, the writings of Jung, the best way to straighten hair, the invention of biographies of imaginary horses, and a method to keep fireflies alive. During the firefly phase, she condemned hundreds of insects to death in her collection jars while she unsuccessfully sought a solution. When she repented of the massacre, she tearfully conducted a memorial service in the backyard at which she required the attendance of her parents, her grandfather, Uncle Bill, and her best friend. Her longest passion had been for Greenland, during which she learned pretty much everything there was to know about the country, including the height, width, and depth of its major glaciers. She wasn't a pretty girl. Not ugly. Just average. But when she smiled, her face lit up like a Christmas tree. Although he supposed that wasn't an apt description for a Jewish girl. Like Leah, her face was somewhere between round and oval, with a defined chin. She had very light reddish-blonde hair and straight eyebrows that were nearly white. Her resemblance to her father came in her tall, spare figure and almond shaped eyes.

"I can make you a fairly substantial bet Rebekah will be here tomorrow or the next day," Laskey said, ". . . and you'll be laughing at the mix-up."

"Her fiancé arrives tomorrow. We're meeting him for the first time."

"I didn't know she was engaged. Congratulations."

Fritz bent down and stubbed out his cigar on a flagstone and then pocketed the remainder. "Shall we?" He held his palm toward the kitchen.

While Laskey did the same with his cigar, he saw Leah and Zuela busy in the kitchen and heard the hum of their conversation. Leah was setting coffee cups on the horseshoe-shaped island in the middle of the kitchen while Zuela placed slices of cake on dessert plates. The blue and white pottery decorated with flowers, belied the state-of-the-art kitchen with its austere off-white walls, stainless steel appliances, and silver-gray slate floor. Laskey gave an inward laugh; the room was almost the size of a pickle-ball court and as sleek and efficient as a rocket, yet Leah had flowery dishes. Gzel pottery from Russia, she told him once. But he wasn't complaining; he'd had many an excellent meal on those plates.

"Two desserts. Good heavens," he exclaimed as they walked in. He slid onto one of the stools at the island.

"Are you complaining?" Leah asked, setting a cup of coffee down in front of him.

"Not on your life." Unfortunately, he could finish both desserts with no problem. Not as trim as Fritz, he needed to watch it. The flesh on his bones was no longer all muscle. A little flab had started to creep on, but he wouldn't admit that tonight. Not when a slice of Sachertorte sat enticingly in front of him, not to mention the apple cake which probably emitted the best aroma of any food in the world. He dived in, starting with the Apfelkuchen, while Zuela, enjoying hers more slowly, kept a steady stream of conversation going. Fritz nibbled, and Leah, ignoring the sweets altogether, picked absently at her napkin, tearing it to shreds.

Laskey leaned toward Zuela. "Did you hear that Rebekah is engaged?" When he saw Leah perk up, he knew his question had the effect he'd intended of distracting her for a moment.

"I did. Fabulous news." Zuela looked pointedly at their hosts. "But you didn't tell us anything about him yet."

"Exceptionally good-looking, we're told," Leah said. "He's from Argentina."

"South America?" Zuela stopped her fork halfway between plate and mouth.

"I believe Argentina is still in South America," Laskey quipped. "Unless an Antarctic ice shelf has broken away and severed Argentina from the rest of the continent."

"Oh, shut up." She gave him a playful slap on his arm. "How did she meet someone from South America when she's living in Jordan? Does he work for Doctors Without Borders?"

"He's a journalist. He's doing a documentary about the refugee camps."

"There might be something in this for us," Fritz said in a droll voice. "Carlos' family has a vineyard. They're one of the big producers of Malbecs and Bonardas in the Mendoza area."

"This sounds better and better." Laskey smiled at his friend. "I'm sure Rebekah will show up by the time her fiancé does. Maybe they're coming in together, and she didn't get the message through to you."

"That could be what's happened." The lines in his face relaxed. "Carlos is renting a car at the airport and should get in around nine in the morning. I'm sure everything is fine. Just fine. She'll be here tomorrow morning for sure."

Laskey frowned down at his plate, empty except for a few crumbs. He didn't want to admit to the possibility that something dreadful had happened to Rebekah, so why the uneasy feeling? He pushed his plate aside. "If she doesn't arrive with Carlos, or before, call me."

Saturday

October 20

Vienna, Austria

"Cover my knees, Elke," the man said. "I'm cold."

"Of course." Rising from the desk where she'd been doing his correspondence, she brought a small blanket to his chair next to the window. "I think we're going to have an early winter," she said as she spread the blanket across his lap and then tucked it around his legs. She reached over his shoulder and flattened her palm against a pane. "It's like ice. Shall I call someone to repair the caulking?"

"As you like." Winter, caulking, icy panes mattered little to him anymore.

"You're full of smiles today." Hugging herself, she rubbed her upper arms to warm them. "Are you pleased about something?"

"Yes, pleased. And I'd be more pleased if you got back to work and let me sit here in peace to think about what it is that pleases me." He waved her away. "Full of smiles," she'd said. Yes, he was full of smiles; a little light had penetrated his darkness. The first part of the plan with the girl had been successful. He ached to hurry things along, but the undertaking would take a few days, and so he must bide his time.

Chapter Three

Careful not to wake Leah, Fritz slipped out of bed and tiptoed from the room, phone in one hand and slippers in the other. The floors of the bedroom and the hallway numbed his feet; the tiles in the kitchen were even colder. Shivering, he sat down at the kitchen desk, put on his slippers, and began rummaging through the drawer where Leah stuck old grocery lists, receipts, coupons, and a host of other items including an old fashioned address book. Neither he nor Leah had bothered to put certain numbers in their cellphone contacts.

He found the red-bound book and flipped to the L section. Annemarie Leitner, also an epidemiologist with Doctors Without Borders, had arrived in Jordan five years ago at the same time as Rebekah. She and Rebekah had become good friends and often took their leave at the same time. Sometimes they spent two or three days at a resort recuperating from their rigorous schedule before heading home. Annemarie, a native of Vienna, had come twice to visit them in Goose Bend, and Rebekah had gone several times to Vienna to visit with Annemarie's family. In deference to his father, Fritz had never traveled to Austria or Germany, but he hadn't burdened Rebekah with the onus to stay away, especially when she'd been curious about her grandfather's place of birth on the outskirts of Vienna.

About to key in Annemarie's number, Fritz stopped. Vienna was not a place he could think of without a clash of emotions. He wanted very much to see the Vienna his father enjoyed as a youth − the Vienna of the Prater, the Spanish Riding School, the Saint Stephen's boys choir, the Belvedere Palace; the Vienna where musicians played in the streets; the Vienna adorned with Romanesque and Baroque architectural masterpieces.

But there was also the other Vienna: the one filled with the horror that drove his father away. His father made an effort to describe his life during that awful time in a matter-of-fact manner, trying not to swim in the tide of hate in which he could understandably have been swept away. Only when his tales strayed to his former business partner, did Fritz hear the tell-tale note of despair and regret in his father's voice.

That had nothing to do with now, however. He tapped out Annemarie's number in Vienna, where it was a little after ten, waited while the phone rang nine times, and then left a message for her to call him right away.

Next, he found the number for Dr. James NacNeish, Rebekah's supervisor. Rebekah had given them MacNeish's number in case of an emergency. "It's his private number since you might have a hard time getting anyone at the hospital, and you definitely won't get anyone at the refugee camps," she'd said. It was five a.m. in Goose Bend, chilly and still dark outside. In Amman, Jordan it was eleven, and almost certainly sunny and warm.

Surprised when someone picked up after the second ring, Fritz waited while the person on the other end, Dr. MacNeish he presumed, cleared his throat, coughed, and then blew out a puff of air.

"Hello," a gruff voice finally answered.

"Dr. James MacNeish?"

"Aye. Who's calling?"

"Fritz Herschmann. Rebekah's father. Rebekah Herschmann. You know . . . ."

"Aye, I ken Rebekah," MacNeish snapped.

"She gave us your number in case of an emergency . . ." Fritz felt like he'd been punched in the stomach, not because of MacNeish's gruffness, but because he realized it *was* an emergency. Rebekah had disappeared.

"And?" Dr. MacNeish asked impatiently.

"Rebekah was supposed to fly into Philadelphia Thursday afternoon, but she didn't arrive."

"I'm supposed to keep track of your daughter?"

Rebekah had to work with this rude man? "I'd hoped you could help us find out what's happened to her." Fritz fought to control his ire. "Do you know if her travel plans changed?"

"I only know she meant to leave Thursday. Around the same time as her friend Annemarie, I think. That's Dr. Annemarie Leitner, in case you don't know."

"I know Annemarie; she's visited here."

"Then call her. If I hadn't been on my way to the lavy, I wouldn't have answered. I'm in charge here, and we have limbs to amputate, ripped guts to close, head wounds . . . . You get the picture." He hung up.

Dr. James MacNeish's rudeness left a vile taste on his tongue. Fritz went to the sink, rinsed out his mouth, and then punched the "on" button to the coffee maker.

He pressed his hands to his throbbing head as he leaned back against the counter to wait. Rebekah had sounded happy when he talked to her last week, in love, and eager for him and Leah to meet Carlos. Carlos Vientos. Not only a journalist, but the author of a novel, *Living in Space,* which had nothing to do with space, but rather tells the story of a young man who withdraws to live as a hermit in the Andes and later returns to his father's vineyards in disguise to work as a laborer. Fritz hadn't read the book. It arrived yesterday from Amazon and lay on the table beside his chair in the living room. He needed to like it for Rebekah's sake, but was afraid to read it in case he didn't.

His heart thumped erratically. "Calm down, calm down," he whispered, putting his hand over his chest and forcing himself to breathe slowly. "Rebekah will show up today." He and Leah would laugh, relieved, but they wouldn't tell Rebekah why they laughed. Whatever delayed her arrival would be a subject they discussed calmly at a later time.

The coffee machine hissed and emitted a sputter — a little explosion of sound that tapered off in a rapid decrescendo telling him the coffee was done. The aroma of Jamaica Blue Mountain filled the kitchen. He went over, reached into the cabinet above the desk, and found the bottle of Tylenol. After taking one and, on second thought, another, he poured himself a cup of coffee and sat down at the island. The two Tylenol and the caffeine would kick in shortly, and he'd feel better, ready to welcome his daughter and prospective son-in-law. Carlos was renting a car at the airport. They should arrive around nine. Rebekah would be upset and penitent when she discovered her message hadn't gotten through.

Chapter Four

L askey heaved Jacob's ice chest into the back of his Sequoia. "Good God! What do you have in there? Bricks?"

"Just the usual, including a day's supply of beer." Jacob threw his wading boots on top of the chest. They were already wearing their fishing vests.

"Enough for a platoon, judging by the weight." Laskey wiped his brow. "And why am I the one doing the lifting? You're the ex-football player."

"If you hadn't been in such a hurry, I would have done it ."

"Of course, I'm in a hurry. We haven't fished together in five years. Do we have everything we need?" He stood back and examined the pile of gear.

"I think we have it all. Tackle box, rods, reels, extra flies, lunch, water, and . . . ." Jacob grinned. ". . . plenty of Krombacher and Schlitz."

"And there must be a god; one who appreciates fishing." Laskey swept his arm around indicating the promise of a perfect day. The sun, hovering just above the horizon, had risen bright, and the night chill had already begun to seep away. A breeze carried the scent of fall: dry leaves and chimney smoke, whiffs of goose droppings, sour apples — Laskey wasn't sure if he actually smelled sour apples or just anticipated the fresh cider that came with the season. He closed the hatch. "How are you fixed for leaders? I'm low."

"I have extras. Do you have your sunglasses?"

Laskey patted his shirt pocket where the glasses bulged. "Let's go."

They got in, and Laskey cranked up the old SUV. It sputtered to life with a groan and a rattle, and they headed down Jacob's lane toward the main road, bouncing over holes and ruts.

"You're going to do something about these pot holes, aren't you?" Laskey pointed over the top of the steering wheel to the lane.

"It's way down the list. Any idea how many things need repairing and replacing in an old stone house?"

"Mostly everything, I'd guess." Six months ago, Jacob had moved into the house he'd inherited from an uncle. Laskey wondered if his godson had any idea that after he'd fixed and repaired everything on the property, he'd have to start all over again. It was never ending: repair, replace, repair, replace. Get one thing fixed, and then another breaks. But Jacob would learn soon enough, and far be it from him to throw a damper in his optimism.

Laskey stopped at the main road for a tractor puttering along, pulling a load of hay.

"How was dinner last night with Aunt Zuela?" Jacob asked.

Laskey frowned as he turned onto the road and, after passing the tractor, headed in the direction that would eventually take them north to the Susquehanna.

"Did something go wrong?" Jacob narrowed his eyes.

"Not with Zuela and me."

"What then?"

The uneasy feeling that had bothered him yesterday evening while he was stuffing himself with Sachertorte had returned. "You know Rebekah Herschmann?"

"Yeah, she was two years ahead of me in school. She's in the Middle East working with Doctors Without Borders. Why do you ask?"

"She was supposed to fly in from Jordan on Thursday, but she didn't show up."

"Missed her plane?"

Laskey shook his head. "Don't know. They haven't been able to reach her."

"Technology fails on a regular basis in some parts of the world. Believe me, I know all about that. Cell phone service blacks out; electricity goes off; internet connections fail. She probably got hung up and hasn't been able to contact them."

"I'm sure you're right." He passed a U-Haul van. That's exactly what it had to be: failed communication. So why was he worried? Any minute now Fritz would call and report that Rebekah had arrived home safe and sound. "She's engaged, you know?"

"That's great." Jacob stretched out his legs. "Someone she met over there?"

"Someone named Carlos from Argentina. A journalist with a rich wine-making father. Carlos was in Jordan working on a documentary about refugee camps. He's arriving today to meet the Herschmanns for the first time."

"Maybe she's arriving with him.'

"I'm hoping that's the case."

THEY WERE ALMOST to the Susquehanna when Laskey's phone rang. Somehow, he knew it was Fritz. He yanked the phone from his pocket, answered, and listened for a few seconds. "Be there in an hour," he said. Jamming on the brakes, he screeched to a stop at the side of the road and then swung back out, did a u-turn, and headed back toward Goose Bend.

"Carlos has arrived, but not Rebekah," he said and set his lips in a tight line.

LASKEY JOLTED his vehicle to a stop in front of the Herschmann's; he'd broken every speed limit between the Susquehanna and Goose

Bend. Bump Herrington's mud-splattered Plymouth Voyager was parked in the drive-way. Bump, the Goose Bend police chief, sometimes showed up at Fritz's for a rousing political discussion, but Laskey knew they wouldn't be discussing politics today. A silver BMW with an Enterprise sticker on the window was parked next to Bump's voyager. Carlos' rental car, Laskey surmised as he and Jacob headed for the front door.

Bump, a big boned man carrying an extra thirty pounds midbody, opened the door and then moved aside for them to enter. "Don't know what to think," he said, running his hand through his fading red hair. He wore a Gander Mountain jacket, faded jeans, and a fishing vest.

Laskey stopped to wipe his feet on the doormat as Jacob brushed past, then the three men moved into a huddle.

"Fritz called you?" Laskey asked Bump. He kept his voice to a near whisper.

"No. I got a report that the alarm in the factory was going off. We went over and checked. It was just a blown fuse. Then Fritz told me about Rebekah not showing up." He nodded at their vests. "I see you two were about to wet your lines, too."

"We were on our way to the Susquehanna."

"Do *you* have any guesses as to why Rebekah didn't show up?" Jacob asked Bump.

Bump shook his head. "I'm sure it's just a mix-up of some sort. They're pretty upset, but there's not a damn thing I can do. Can't file a missing person's report. Can't initiate an investigation. FBI won't do anything at this point. According to the FBI, as an adult she's allowed to go missing." He looked at Laskey. "I don't know why I'm telling you; you know better than me what the FBI will and won't do." He jerked his head in the direction of the kitchen. "They're back there."

They followed Bump through the dining room and into the kitchen. Leah and Fritz, seated at the island, looked up with drawn faces. Leah had the look of having started the day with styled hair only to dishevel it by running her hands through it. Sunlight flooded through the windows, but the overhead lights were still on as though no one had taken the time to notice they were no longer needed. Laskey observed the cups of stale-looking coffee that sat in front of them, along with the plate of untouched croissants and the butter that had gone soft. The room smelled of slightly burnt coffee from the carafe sitting too long on the heated base of the coffee maker.

Fritz rose. "Thanks for coming," he said to Laskey in a subdued voice, and then extended his hand to Jacob. "You, too. I haven't seen you since you got back from Africa. Welcome back. And if you've come to help . . ." he swallowed, ". . . I appreciate it."

"I'll help any way I can." Jacob grabbed his hand.

Leah's eyes were damp. "Carlos couldn't sit still," she said. "He's pacing around the backyard, trying to get through to the American Embassy. Thank goodness, he's here."

Laskey noted the beige corduroy blazer and red tie flung carelessly over the back of a stool. Jacob had wandered over to the windows and was peering out, presumably trying to catch a glimpse of Carlos.

"I already explained why we can't do anything officially," Bump said, leaning against the counter near the coffee maker. "Laskey will back me up on that." He looked over at Laskey who nodded. "But rest assured, we won't let red tape stop us from tracking her down."

"I don't understand why if she's missing, you're not allowed to . . ." Leah stopped when Fritz squeezed her hand.

"Let's just listen, dear," Fritz said.

Laskey pulled out a stool and sat down. "We'll find her. That's a promise." He whipped out the frayed spiral notebook he kept in his shirt pocket. Even on fishing trips it was there, and today was a good example of why. He pulled a pen from the same pocket and opened the notebook. "Let's start with flight numbers." He glanced up at Jacob, still at the window. "Jacob, you can help," he said, and tapped the stool next to him.

Jacob came over and sat down. "Tell me what to do, and I'm on it."

"Count on it." Laskey looked up at the Herschmanns. "Give me her flight number."

When they looked at each other, a question in their eyes, Laskey realized they didn't know. What should have been an easy job was going to be more complicated.

"She didn't tell us." Fritz looked embarrassed.

Leah patted him on the arm. "Fritz no longer picks her up at the airport, so she doesn't give us her flight information. She just tells us when to pick her up at the train station in Lansdale. Unless Totsy is picking her up."

"Totsy?" Laskey asked.

"Her best friend from high school." Leah looked at Jacob. "You know Totsy, don't you?"

"Totsy Love," Jacob said. "Next great actress of stage and theater. Or has she moved on to other things?"

"She still aspires," Fritz replied in a dry voice, "Meanwhile she supports herself working as a receptionist in Dr. Wallace's office and lives with her mother."

Leah ran her finger absently around the rim of her coffee cup. "She takes acting lessons on the side. Four years ago, she moved to New York. She seemed to think she was going to be the next Meryl Streep, only prettier."

Fritz, in spite of the worry that molded his face, gave a sound like the aborted birth of a laugh. "Totsy is right about that. What she lacks in brains and good sense, she makes up for with looks." He shrugged. "She and Rebekah are about as unlike as any two humans can be, but we like Totsy anyway."

"Totsy lasted all of seven months in New York." Leah pushed the coffee cup away, leaned back, and let her hand slide off the counter to rest on Fritz's thigh. "Now she's saving money to go to Hollywood. She thinks her physical attractions will be more of an asset on the big screen than on Broadway. To tell you the truth, that girl's so focused on her big career plans, even if Rebekah said anything to her about coming home, I doubt if Totsy would remember."

"You say Totsy picks her up at the train sometimes?" Laskey realized they were rattling on about Totsy in order to push aside their fear for a few seconds.

"She's picked her up several times," Leah said. "Especially since Fritz's heart attack.

Laskey made a few scribbles on the page. Fritz didn't like for anyone, especially Leah, to remind him of the attack. "Which airline does Rebekah usually fly?"

Bump, who had helped himself to a cup of stale coffee, wandered over to sit beside Jacob. Fritz squeezed his forehead between his thumb and fingers. "She flew various ones depending on connections, or if she was stopping off someplace for a day or two before coming home. She's flown US Air, but she's also flown Emirates and Jordan Air, and British Air at least once. Last year she had a conference in Virginia and took Qatar Air into Dulles." He raised his shoulders in an I-don't-know gesture. "I'm supposed to be an educated man; I run a successful business; and yet I don't ask which airline my only child is flying in on."

"It's okay," Laskey said. "We'll check them all." This wasn't going to be simple.

"Can I help with checking airlines?" Jacob asked.

"Not with the new security regulations. I have a different job for you." He gave Jacob a *do-not-ask-look*.

Laskey filled in several pages of his notebook as he and Bump threw questions at Fritz and Leah. Names and phone numbers of friends. Passport number. Places she'd stopped off in the past, even though she hadn't meant to stop over anywhere this time.

"Rebekah got mixed up in some protests against pharmaceutical companies," Leah said. Absently, she pinched an end from a croissant and rolled it between her fingers.

Laskey glanced at Fritz who had already told him this. Fritz was rubbing the vertical frown line between his brows.

"The first was against Pfizer," Leah said. "A bunch of people from Doctors Without Borders staged a sit-in over the cost of pneumonia vaccine in India. She participated in that and in a couple other protests. Actually . . . ." She let out a sigh before continuing in a peeved voice, "I think Rebekah was one of the people doing the organizing. I wish she'd just stick to her job." She looked down at the croissant piece as though surprised to see it in her hand and then set it down on the saucer beside her cold coffee.

"If pharmaceutical companies had people arrested, which I don't believe they can for protesting, we'd know about it," Laskey said. He turned to Jacob. "Am I right?"

"Big pharmaceuticals don't want the kind of publicity they'd get if protestors were imprisoned. That would call attention to the very thing protestors want people to know. Besides, with the control those companies have over our congressmen and the amount of money they're raking in, they can afford to ignore a few protestors."

"Is that true outside the United States?" Leah raised her eyebrows at Jacob.

"I don't think you need to worry about that."

Laskey was trying hard to maintain a neutral expression, but the dark hound of worry nipped at his heels; something was amiss. He hoped he was wrong, but hope was fading fast. "Can you give me a picture of Rebekah?" He addressed his question to Leah, guessing she was the one that kept track of photographs.

"I'll get one," Fritz said. He slid off the stool, went over to the desk, and rummaged in the middle drawer. He pulled out a nine by twelve envelope, removed two pictures, and handed them to Laskey. "These are smaller versions of a formal portrait we had done when she graduated from med school."

Laskey glimpsed at the photos and then stuck them in his shirt pocket. He was about to ask Jacob to go out and ask Carlos to come in, when he heard the bang of the back door closing, followed by the sound of footsteps coming through the mudroom. Carlos, his eyes full of wild energy, burst in, phone still in hand. Tall and toned, he had square jaws, olive-skin, and a thick mane of dark, wavy hair that fell below his ears. Even from several feet away, he smelled of cigarettes. He stopped short when he saw them.

"You help us find her?" Carlos slipped his phone into his shirt pocket. "It's a mex up . . . a miiix up of some sort," he said, struggling to make the "i" sound. "But we . . ." He gestured to Fritz and Leah. ". . . .are worrying ourselves to death if we not find her soon." His tone was a cross between demanding and frightened.

"I assume you were familiar with Rebekah's plans," Laskey said after Bump had introduced him and Jacob to Carlos.

"She supposed to arrive on Thursday. I was at home in Argentina for a few days." He paced as he talked. "Her friend, Annemarie Leitner, rode with her to airport. A taxi, I think." He stopped and held out his palms in a show of helplessness. "I'm calling Annemarie, but can't get her."

"Do you know if Rebekah and Annemarie actually got to the airport?"

Carlos shook his head. "My camera man going over to her apartment to check if she's still there, and I talked to American Embassy. They sending someone over."

Laskey rose and handed Carlos his card. "You'll call me right away when you hear from your camera man?"

"Of course. Where you going now?"

"To the station. To come up with a plan of action."

"I come with you." He grabbed the corduroy blazer he'd flung over the back of the stool. "Rebekah wouldn't just disappear like that."

"You could help by taking charge here," Bump said, rising. He held out his palm, indicating Fritz and Leah. "They're worried half to death. They need you. "

Laskey saw that Carlos was about to protest, but Bump cut him off. "You're the logical person to man the home front."

Laskey smiled inwardly. He couldn't have done a better job himself taking care of an over-anxious fiancé who was likely to get in the way.

LEAH WIPED AWAY a spot of coffee from the counter and then crumbled the napkin and tossed it aside. Fritz, still seated beside her, stared off into space. With the others gone and Carlos having shot back out into the backyard for another smoke, her imagination was going places she didn't want it to go. She squeezed her eyes shut trying to control her thoughts, but the awful images were still there:

visions of Rebekah mugged, arrested, raped, a victim of human trafficking. She leaned toward Fritz until their shoulders touched. Her husband's body brought physical warmth, but not the assurance she wished for.

"You didn't want her to go to Jordan in the first place," she said.

"I was just being a father. Fathers don't want their daughter going off anywhere, certainly not half a world away." He laid a hand over hers.

"You were worried about her being Jewish in a Muslim country."

"I haven't heard of any violence against Jews in Jordan. It's a stable country."

"You're telling me that, but I know you've been concerned. And I don't care what they say; I still worry about her participating in those protests."

He patted her hand. "Everything's going to be okay, Leah. She's alive and well somewhere and aggravated to death that she can't call us. She probably lost her phone."

Maybe she did lose her phone, Leah thought as she began clearing away cups and crumbs. But she could have bought another, or borrowed one. She stacked the dishes, took them to the dishwasher, and stuck them inside. Laskey and Jacob had been about to go fishing, she knew. And Bump, too. They all wore their fishing vests with flies attached to the Velcro on the pockets. Something about interrupting their day of recreation made the whole thing more terrifying. Like . . . . well, like finally admitting that something had gone horribly wrong.

Chapter Five

Laskey followed Bump as they headed for the police station. The day had fulfilled its promise of being warm and sunny, so he was sorry on more than one count that he and Jacob weren't casting their lines in the Susquehanna.

Jacob slumped in the passenger seat, his face turned to the window, alternately biting his lip and then running a forefinger over said lip. "Carlos isn't Rebekah's type," he said finally. It was the first time he'd spoken since they left the Herschmann's.

About to turn onto Fifth Street, Laskey stopped for the longest stream of traffic he'd ever seen in Goose Bend – five cars – to pass. Then he remembered there was a Saturday farmer's market down by the river. "What's her type?"

"Not a prick who looks like he stepped off the cover of a romance novel."

Laskey threw Jacob a quick glimpse. Jacob wore the expression of a rooster bested in a cockfight. Had the situation not been so serious, he would have been amused. "You've known Carlos for less than twenty minutes. How did you decide he was a prick? Was it the smoldering sex appeal? I'm told women like that dark, disheveled look. Five o'clock shadow. Hooded eyes. Tight pants. Why would Rebekah be different from any other woman?"

"Obviously, she isn't." Jacob crossed his arms and looked straight ahead, clearly not amused. "You said you had a job for me."

"I want you to call hospitals and morgues." Seeing Jacob shiver at the mention of *morgues*, he added, "We have to check the improbable. When you were a boy, you lathered at the mouth wanting to help me solve crimes. Here's your chance."

"I bloody well hope it's not a crime."

"True." The thought that it might be more than just a communcations mix-up, sobered him.

Three minutes later they arrived at the police station, a one-story frame structure located a few hundred feet from the intersection of Fifth and Main. The building sported a new grey, rib-steel roof, but needed a paint job. Narrow rectangles, a lighter yellow than the rest of the building, indicated where shutters had once hung.

Bump pulled into the gravel parking lot ahead of them, got out of his SUV and, hiking up his pants with one hand while running the other across his forehead as though wiping away sweat, waited to lead them in. Nodding at the dispatcher, the police chief took them down the hall to his sparsely appointed office, motioned them in, and closed the door. He gestured toward the visitor chairs in front of his desk and then shuffled over to a side table and pushed the "on" button of a Kuerig machine.

"This is worrisome," Bump said.

Laskey nodded. Even though they didn't know if a crime had been committed, Laskey knew that in someone else's turf it was good to keep quiet in the beginning. By guarding his words until the right moment he'd avoided many a jurisdictional battle. This was not an investigation, at least not yet, but habit exerted itself. He propped his elbows on the chair arms, leaned his chin onto templed hands, and narrowed his eyes. Thought mode. Beside him, Jacob stretched out his legs, folded his hands across his stomach as though lounging on a sunny Carribbean beach, but judging by the look on his face, Laskey surmised that Jacob still puzzled over Rebekah's choice of a mate.

The light on the Nespresso Keurig stopped flashing, indicating that the device was ready. "Coffee?" Bump rotated his eyes between Laskey and Jacob.

"No, thanks," Laskey said.

"Me neither," Jacob echoed.

"Don't know what to think." Bump stuck a capsule in the machine, pushed the button, and the machine spewed out a black stream into the mug beneath the spout.

"Fritz has tried calling her repeatedly, but her phone appears to be dead," Laskey said. "They have a family plan so he can see her calls. She made her last call Wednesday evening in Amman."

"If the battery is dead or been removed we won't be able to trace the phone." Bump dumped creamer in the mug and then moved over to his desk, bringing with him the scent of French vanilla and Ristretto. He sat down, extracted a pair of glasses from his shirt pocket and put them on. He peered over the lenses at Laskey. "You're the one with the most experience. Tell us what to do." He took a sip of coffee and then directed his attention to Jacob. "I know you have to go to work on Monday, but until then . . .?"

"Count me in. I want to help." Jacob straightened.

"Good," Laskey said, glad that Bump readily conceded the lead to him, and that Jacob was available to lend a helping hand. Bump had recused himself in a murder investigation a few months ago because one of the prime suspects had been related to him, and Laskey had been called in to take charge. Bump had provided help and information when asked, and had proven to be an amicable colleague during the process, so Laskey was happy to work with him again.

Within a few minutes, he'd laid out a plan. He'd check flights to find out which one Rebekah was on, or *supposed* to have been on. With the new security regulations he'd have to go to the airport and do it in person. Carlos would contact people he knew in Jordan to see if anyone there could find out anything. Thanks to Carlos, the embassy had been alerted. Jacob would call area hospitals and morgues as well as get in touch with Rebekah's friend, Totsy Love, to see what she knew about Rebekah's travel plans.

He handed Bump the photos Fritz had given him. "Since the regular passengers won't be commuting on the weekend there isn't much point in going to the train station today to see if anyone recognizes her, but if by Monday we haven't . . . ." He rubbed his hand over his forehead and let out a long sigh. It was a long time until Monday.

Bump stuck Rebekah's photos in an envelope. "I'll check with the people getting off the four o'clock train on Monday and stay for the five o'clock, too. Unless, of course, you discover she didn't get on the plane in the first place. What about today?"

"Maybe one of those people at the check-in kiosks along the terminal curb might recognize her picture. You can also check with car rental agencies in case she changed her mind about how she was getting home."

It was noon when they finished. Laskey drove Jacob back to his house, opened the hatch of the Sequoia and, preoccupied with his afternoon agenda, stood by absently as Jacob fished out his gear and piled it on the ground near the back door steps.

"Keep in touch," he said when Jacob finished unloading. Without waiting for a response, he climbed into the SUV and drove away. He'd been so busy reassuring Fritz and Leah that nothing had happened to their daughter other than a snafu with communications that he'd half believed it himself. But now he wasn't so sure.

⸻

JACOB THREW his waders over his shoulders, grabbed as much gear as he could carry, and lugged it into the mudroom. He stacked it in a corner and then went back for the rest. He'd forgotten and left the ice chest with their lunch in the back of the Sequoia. He threw together a ham and Swiss on rye and headed for his office upstairs, eating the sandwich on the way, and dreading what he was about to do. The worst job of the afternoon had fallen to him.

He slipped out of his fishing vest, threw it across the back of a chair, and after booting up the computer, pulled up a list of hospitals and morgues in the greater Philadelphia area. While he waited for the list to spit out of the printer, he went to stand in the sun shafting through the room's single window and called Totsy Love.

There was no answer.

He began calling hospitals, starting with those nearest the airport. "Have you admitted a woman named Rebekah Herschmann or any unidentified white female around the age of thirty-three in the past forty-eight hours?" he asked hospital after hospital. While someone searched through admissions records he paced from window to door to desk, and then repeated the circuit, but always in the patch of sun that reached two-thirds of the way across the room. The patch petered out at the foot of the sagging armchair he'd bought at Goodwill. Stacks of musty-smelling books which he kept meaning to sort through lined the edges of the room: law school texts, the set of classics from his grandmother, dissertations on fracking, his Dumas collection. He continued to pace as he listened to the sounds coming from the receiver — breathing, the shuffling of papers and folders, extraneous conversation, beeps, phones ringing. Each time, when the answer was "no," he breathed a sigh of relief.

Two hours later, after dealing with the last hospital, he looked with trepidation at the list of morgues. What he wanted most right now was for Laskey to call and say Rebekah's plane had been diverted to some god-awful place where there were no cellphone towers or internet connections, and that the plane had been grounded while they waited for parts to be flown in.

He tried Totsy again. Still, no answer.

Thirsty and stiff from being wrapped around the phone — that's what it felt like, *wrapped* around the device in a back-stiffening knot — he went down to the kitchen, filled the cat bowl with clean water, and then grabbed a coke and a cylinder of Oreos.

He slipped out the back door and sat on the steps. The day was warm enough for nothing more than a sweat shirt, but the concrete steps were not, and the cold seeped into his backside and thighs. The elm tree near the southeast corner of the house had stubbornly held onto its leaves while the other trees dropped theirs, but autumn was finally winning out and elm leaves were drifting down to join the others. Only the occasional splashing of the geese broke the silence of the afternoon. There were no tractors plowing, no roosters crowing, and no dogs barking on neighboring farms.

His mind was anything but silent, though. He'd never been able to figure out why Totsy and Rebekah were such good friends. Totsy was silly and boisterous; Rebekah was MENSA material. Sometimes Totsy barely passed her courses. Once, she didn't and had to go to summer school to retake algebra. Rebekah led organizations, not because she pushed herself forward, but because people had confidence in her. Totsy, on the other hand, thrust herself into the center of attention anywhere and anytime she could. Totsy's goal was to become a famous actress, while Rebekah revered Dr. Albert Schweitzer as an exemplar. Rebekah was achieving her goal while Totsy still hung around Goose Bend planning to break into movies some day. One day. Sooner or later. Eventually. Hell, at age thirty-three, if she hadn't already done it, her chances were about zip.

And now Carlos. Jacob took a bite of an Oreo, and then popped the whole thing in his mouth. Obviously, he didn't know Rebekah as well as he thought he had. But like Laskey said, how could he judge a man in twenty minutes? Maybe it was a custom in Argentina for men to define their male equipment with skin tight pants instead of competing in pissing contests like boys on the northern continent.

He popped another Oreo in his mouth and went inside. "Get it over with," he muttered as he clomped up the steps, bringing the cookies with him. A knot had formed in his stomach, but he put aside the temptation to call the hospitals again in case someone had mistakenly given him the wrong answer. A *yes* at a hospital was preferable to a *yes* at a morgue.

An hour later, he'd gotten no *yeses*. "Cheers," he said by way of celebration, and held up an Oreo.

After another unsuccessful attempt at calling Totsy, he called Laskey.

"Anything?" Laskey asked by way of answering.

"Nothing."

"And Totsy?" Laskey sounded tired.

"She isn't answering. How're you doing with airlines?"

"I didn't find her on the flight manifests of any of the domestic airlines. I still have to check foreign flights. There's no one here from Royal Jordanian or Emirates for a couple hours yet. So it's going to take a while."

"What else can I do?"

"Check in on the Herschmanns."

THE HERSCHMANNS' front door stood ajar, so Jacob rapped lightly and then entered without waiting for someone to answer. Carlos and Leah were seated side by side on the living room sofa, their heads bent over a photo album. They looked up in surprise when he appeared in the archway.

"I thought you were Fritz coming back from his walk," Leah said. "Has Laskey . . . .?"

Jacob shook his head. "He's checking flight manifests. He'll let us know as soon as he finds out anything."

Carlos, a look of relief on his face, had stood as soon as Jacob entered the room. Jacob understood the look of relief. He couldn't think of too many things more boring than being pinned down to look at scrapbooks, especially when you'd rather be actively pursuing the disappearance of your fiancé.

Leah's eyes were full of questions. "I'm glad you dropped by, Jacob," she said. "Have a seat. We made Fritz take a walk. He needed some exercise." She nodded at Carlos, indicating that he was part of the *we*.

Jacob, about to sit, remained standing when Carlos took a step toward him.

"How long will it take?" Carlos's face had the look of a dog begging for a bone.

"Security regulations are slowing Laskey down. My guess is he'll know more by tomorrow morning." He wouldn't tell them he'd spent his afternoon calling hospitals and morgues.

Carlos rubbed his fingers hard across his forehead, leaving streaks of white. "I contact everyone I think of. My news agency people in Amman suggesting she might have stopped off somewhere on the way home. I don't think she did that." His speech had a staccato quality to it.

"She most certainly would not have stopped on the way home. Not this time." Leah closed the album with a bang. "The idea is absurd."

Jacob nodded, agreeing with her. He noticed that the top two buttons of Carlos' shirt were unbuttoned, revealing a tuft of black hair and a small gold chain.

Carlos touched the chain. "A geft from Rebekah. A giiiiift, I mean. My English getting better, I think. It's a work in progress." He was still fingering the chain and looking at Jacob from beneath half-lowered lids. "We Latins are more into gold chains than you Americans." He strolled over to a window. Leaning one shoulder against the panes, he riveted his gaze at a spot on the opposite wall. The afternoon's last rays streaked his hair with gold and bronzed the side of his face tilted toward the window. The other cheek and brow were shadowed. "Maybe she was sick or dead tired. I sure she told you and Fritz how hard they work." He looked at Leah.

Leah nodded and touched her fingers to her forehead as though she had a headache.

"She might have checked into one of those airport hotels somewhere," he continued. ". . . and not realized how much time has passed. Do you have any idea how hard those doctors over there work?" He lifted his brows at Jacob.

"Abominably hard, I imagine." Jacob walked over and picked up Carlos' novel from the table beside Fritz's chair.

"Or how many contagious illnesses they're exposed to?" Carlos asked.

"Sounds tough." Jacob turned the book over to look at Carlos' photo on the back. It wasn't the usual author's picture, but showed Carlos in profile in the act of climbing a cliff.

"My documentary . . .," Carlos said, ignoring Jacob's examination of his book, ". . . is meant to show what those doctors and nurses experience."

"I look forward to seeing it." Jacob pointed to the picture on the back of the book. "You like rock climbing?"

"Since I was fifteen. You?"

"Never tried it."

Carlos shoved his hands in his pockets. "When this is over, want to give it a shot? I could teach you the basics."

"Thanks for the offer. Maybe I'll take you up on that." Jacob looked over at Leah. "Anything I can do for you while we're waiting to hear from Laskey?"

"You already have just by being here. And we're grateful."

"Wait," Carlos said, holding out his hand to stop Jacob as he turned to leave. "I should be on knees thanking you for your help." He swallowed. "But all I capable of right now is worry. Please forgive me."

"Not a problem," Jacob replied. "I'll see myself out."

DUSK HAD PAINTED the world gray, melancholy, and depressingly baffling when Jacob descended the Herschmann's front door steps and then plodded through the bloodless twilight to his car. The shadow of the house consumed a large portion of the front lawn. Silhouettes of two large oaks shrouded most of the remainder.

He got into his Subaru, rested his hands on the steering wheel, and wondered what to do. He didn't want to go home to a dark, empty house. He needed company other than his cat, and it was supper time. There was only one thing to do. He cranked up and headed toward Aunt Zuela's. She'd been his *default* often enough; what was one more time? Besides, he'd promised to hook up her new printer and the sooner he did, the sooner she'd be off his back.

He smiled. When it came to technology she was like a little kid standing in front of a big, scary rhino: she trembled. *"I'm a techno-idiot, Jacob, I need you to do it for me." "Read the instructions, Aunt Zuela." "I did; they're written for people who already know how to do it." "You have a*

PhD; I'll bet you could figure it out." "No, you're wrong. The directions are written in a different language. It's like taking Greek 201 before you take Greek 101. Do you want me to have a nervous breakdown?"

It was a losing battle. Why did he even argue with her? He could save himself a lot of grief by doing it and getting it over with instead of trying to convince her she could accomplish something as simple as hooking up a printer. But that was what she wanted, wasn't it? For him to stop arguing and just do it.

A few minutes later he pulled into her driveway. He didn't really mind hooking up her printer, or any of the other tasks she found for him. And there was always something. Protesting was a habit left over from his teenage years, and he still got a kick out of baiting her. Actually, he rather enjoyed the company of his mother's best friend. Especially when she had something good brewing in her kitchen.

"And tonight it must be . . . ." he mumbled as he opened the front door. "Saw dust and tomato soup." He hoped it was Trader Joe's roasted red pepper and tomato soup. A couple times a year, she drove up to Allentown to the nearest Trader Joe's to stock up. But the sawdust?

Past the shadowed gloom of the living room, through the archway into the brightly lit dining room, he saw the source of the smell. A few boards and a saw lay on the floor in front of newly constructed shelves. Two paint cans, a level, and a hammer sat on a tarp in one corner. Books were piled everywhere — on the floor, on the table, on chairs. She'd been threatening to build shelves in the dining room for the past twenty-five years, and she'd finally done it.

Sawdust footprints marked out a path to the kitchen and another toward the rear of the dining room where a door opened into a short hallway. He heard a clank from the kitchen and the hum of a tune he didn't recognize – actually it was only the semblance of a tune; singing in key wasn't one of Aunt Zuela's talents. He stepped over a board, skirted a couple piles of books, and went to join her.

"Shit," she said and dropped two slices of pumpernickel on the floor. "I didn't hear you come in, Jacob Gillis. You scared the crap out of me."

"Sorry." He bent over and picked up the bread. "Thirty-second rule," he said, handing them back to her.

She blew on them.

"Blowing off the germs?"

"Yes. My breath is more sanitary than the floor. Interested in tomato soup and grilled cheese? I was going to eat from a tray and watch a movie. I need something to pass the time, otherwise all I'm going to do is sit around and worry about Rebekah."

"I know what you mean. What movie?"

She put the two slices down on the counter and began cutting more from the loaf on the cutting board. "I don't guess you'd be up for *Dr. Zhivago*?"

"Probably not."

"*Probably*?"

"Okay, I'm *not* up for *Dr. Zhivago*. Don't you have a movie that's a little more up to date?"

"Since when did romance go out of date?" She reached into the refrigerator for more cheese.

"I'll watch *Dr. Zhivago* if you like." His voice had gone quiet.

Leaving the refrigerator door to close on its own, she narrowed her eyes at him. "You're really worried?"

He nodded.

"Me, too. Leah called a few minutes ago and brought me up to date, which is to say that there was absolutely nothing to be updated on."

She unwrapped the cheese and cut pieces to fit the bread. Butter was already bubbling in the frying pan. Shaking her head, she put the two sandwiches in and slid them around with the spatula. "I don't have a good feeling."

"I don't either."

"But worrying accomplishes nothing. Go get a movie ready."

Anything but *Dr. Zhivago*, he thought as he returned to the living room to choose something. Not only were there books in the dining room, but her living room contained three bookcases stacked haphazardly with volumes of all sizes and conditions, ranging from new to falling apart. The subjects varied widely, too. A volume on growing tomatoes and another called *The Theory of Literature* were mixed in with Agatha Christie novels. He supposed every English writer worth a dime was represented either on these shelves or ones somewhere else in the house. There were complete sets of Jane Austen, Charles Dickens, and Thomas Hardy, along with more critique books on Hardy than there were novels. Lacking the precision of a library, the spines stuck out unevenly.

Aunt Zuela had placed the TV she seldom watched on a cabinet between two bookcases. He rummaged in the cabinet, rattling the DVDs around as he went through them twice. She didn't have a single one he cared to watch this evening, or any other evening for that matter. Sighing, he pulled out *Dr. Zhivago* and inserted it in the player. It was also his mother's favorite. What was it about old women and that movie? Then he chastised himself. Neither his mother nor Aunt Zuela was old. They were both sixty-five – the new fifty-five, they claimed.

The DVD player set to go, he fished out his phone and tried Totsy's number again. Still, no answer.

"So you didn't get to go fishing today." Aunt Zuela walked in and handed him a tray with soup, sandwich, potato chips, and coke.

"We'll go next week. Or the week after. We'll get there." He placed the tray on the table next to the chair which he always claimed as his, and then sat down while Aunt Zuela returned to the kitchen for her tray.

"I've been trying to get Totsy all afternoon," he said when she returned. "I thought she might know something about Rebekah's travel plans."

Aunt Zuela set her tray down on an ottoman. "What would she know that Fritz and Leah don't know? Or that Carlos doesn't know?"

He shrugged. "Probably nothing. But like Laskey says, *That's just another rock to look under.*"

"Well, I don't think you're going to find anything under that rock. Shall we?" She nodded at the TV.

IT WAS NEARLY ten when Jacob's phone rang. They'd just finished the movie. Zhivago's presumed daughter, Tanya, had said goodby to his brother Yevgraf and gone off with her boyfriend, balalaika flung over her shoulder. Aunt Zuela had wiped away a tear and was bending over to collect her tray.

"It must be Laskey." Jacob grabbed his jacket, snatched the phone from a pocket, and hit the "on" button. Aunt Zuela straightened, the anticipation on her face equal to what he guessed was on his own. "What did you find out?" he asked Laskey.

"I'll drop by your place first thing in the morning to talk to you," Laskey said and hung up.

"Well?" Aunt Zuela raised her hands in a question.

Jacob shook his head. "He didn't tell me anything. Just that he's dropping by early in the morning." A chill ran through him. What was Laskey not telling him?

Sunday

October 21

Vienna, Austria

On Sundays, the man's son came to check up on him and to play a game of chess.

"Think you can finally beat me?" the man always asked when they sat down at the games table.

Karl invariably replied, "I can hope."

The man usually won in less than twenty-five minutes but today his mind wandered. They'd been maneuvering for almost an hour, and he still hadn't checkmated Karl's queen. Joseph Herschmann, the younger, had been the only person able to beat him at the game. The man frowned at the memory of young Joseph. Brash. Over-confident. Irritatingly intelligent.

"Are you stuck then?" Karl asked.

The man noticed the beam of hope on his son's face. "No, I'm not stuck." He looked back down at the chessboard and, seeing what he should have seen before had he not been so preoccupied, moved his bishop to breach his son's defense.

"At least you didn't beat me so quickly today. That's progress, I suppose." Karl sat back and stretched out his legs beneath the table.

"I'll always win."

Now that the game was over, he wanted to drag himself to the window, but he refused to put his weakness on display for his son. Damn the Parkinson's that afflicted him!

Karl, who still had two good legs, rose and went to look out. "I envy your view," he said.

"Yes . . . it's pleasant." The vista looked toward the village of Pöchlarn which lay at the western edge of the city, beyond the sprawl of the newer sections, beyond the Ringstrasse. It was where he and Joseph had grown up, playing and raising hell together, and then working together just as their fathers had, until . . .

"I want to go to Pöchlarn," he said and began to put the chess pieces back in their home positions.

"I'll arrange to have the driver pick you up." Karl turned away from the window to face his father. He sighed. "Why must you go? It will only remind you of things you want to forget."

"I don't want to forget; I want to remember." He placed the black bishops in their places, and the black queen in hers, and smiled. Joseph Herschmann might have beaten him at chess, and at other things including trickery and deception, but the final victory would belong to him, Gustav Fuchs. Yesterday, the girl had walked into the trap. Today: step two.

Chapter Six

Laskey swung his legs out of bed, shaved, dressed, fed his three cats, and by six-thirty was headed for the 7-eleven, mystified over what he'd learned yesterday. He'd grab some donuts and then shoot out to Jacob's to talk it out.

He'd begun to bounce things off his godson while Jacob was growing up. Careful not to give away things he shouldn't be telling an outsider, ideas, problems, questions were all presented to Jacob as hypothetical situations. His colleagues were too prone to offer prescripted solutions when all he wanted was someone to listen. In the beginning, Jacob had persisted in expounding his own wild theories, but eventually he'd learned to let Laskey talk, bottling up his own comments until he sensed Laskey was ready for them. The seven years Jacob had spent in college and law school had left them little time together, and then his five years in Africa had left Laskey completely bereft of his company. Truth was, he'd missed Jacob something fierce during those years. Jacob was family. The son he didn't have. He dreaded the day Jacob became too busy with his own career and family to spend time with him.

This morning Jacob would know it was not a hypothetical situation. And it was a real puzzler. His colleagues teased him about his success rate with puzzlers, joking that as a Quaker Laskey had a direct line to the *Inner Light*. They teased, but sometimes he thought having been brought up in the practices of the Religious Society of Friends did have a certain advantage; he knew how to talk things through with someone like Jacob and then to sit quietly and wait for details to settle and answers to come.

Black clouds furrowed across the sky as he dashed into the 7-eleven. He tossed half a dozen donuts in a bag and then went to stand in the check-out line. Jacob would have coffee. Then he remembered how much Jacob hated grocery shopping and decided Jacob might *not* have coffee. He got out of line and poured two large cups of Columbian Intense.

Several people had jumped in ahead of him when he returned to the line. Something had gone terribly wrong with his friend's daughter, yet he had to cool his heels while a man in an expensive business suit counted pennies from his pocket to purchase a bagel, and then while a woman rummaged through a luggage sized purse in search of her credit card.

Nor did the lack of sleep help his mood. Last night, as hard as he tried to erect road blocks in his mind, one thought kept popping into his head. *Farfetched*, he tried to convince himself. But was it?

"Can I help you?" The cashier, a tired look in her eyes, stood slump shouldered as she waited for him to set his purchases on the counter.

LASKEY PULLED around Jacob's house to park in the back. A cold wind snapped at him as he made his way across the yard, and a pain caused by humidty shot through his arthritic left ankle. Black clouds amassed overhead, thickening the gloom. Then Jacob's backdoor swung open and the welcome glow of house lights poured out to greet him. Jacob, bristly-cheeked, waved him in.

"You sure know how to keep people in suspense," Jacob said, stepping back for Laskey to enter. Jacob was dressed in a pair of torn jeans and an old sweat shirt. "Tell me everything's all right."

"It isn't." Laskey handed Jacob a cup of coffee and the bag of donuts. "Let's sit down and we can talk. Do I smell a fire, or is that the remains of an old one?"

"I just started a fire." Jacob led the way into the kitchen. "Want me to warm your coffee?" He nodded at the 7-eleven cup in Laskey's hand.

"It's empty. If you have any brewed, I'll take a fresh cup, or three."

He ignored the impatience and curiosity in Jacob's eyes and meandered over to the fireplace while Jacob poured him a fresh cup. The kitchen occupied one end of a long room. At the other end was a sitting area where flames licked at the old cheeks of the fireplace. He sat down in one of the two rocking chairs, leaned over, and held out his hands toward the flames. The hickory logs smelled like ham baking. He leaned closer and took a long, deep whiff.

"You're going to keep me guessing?" Jacob called from the kitchen area.

"I'm not doing it on purpose." He held his hands closer to the fire. "I just haven't been able to wrap my mind around things, yet."

Jacob walked over, set the bag of donuts on the hearth, and handed Laskey a cup of fresh brew. He popped another log on the fire and then sat down in the other rocking chair. "Tell."

"Rebekah boarded Lufthansa flight number 693 at Queen Alia International Airport in Amman, flew to Frankfurt, and then boarded flight 426 to Philadelphia." He reached over and took a donut. "Her name is on the manifest of the flight leaving Amman as well as on the one from Frankfurt. It looks like she arrived in Philadelphia on Thursday like she said she would."

"So . . . . Where is she then?"

"What's the first thing that pops into your head?"

"Why would she be here and not go to her parents? I find it hard to believe that someone could abduct her from the airport or the train. If I let my imagination run wild, I'd wonder if someone stole her identity and came in her place."

Laskey closed his eyes and nodded. When he opened them, Jacob was searching his face. "That's one possibility," Laskey said.

Jacob took a chocolate donut from the bag. Frowning, he stared at it for a few moments as though looking for an answer there. "If it was just a matter of someone stealing her documents, she would have reported it to the authorities and called her parents."

Laskey nodded again. If a woman, or a man dressed as a woman, had come here in her place, it could be a terrorist or someone just wanting to slip into the United States. They would probably have incapacitated Rebekah, either temporarily or permanently. They wouldn't want her to report that her documents had been stolen. The best case scenario would be that she was being held alive and unhurt until the other person had disappeared into the U.S.

"So, what now?" Jacob raised his palm.

"I'm going back to the airport to watch videos. If she doesn't appear on the deplaning video, then I'll know someone else came in her place. We know which seats she sat in on both legs of the trip. I can try to get a description of the person sitting in that seat from the plane personnel, if they can remember. And it might take me a week or more to track the personnel down. What would I do with a description anyway? If Rebekah does appear on the videos, then we have to figure out what happened to her after deplaning."

"Maybe she had second thoughts about Carlos."

Laskey gave him a sharp look. "Why would she do that?"

"He isn't her type."

"You said that last night."

Jacob ran his hand over the bristles on his chin. "Rebekah is . . . Well, she isn't the type to attract a man with movie-star good looks. Carlos could probably have any Barbie doll he wanted."

His eyes on Jacob, Laskey drank his coffee. Jacob wasn't bad-looking, and there'd never been a shortage of girls chasing him. The blonde curls he'd had as a boy had become slightly darker blonde waves, the kind, he was told, that girls like to run their fingers through. He was fairly certain that numerous fingers had plowed rows through Jacob's. He was a well-built, athletic specimen who also happened to have a sharp mind and a promising career. Sometimes he thought Jacob didn't recognize his own assets.

"You make it sound like good-looks is a detriment to a sound mind," Laskey said. "Obviously, Carlos is smart enough to recognize quality when he sees it. I think you're misjudging him."

Jacob shrugged. "I'm sure you're right."

Laskey drained the last drops of coffee and then let his head rest on the back of the chair. He had no right to accuse anyone, including Jacob, of misjudging someone. Not after his own brush with disaster which had left him with a lame foot and a deficit in the trust department.

A crash of thunder rattled the glass in the windows. He rose, walked over, and looked out at the fingers of incandescent white shredding the western horizon. When he was a child, the jagged streaks of lightning made him think the devil was paying them a visit. He shuddered. The feeling of being surrounded by evil wasn't so much different right now.

"More coffee?" Jacob asked as he came to join him at the window.

"No, thank you." He handed Jacob his empty cup. "I haven't told Leah and Fritz about Rebekah's name being on the flight manifest."

"This is going to shake them."

"It shook *me*."

"What are you going to say to them?"

"Nothing yet." Staring out at the gathering storm, Laskey wondered. What *would* he say? There was nothing, nothing at all, that wouldn't rock them to the core. "I have to go," he said, looking at his watch. "They'll have the videos ready for me in another hour."

He walked over to the fireplace and grabbed another donut. "Lunch," he said, holding it up. Then he headed for the door. "I'll know more in a couple hours."

Chapter Seven

L askey leaned closer to the monitor. The door of Lufthansa flight 426 swung open and the video showed an attendant moving just inside the plane. A few seconds later, he disappeared. An interminable period ensued while Laskey waited for passengers to deplane. Finally, a tall man dressed in a business suit and carrying a briefcase exited, followed by other passengers close on his heels, many with heads down as they checked purses or phones. They walked toward the camera and then disappeared as they passed beneath.

The agent operating the video sat beside him drumming his fingers on the table, beating out a rhythm of boredom. A couple other agents milled around, monitoring the rows of screens crammed against the walls of the long room. Windowless, the ill-lit space had an astringent smell.

A couple times, thinking he'd spotted Rebekah, Laskey asked the operator to stop the video, but each time, when he looked closer, it wasn't her.

His stomach was in knots. If she weren't on the plane, someone had taken her place.

Even if he saw her exit the plane, where did that leave them? A grown woman disappearing between the airport and the Lansdale train station? At no place along that route would she have been alone; there would have been other commuters every step of the way. Another thought occurred to him. The train made a couple stops before it reached Lansdale. Fort Washington, for one. Also somewhere in North Philadelphia. Germantown, maybe? She could have gotten off in one of those places by mistake and had something happen. Or she could have fallen asleep and, instead of getting off in Lansdale, continued north to Allentown, or Wilkes-Barre, or any of several other towns. A bead of sweat dribbled down his forehead. He couldn't think of any scenario that gave him hope. It had now been two-and-a-half days.

The agent leaned his chair back on its hind legs and clasped his hands behind his head. Two others carried on a conversation a few feet away. Laskey fought the urge to ask them to be quiet.

A family with three small children struggled off the plane, the mother carrying a boy toddler and the father attempting to corral a fight between two older boys. Behind the family was . . . .

"Stop the video," he slapped the table.

The agent flopped the front chair legs back to the floor, hit the pause button, and then backed the video up a few frames.

Laskey stood and, propping his hands on the surface of the table, leaned toward the monitor. There, behind the family, was Rebekah frozen in the act of brushing back her hair. Her head was tilted down as though looking at her feet. She wore a pair of jeans and a rumpled blue-striped shirt. A gray sweat shirt was tied around her waist, and a red back pack hung from her shoulders.

"That's her," he said to the agent and pointed. "I want to see her walk through the airport." The flood of warmth that had coursed through him when he first saw her turned quickly to ice. He'd be able to follow her through the airport on a series of videos until she vanished, but somewhere she'd done just that. Vanished.

He sat back down. He'd learned to deal with the aftermath of violence, or the likelihood of violence, by putting his emotions on ice and coring himself down to the logical, observant detective. He tried to do that now, but knowing the victim made it difficult. He gave a start when he realized he'd labeled her a victim.

The agent restarted the video, and Laskey watched Rebekah trudge toward the camera, shoulders drooping as though in exhaustion, but every now and then, she straightened and he thought he caught a look of joy on her face. A series of segments showed her striding along the corridor toward the baggage claim, the walk seeming to energize her, but each time she came to a moving walkway, she leaned on the rail of the moving belt, her body slumping. Once, she lifted her hand from the rail and pressed her palm to her face, covering forehead and eyes. A fifteen hour flight could deplete, but he thought it was more than the flight. She must have been either unusually exhausted when she boarded the plane, or sick. Or both.

She stopped off in a ladies room, and the agent switched to a video aimed at the door. Ten minutes later, Rebekah still hadn't come out, and Laskey found himself holding his breath again although he didn't think could have happened to her in the toilet. Other women had gone in and come out.

She exited finally, hair combed and wearing a light blue jacket. The sweatshirt had disappeared, probably tucked inside her backpack.

Several more clips brought her to the baggage area. She stopped in front of the carousel, already circling with suitcases, and then she took a couple steps to the side and disappeared from view.

"The camera is stuck," the agent said. "It isn't swiveling from side to side like it's supposed to." He frowned down at the equipment.

Rebekah moved back into view and stood there for a few seconds, leaning forward occasionally to better see the luggage on the belt. Then she moved aside again and disappeared.

"Is there another camera?" Laskey was losing patience. "No, wait." Rebekah had reappeared. She looked down at her purse, removed her phone, and held it to her ear. She broke out in a smile. A few seconds later, she hit the "off" button and, still smiling, headed toward the terminal exit without retrieving her luggage. The way to the trains lay in a different direction. She approached the terminal exit and then disappeared as she walked beneath the camera.

Laskey's stomach fluttered at the promise of discovery. Someone was picking her up. He tried to contain himself while the agent fiddled with the equipment. When nothing happened, he turned to the agent. "Well?"

The agent creased his brow as he flipped the control bottons on and off, trying to make something happen. "The system was supposed to be serviced a couple months ago, but the company never showed up," he said. He flipped a couple more switches, and then hit the "play" button again. "Here it is . . . Oh, crap." Looking defeated, he sank back in his chair.

Laskey felt something raging inside. Only the tops of cars were visible, and not enough of the tops to identify their makes. The camera had been knocked askew. "Do you have another camera focused on this spot?"

The agent shook his head. "I'm afraid this is the only one."

"NO, we have no unclaimed luggage from Thursday's Lufthansa flight." The attendant looked up from the monitor. "You lost yours?"

"I'm trying to locate a friend's luggage." Laskey held out his ID.

The attendant raised his brows. "I'll recheck." He frowned at the screen as he hit tabs and keys, shuffling through lists. "Nothing here from that flight," he said finally. "Maybe somebody stole it off the carousel, but it's been three and half days. Why are you just now looking for it? Can you describe the luggage? Color? Size? Brand?"

"I'll have to get back to you on that. Thank you for your time." Laskey turned and walked away. Leah would know what kind of luggage Rebekah had. He'd find out and then force the baggage attendant to watch the films to discover who'd taken it.

He left the terminal, strode over to the parking garage, and was about to open the door of his car but let his hand slide away from the handle. According to the log on Fritz's phone, Rebekah's last call had been on Wednesday while she was still in Amman. The call she'd received at the airport hadn't shown up. And that led to another question: if she'd bought a new phone, how was it that she'd informed whoever called her of a new number, but had let neither her parents nor her fiancé know?

FRITZ TOOK Laskey's umbrella and raincoat and hung them on the coat tree beside the front door. Laskey took his time brushing his feet on the doormat, and then he examined the edges of his soles, checking to see that they were clear of mud. He picked up a leaf he'd trailed in and stuck it in his pocket. He was conscious of his every movement, his every excuse to delay. His stomach had all but twisted into a pretzel during the hour's drive from the airport to Goose Bend. Finally, unable to hold off any longer, he met Fritz's eyes.

"Is it Uncle Bill?" Leah called from the living room. When Rebekah started calling him that, Leah had followed suit.

"It is," Fritz called back, his gaze still fastened on Laskey.

Leah appeared in the archway. "You've found out something?" It was past lunchtime, but she wore a fluffy blue housecoat. Her hair was tousled and her skin blotchy without make-up.

"She was on the plane," Laskey said, without looking directly at either of them. "Lufthansa flight number 693 from Amman to Frankfurt and then flight number 426 to Philadelphia. She landed in Philadelphia on Thursday as scheduled."

They stared at him.

"She couldn't have been on the plane, or she'd be here." Fritz said at length, his face ashen.

"I watched the security videos and saw her exit the plane and go to the baggage area." He was about to suggest she might have gotten into a car with someone, but stopped. It was possible she'd crossed over to the parking garage opposite the terminal instead, intending to meet someone there and been accosted. The person she was supposed to meet might have given up and left when Rebekah didn't show.

Fritz held out his palms in bewilderment.

"They were having problems with the airport cameras so the last I saw of her was at baggage claim," Laskey said. The lie jolted.

Leah had begun to cry softly. Fritz, put his arm around her shoulders and drew her closer. The furrows in his forehead had deepened to channels.

"When you last talked to her, did she mention anything about meeting someone at the airport?" Laskey asked.

Both shook their heads.

"Did she seem worried about something?"

"Just the opposite." Leah took a tissue from her pocket and wiped her eyes. "She was happy."

"Why don't we sit down?" Fritz's voice sounded mechanical, as though his words were disconnected from his soul. He dropped his arm from Leah's shoulder, led the way into the living room, and collapsed into his chair. Laskey sank into a chair near a side window. Leah, one hand over her mouth, the other clutching at the lapels of her housecoat, sat down on a sofa.

Fritz squeezed his forehead. "If what you say is true, someone who didn't know her might think she ran off with one of her friends for a holiday without telling us. She'd never do that. Not in the past. Not now. It doesn't make sense. Especially with Carlos here." He let go of his forehead and gave Laskey a haunted look. "Something is terribly wrong."

Laskey shifted uneasily. Fritz and Leah were hanging on his every move, his every breath, waiting for something hopeful to come out of his mouth. What he wanted most was to tell them there would be a good ending. That he and Bump would figure it out. That Rebekah would come home safe and sound.

"You said her last call was one she made in Amman on Wednesday?" Laskey asked.

Fritz nodded. "To Annemarie Leitner."

"That was an outgoing call. Does your phone log also show incoming calls?"

Fritz nodded again. "The last one was on Tuesday evening from Carlos. I called her several times Thursday, and everyday since then, but none of those show up."

"Can you ask the phone company to provide you an official log? I can't request that without a warrant."

"She must have lost her phone and gotten a new one," Leah said. She held one of the sofa cushions to her chest, crushing it against her bosom. "But she would have told us."

"That's a possibility. What kind of luggage did she travel with?"

"Just a backpack," Leah said. "She has clothes here so she didn't need to do a lot of packing. Unless she was bringing gifts. Then she just threw them into one of the old suitcases she had there. I can't even remember what they looked like. Why do you ask?"

"Just wondering." Disappointment shot through him with another tiny hope of discovery crippled. "Have either of you gotten in touch with Totsy?"

"She isn't answering." Fritz said. He was leaning over, forearms propped on thighs, hands dangling between legs. "I'm not sure how much help she'd be even if Rebekah talked to her about her plans. Totsy's a little . . . ."

"Wifty." Leah supplied the missing word. Shivering, she hugged the sofa cusion tighter. "We like Totsy anyway. We always felt a little sorry for her."

Laskey heard the squeak of shoes crossing the foyer, and looked up to see Carlos appear in the archway, package of cigarettes in one hand, while brushing rain from the sleeves of his corduroy blazer with the other. Drops of water pearled on his forehead where a damp curl stuck to his brow.

"What have you found out?" Carlos asked.

"Rebekah arrived in Philadelphia on Thursday," Laskey said.

Carlos' face darkened. "I don't believe that."

"I saw her on the airport security videos."

"I don't understand." Carlos came into the middle of the room so that Laskey had to look up. He smelled the musk-jasmine scent of Carlos' aftershave.

"When did you talk to her last?" Laskey asked.

"How could she arrive and not be here?" Carlos ignored Laskey's question.

Laskey rose and repeated his question. "When did you talk to her last?"

"Tuesday evening. I was in Buenos Aires. I tell you that already. My cousin was getting married. I didn't call Rebekah on Wednesday because of wedding, and Thursday because I know she's traveling. I try every day since. I think maybe her phone charge run down. Or maybe she too busy with her parents."

Too busy to talk to her fiancé? Laskey doubted it. "Did she sound normal on Tuesday?"

"Yes, she sound normal; meaning exhausted. It was bad in those camps before, but when war in Syria began, *bad* turned to *hellish*. Doctors without Borders should win a prize for what they do."

"They did. The Nobel Peace Prize."

"I'm aware of that. Do you know what kind of salaries they get?"

"Not much, I imagine."

"Less than a thousand dollars a month." Carlos shook his head. "Unbelievable."

"What did you and Rebekah talk about?"

"Driving up to Poconos to see leaves? Spending a day on South Street? She was

taking me to Amish country one day. And we talked about things lovers talk about which I'm not sharing." He flopped into the chair nearest the door, propped his arms on the chair arms, and hung his head. "I talked to American Embassy again." His voice broke. "They sent someone to check on her, but her friends say she left Thursday morning."

Laskey flickered his gaze at Leah. Her face was drawn, and she was biting her lips. He turned back to Carlos. "Did Rebekah tell you how she was getting to Goose Bend from the airport?"

"You know that already." He looked up with a hard glint in his eyes. "She was taking the train into . . . Whatever that town is called. Lans . . . something."

"Lansdale."

"When she didn't arrive on Thursday, we sort of hoped she'd changed her plans to arrive the same time as you and forgot to tell us," Leah said.

Carlos shook his head. "No, that wasn't in plans."

"Which flight were you on?" Laskey asked.

Carlos shrugged. "I forget flight number, but I flew Delta out of Buenos Aires. I had an hour stopover in Atlanta, and then . . . Wait. I *can* tell you flight number; I forget for a minute, but here. . ." He groped in his jacket pocket − the opposite one from where the package of cigarettes bulged, pulled out a couple wadded papers, and handed them to Laskey.

Laskey smoothed out the boarding passes, one for flight 110 from Ministro Pistarini to Atlanta, leaving Buenes Aires at 8:20 P.M. on October 19, and the other for flight 2273 from Atlanta, arriving in Philadephia the next morning. It would be easy enough to check if Carlos had actually been on these flights. He folded the passes and stuck them in his pocket.

Laskey glanced at Fritz, and an alarm ricocheted through him. He sprang up, took two steps over to his friend, and put his hand on his shoulder. "Are you okay?" One side of Fritz's mouth was drawn back, and the other end drooped while he looked off into space, his eyebrows knit together.

Fritz jerked to attention. "No, I'm not okay. My daughter is missing, I'm scared, and I don't know what to do."

"Fritz, I will not leave you alone in this."

"I know," he said. "I know."

ON HIS WAY OUT, Laskey stopped and turned to Leah who had followed him into the foyer along with Fritz. "Why did you say you felt sorry for Totsy?" Laskey asked.

"They've had a hard time. Her mother is a waitress, not that there's anything wrong with that. But they barely squeaked by at times. To make things worse, Totsy's mother has been sort of ostracized because of being a white woman who got pregnant by a black man. He disappeared before Totsy was born." Leah seemed relieved to talk about something else. "And Totsy wasn't gifted with . . ." She looked at Fritz for help.

"Totsy was neither brilliant nor industrious as a student," Fritz said. His voice was subdued. "Rebekah helped her get through high school. She kept at Totsy until she got her grades high enough to get into Moravian College." He stretched a corner of his mouth into a rueful half-smile. "At Moravian, *without* Rebekah's help, she flunked out first semester. I have no idea why those two were such good friends but if anyone other than us knows what Rebekah is up to, it would be Totsy."

"I'll track her down," Laskey said.

Chapter Eight

Laskey limped through the soggy leaves littering the Herschmann's sidewalk. The rain, which had been like needles of ice when he arrived, had stopped for the moment, but a cloying dampness hung on. The arthritis in his foot had flared up making it feel like an elephant had stepped on it, and his shoulders sagged. The smell of wet earth and rotting leaves reminded him of dank, dark cellars. He wanted to see one tiny little ray of sun, one beam of hope, but judging from the color of the sky more bad weather was yet to come.

He crawled into his Sequoia and reconsidered his previous idea. Could Rebekah have gotten on the train, fallen asleep, and then detrained somewhere other than Lansdale? If she got off at some other station disoriented, she might have left her purse with identification on board or dropped it somewhere. It was entirely possible she'd contracted one of the diseases she treated and was in a semi-conscious state. The idea was far-fetched, but he was grasping for any explanation at this point.

After calling Bump, he rang Jacob. "Did you check hospitals at the end of the line?"

"No. But now that you mention it, I should have. You saw the videos?"

"Yes. She was on the plane." He explained the sequence of events up until she left the terminal. "It's possible she didn't get into someone's car as I thought at first, but went to the parking garage, met someone briefly, and then got on the train. She could have fallen asleep and gotten off at the wrong station."

"I'll call hospitals along the line past Lansdale now."

"Thanks. Bump is headed for the airport with her photo to look for anyone who might have seen her leave the terminal."

Laskey hung up and pulled into the street. His stomach in knots, he headed toward the center of town. The pain of losing an only child, or *any* child, clawed at him. Tomorrow, he'd ask for time off from his job. Emotionally involved or not, he had no intention of bowing out until Rebekah was safe at home or . . . . He shuddered.

Approaching the intersection of Main and Fifth, he realized he was starving — donuts for breakfast didn't cut it. His vehicle, of its own volition it seemed, headed in the direction of Zuela's. Showing up at her front door, unannounced and uninvited, was definitely not the right thing to do, but the Sequoia kept going.

He pulled up to the curb in front of her house, switched off the engine, and then realized that showing up uninvited would also conjure up the idea they were more than just friends. They weren't. And he doubted his ability to explain that he simply needed the company of another human being right now, one who would give his mind a break from what it had been going through for the past twenty-four hours. Could he explain, without his explanation being taken as more than he meant, that sometimes he wanted a woman's company because women were better at going on about inconsequential subjects, leaving a man free to stew? Or maybe it was because he had four sisters that he *thought* women were better at that.

Jacob had teased him about being spoiled. *Four older sisters running your world while you were growing up? No wonder you have to have the table set just so, with cloth napkins and the flatware layed out correctly. And I'm guessing your sisters probably waited on their little brother hand and foot.*

Well, crap, he liked order. Order in his surroundings created order in his mind. So, yes, he liked the table being set correctly, and he liked other things women did that most men didn't bother with. Making beds. Hanging laundry on the line because it smelled better. He smiled. It felt good to ease the tightness in his face. Who knew, it might be his last smile for a while, so he let it linger. And yes, his sisters had spoiled him. He wished one was here with him now.

Zuela Hay, in spite of being brash and opinionated, had a softness, too, but she hid it beneath an armor of flippancy. Protection against hurt, he supposed. According to Jacob, her professor husband had deserted her for a coed.

He turned the engine back on. Soft or brash, no matter, he couldn't show up unexpectedly at her door at lunch time on a Sunday, or any other day for that matter. If nothing else, she'd be furious at him for making her answer the door if she hadn't penciled in her eyebrows. That was something else he'd learned from his sisters.

As he prepared to pull back into the street, someone tapped on the passenger window. Caught! He clasped his forehead in a vize of thumb and fingers for a few moments and then lowered the passenger side window.

Zuela poked her head through. "Are you stalking me?" She had a 7-eleven bag in one hand and an umbrella in the other.

"I am indeed. Damn, you caught me."

"I'll have to report you to the local authorities. What *are* you doing here? Don't tell me you've developed Jacob's habit of showing up at meal times?"

"He does that?"

She rolled her eyes. "You have no idea."

He sensed that she rather enjoyed Jacob showing up.

He turned off the motor. "Truth is, I'm worried, and I need a few minutes conversation about something not so dire to get my brain back in working order. You wouldn't by any chance like to run out to the diner?"

"It'll be crowded after church. Why don't you come inside. I'll fix something."

HE SMELLED the sawdust as soon as he stepped inside. Looking through the arch into the dining room, he saw the new shelves, the saws, the paint, the extra boards, the stacks of books.

"Too many books," she said. "I've put off building shelves for years; I finally decided I might as well get it over with."

"So you'll be dining in a library."

"If I can ever get my guests out of the kitchen."

She hung her jacket and umbrella on an old-fashioned hat rack near the front door, motioned for him to do the same, and then led the way to the kitchen. "I can offer you a tuna salad sandwich, chicken salad, or left-over chicken pot pie," she said setting the 7-eleven bag down on the counter. "The pot pie is *so-so;* it isn't home-made. I also have potato salad, cole slaw, and sliced roast beef. You can have beef on a bun if you like."

"No wonder Jacob drops by at mealtimes. I'll take beef on a bun and potato salad. Thank you."

"Have a seat." She nodded toward the table in the corner and then opened the refrigerator and pulled out beef wrapped in butcher paper, potato salad, a tomato and lettuce, and two kinds of mustard. "French's or Grey Poupon?" She asked, holding them up.

"French's." He sat down and looked around, taking in the white cabinets, red countertops, and the dishes imprinted with cardinals. She set about making sandwiches while she chatted about the weather, the latest issue with the library board of which she was a member, the neighbor next door who wouldn't mow his lawn. She stopped occasionally to wave the top of a bun or a mustard encrusted knife as she made a point, or she propped her hands on her hips while she went on about something, or she paused in her sandwich making to clean up bits and pieces of beef and tomato she'd dropped on the counter or floor. When she pulled a bag of chips from the 7-eleven bag, she changed the subject to problems with the workmen building her shelves.

"They were supposed to come Friday, but didn't show up," she said, ripping open the bag. "After a little *conversation* with them, they agreed to come yesterday."

Laskey could imagine the gist of the conversation if she'd persuaded them to come on a Saturday morning.

"The question is . . . ." She set a plate with sandwich and salad down in front of him, "Will they actually show up Monday to finish painting?" She propped her hands on her hips, and stared at the refrigerator. "What do I have here to drink? Hmmmmm. Water, coke, ginger ale? I can make coffee or tea. I think that's about it. Unless you want a gin and tonic."

"A coke, thanks. I'll have the gin and tonic another time."

She filled a glass with ice and handed it to him along with a can of coke. Then she set down a plate of food for herself and sat down.

"Do you know Rebekah's friend Totsy Love?" he asked.

"Not really." She flapped her napkin open and put it in her lap. "Totsy's the receptionist at Dr. Wallace's office, so I've seen her a few times. She's acted in several local drama productions. Friends keep trying to get me to go, but I can't think of many things as dreary as an amateur drama production." She took a bite of her sandwich and then wiped a fleck of mustard from her lips. "The local gossip is that Totsy went to New York planning to make it big on Broadway, didn't, so she came home to save money to take on Hollywood. And that's all I know about Totsy Love. We don't exactly move in the same circles."

He grinned. "Which circles do you move in?" He watched her eyes flicker with humor.

"The ones that offer at least a little hope for fun and entertainment. I play bridge fairly often. Do you play?"

"Oh, good lord! Do I play bridge?" He set his sandwich down and picked up his drink. "Imagine having four sisters and not knowing how to play. They used to drag me out of my room or away from wherever I was trying to hide, and sit me down to fill in whenever one of them was off somewhere."

"Were you awful at it?"

"I tried to be. Didn't do any good, though. They kept forcing me to play." The conversation had worked its magic, easing his tension by a few degrees. Finished with his sandwich, he pushed his plate aside. "This was exactly what I needed. A few minutes of good company. Thank you." He rose. "You'll forgive me if I hurry back to work?"

"You're worried," she said. "What have you found out?"

He looked down at his feet, hesitated, but then said, "Rebekah was on the plane."

"Oh, good God." Zuela stood up.

"I'm not sure what that means." He met her eyes. "The answers range from bad to worse."

"Are Fritz and Leah eating?" she asked after an interval of silence.

He frowned. He hadn't even considered that.

"Should I pop over with a casserole later in the afternoon?"

"Good idea. I'll meet you there around five?"

"Sounds good."

He gave a cursory wave and left.

Chapter Nine

Rain pattered on his windshield as Laskey pulled away from Zuela's and headed for the Goose Bend police station. He would have preferred to tuck himself away in the public library in Doylestown surrounded by the musty smell of books and a quiet punctuated only by the occasional beep of a computer, the squeak of a book cart, or the clunk of volumes being set back on shelves. He wanted to sit there undisturbed, and try to make sense of what had happened.

The rain had picked up by the time he pulled into the parking lot. He hurried inside, stopping in the lobby to brush away the wet from his face with a tissue. A few months earlier when he'd been assigned to a murder investigation in Goose Bend, Bump had made one of the offices available to him. He was sure the police chief wouldn't mind him using that office again. The dispatcher looked up from her book and nodded at him as he passed. He nodded back and then made his way down the hall.

The smell of popcorn and stale coffee drifted from the lounge at the far end along with two voices engaged in a friendly argument over the choice of a player the Phillies were bringing up from the minors next season. Ordinarily, he would have gone down and set them straight on the issue, making them aware that he'd received a bid from a minor league team. He would surely have made it to the majors had he been so inclined. Or so he liked to think. Spending his days on a diamond would certainly have evoked less stress than flailing about for the answer to what had happened to his friend's daughter.

He closed the door behind him, and the semi-calm that lunch with Zuela had brought, evaporated. Images he'd tried to keep away bullied themselves into his head: women buried in shallow graves; dismembered bodies; corpses rotting in the woods; young girls with lifeless eyes, their underwear stuffed in their mouths.

He took a few deep breaths, sat down, and reviewed the facts, rapping his knuckles on the desk as he enumerated each item. One: Rebekah arrived in Philadelphia as planned. Two: she got off the plane, made her way through the terminal to baggage claim, stopping once on the way for a stay of a little more than ten minutes in the ladies' room. Three: shortly after arriving at the carousel, she answered a phone call that made her smile. She left the area without her checked luggage and, instead of going in the direction of the trains, she exited to the outside of the terminal where passengers were picked up, or where they could get a taxi. Hotel vans also pulled up in the same area. A parking garage stood directly across from the exit. Either she'd gone back in later and retrieved her luggage, or someone else had gotten it.

And there was the phone call that hadn't shown up on Fritz's call log. He ran his forefinger over his lips. He felt fairly certain that Rebekah would have informed both her parents and Carlos had she lost her phone and gotten a new one.

He took his notebook from his pocket, found the number for TSA Agent Lewis Farley at the airport and dialed. When he began the inquiries into Rebekah's flights, he'd made it clear he might have additional questions, and that he'd call instead of making another trip to the airport. He hoped Farley didn't check and discover that he wasn't on an official case but was acting on his own.

"I need to know if a Carlos Vientos flew in from Argentina, arriving Saturday morning in Atlanta." He gave Farley the flight number. "And if he then took Delta flight 2273 from Atlanta to Philadelphia."

"It'll take a few minutes. Shall I call you back?"

"I'll wait." Laskey arched his back and stretched out his legs beneath the desk. When the waiting became too long, he rose and paced. Five times back and forth across the office. Six times.

"Carlos Vientos was on both flights," Farley said when he came back on the line. "Anything else?"

"Not right now. Thank you."

He opened his notepad to where he'd jotted down phone numbers of Rebekah's friends and realized the room had darkened and that the shower had turned into a downpour. The window was open a couple inches, allowing rain to spatter the window sill and puddle on the floor. He went over and closed the window and turned on the lights.

It was like a fishing expedition, he thought as he tapped out Dr. Jamie MacNeish's number. You never knew what you were going to get, if anything. But sometimes you caught a surprise. What was it that MacNeish had said to Fritz? Something about having limbs to amputate, guts to close, and head wounds to patch? After ten rings, Laskey supposed the good doctor was still busy amputating, closing, and patching. He didn't bother to leave a message.

He called Annemarie's number in Vienna. Presumably, she flew out of Amman about the same time as Rebekah. He had a sinking feeling she wouldn't know anymore than the others. He hung up when her voice mail came on.

Next, he tried Rebekah's high school friend, Totsy Love. If there were anyone who might know of a change of plans, Leah had said, it would be Totsy. Strike three — there was again no answer. He left another message, this time less polite. What kind of young woman didn't check her messages? He went over and leaned his forehead against a pane and closed his eyes. The glass cooled, calming him a mite, but that mite compared to a drip in a deluge. He knew his blood pressure was up, and Fritz's was surely through the roof.

His phone beeped. He straightened and read Jacob's message: *Called hospitals, etc. between Lansdale and end of line. Nothing.*

He hadn't expected Jacob to find her in a hospital; still, he was disappointed. He sighed, wiped away the smudge on the window where his breath had left a cloud, and then sat down and began calling Rebekah's college and medical school friends. There was *someone* out there who knew where Rebekah was.

Chapter Ten

J acob reviewed the list of chores taped to his refrigerator door. *Measure for shelves in study. Sand floors in spare bedrooms. Replace light bulbs. Tighten hinges on front door.* He grabbed a screwdriver from the tool drawer. Easiest chores first. Twenty seconds to tighten the hinges, and then . . . .

He threw the screwdriver back in the drawer, rattling it against the hammers, pliers, and wire cutters, and then slammed the drawer shut. He didn't feel like tightening, measuring, and sanding today. The house needed a mountain of repairs, but they'd have to wait.

He took the stairs, two at a time, went back into his study where he'd already spent a large part of the day, and rebooted the computer. His body pleaded for exercise, movement of any kind, even tightening screws on front doors, but he couldn't get his mind off Rebekah. He'd called every hospital and emergency facility between Lansdale and the end of the line and come up with nothing, and *nothing* left him restless, curious, dissatisfied, and determined to find *something.* What the bloody hell had happened to her?

He clicked on the Safari icon, and the search screen came on, but what was he searching for? He patted his palms against the desk, thinking, until finally, for lack of any other ideas, he typed *Doctors*

Without Borders, the English name for Medicin Sans Frontiere, in the search bar. A long list of sites came up, including the official site of Medicin Sans Frontiere, or MSF.

He chose the official site and read a few lines. Then he clicked on other sites, reading a little here and a little there. The articles impressed, or depressed, depending on how you viewed them. The accomplishments of the organization were nothing short of amazing, but the conditions the medical personnel worked under were enough to deter all but the strongest. Frequently, they worked around the clock, struggling with minimal supplies and drugs. Seeing the kinds of shortages they had to deal with, he understood why Rebekah would become involved in protests. The organization had insufficient personnel who were often in danger, particularly in the Middle East. A case in point: a strike in Kunduz, Afghanistan killed twenty-four patients, fourteen staff, and four patient caretakers. In Syria, just getting to the hospital was dangerous.

Several articles described protests against pharmaceutical companies organized by members of Doctors without Borders, including one against Pfizer. The corporation had refused to lower the cost of pneumonia vaccines in India where large numbers of children die from the disease. Jacob knew that even had Pfizer wanted to get nasty, there was no reason why they would have singled out Rebekah from among a slew of protestors.

MSF had also come out strongly against the Trans-Pacific Partnership. He knew the text of the TPP Treaty included provisions to dismantle public health safeguards and restrict access to price-lowering generic medicines for millions of people. One article pointed out how MSF relied on affordable generic medicines to treat a wide variety of diseases, including tuberculosis, malaria, HIV/AIDS, and a host of others. During his five-year tenure abroad, he'd seen ample evidence of how people in developing countries were required to pay for medicines out of pocket and thus went untreated because they couldn't afford them. He understood Rebekah wanting to protest prices of medicines, but what he didn't understand was her attraction to Carlos. Or to Totsy Love.

He got up, stretched, and went to the window overlooking the back of his property. The sky was still overcast, but the rain had stopped. The Canada geese who used the small triangular pond beyond his unkempt backyard as a stopping place on their twice-yearly migrations, had taken to the water. A stubbly field separated the pond from a shallow woods through which the Pumqua River meandered. Following the shape of the tree line, he ran his finger over a dusty pane leaving a wavy, horizontal streak.

Laskey had told him a little about the Herschmann family history. Fritz's grandfather, Joseph Herschmann I, and a friend had formed a pharmaceutical company in Vienna which produced, among other things, a widely used antibiotic. After the annexation of Austria by the Nazis, Fritz's father, Joseph Herschmann II, had been forced to hand over his share of the company to his Aryan partner. It was ironic that Rebekah would protest against the very industry in which her great grandfather had created a business and in which her grandfather had continued until his flight to America.

He sat down, logged off, and tipped his chair back to rest on its hind legs. Something had been niggling at him all day, and as hard as he tried to force it to the back of his mind, the question kept popping up. Was Rebekah who they thought she was, or had some hidden aspect of her character emerged, propelling her toward a goal her parents and friends had no clue about? Laskey claimed that Rebekah was smiling when she left the baggage area. Jacob imagined her running out, waving someone she knew down, and then dashing back inside to grab her suitcase as though the meeting had been planned from the start. As though . . . .

"Don't be ridiculous," he said aloud and slapped his desk. It was a stupid, stupid idea that Rebekah herself would have something to do with her own disappearance.

Chapter Eleven

Laskey stood on the Herschmann's top doorstep and watched Zuela trying to maneuver her Beetle into a space. His SUV stood in the driveway next to Carlos's BMW rental and, except for a Jeep Cherokee at the end of the block, there wasn't another vehicle parked along the street. Yet in spite of having a half-mile of curb to herself, she couldn't parallel park. With each try, she either had the rear end or the front end too far out, and she kept hitting the curb with whichever end wasn't jutting into the street. A maven at Shakespeare, maybe, but she definitely needed help in the parking department. Finally, she gave up and settled for stranding the Beetle four feet from the curb – a ticket-worthy distance. She slid out, her dress migrating up to expose a pair of shapely thighs, and opened the rear door where he assumed she'd stashed their dinner. Then she turned to face him, propped one hand on a hip, and extended the other in his direction, palm up. *Help needed.*

He strode toward her feeling guilty. He shouldn't be admiring a woman's legs while Rebekah's safety was in question, but it had been a gut reaction.

"Oh, wipe the grin off your face and give me some help," Zuela snapped when he came to where she was. "So, I can't park. I have other talents." She reached into the back seat, took out a Dutch oven, and handed it to him. "Curried lamb stew. I have poppy seed noodles to go with it." She leaned back in to get the noodles.

"You're still grinning like a jackass," she said as they made their way up the sidewalk.

"The glimpse of your legs made my heart sing." Actually, it was the smell of onions, curry, and lamb that made his heart sing. He realized how hungry he was.

"Don't be ridiculous. You're in sad shape if sixty-five year old legs make your heart sing. But I'll pretend the lie is a compliment."

Frivolity vanished when Fritz opened the front door and they stepped into a well-lit entry but an atmosphere of darkness.

"I spent the afternoon calling her friends," Laskey said in answer to Fritz's unspoken question. "Sooner or later . . . ." The despair on his friend's face silenced him.

Fritz nodded at the food containers. "Zuela, I'm glad to see you again. Especially since you're bringing offerings. We'd probably forget to eat otherwise."

"I thought that might happen," she said.

"You shouldn't have," Leah said, joining them in the foyer. She'd shed her housecoat for a skirt and blouse.

"Of course, we should have. But the stew needs warming." Zuela started toward the kitchen, the others in tow.

Laskey set the Dutch oven on the stove, and Zuela, after depositing the noodles on the counter, turned the eye to warm. "Jacob will be along any minute with salad and rolls."

"Oh, my." Leah put her fingers to her cheek. "You're all so good. I don't know what to say."

Fritz turned to Laskey. "I tried to think of anyone else Rebekah might have contacted about coming home, but other than the names I gave you already, I've drawn a blank. I tried Totsy again. And Annemarie Leitner. I finally got someone at the hospital in Amman, but the person knew nothing." He gave a rueful smile. "I even tried MacNeish again hoping he might be in a more helpful mood. He didn't answer."

"Did you get in touch with phone company?"

"Yes." Every muscle in Fritz's body was tense. "They claim there's nothing wrong with my call log; that there have been neither any outgoing nor any incoming calls since Wednesday evening.

A rapping came from the front door, and before anyone could go to open it, Jacob called out a hello and the sound of his footsteps clattered toward them. He walked into the kitchen with a grocery bag just as Carlos strolled in from the backyard.

After a brief nod at Jacob, Carlos directed his attention to Laskey. "My camera man went to Rebekah's apartment and talked to her neighbors. But they not know anything. I . . . ." Noticing Zuela, he stopped.

"Hi, I'm Zuela Hay." She extended her hand. "You're the fiancé, I gather. Glad to meet you." She turned to Jacob. "Make yourself useful and set the table. Carlos, you can help. Find some bowls for the salad."

Laskey waited for her to issue him orders, too, but when none were forthcoming, he leaned back against a counter to watch.

"And Leah, you sit down." Using the spoon she was about to stir the stew with, Zuela pointed to a stool.

"We've been sitting all day; we didn't know what else to do," Leah said and tears welled up, but heeding Zuela's command, she slid onto a stool. "You have no idea how much it helps having you all here." She took a napkin from a holder and wiped her eyes. "Bowls are in the cabinet to the left of the sink," she said to Carlos who was opening and closing cabinet doors.

Fritz wandered over to where Laskey stood and gave a little jerk of his head indicating a request to slip away. Amid Zuela's chatter, and the knocks and clangs of table setting and stew stirring, and the aromas of garlic and curry, they slipped across the hall to Fritz's den. Surrounded by shelves of books and miniature ships, they stood at the window looking out. A light wind had set an eddy of leaves whirling just outside. When the wind held its breath for a few moments, a mosaic of wet leaves pressed against the panes before beginning a slow, wavery slide downwards.

"Can the FBI help?" Fritz asked, watching a maple leaf meander down the glass.

"They can make their Identification Division and the FBI Laboratory facilities available, but right now we have nothing to identify and nothing for the laboratory. Bump has notified the state police and called every law enforcement office in this end of the state. He forwarded her picture along with a description. He also contacted the National Crime Information Center."

Ashen-faced, Fritz squeezed his eyes shut for a few seconds.

"Don't panic," Laskey said. But he, too, was struggling to fight off the cold talons of fear that clawed at his insides.

LASKEY PUSHED HIS PLATE ASIDE. Normally, he would have had a second helping, but concern had curbed his appetite. Leah and Fritz, their faces drawn in worry, hadn't been able to force down more than a few bites.

"Delicious stew." Fritz wiped his mouth and then set the napkin beside his plate.

"I'm sorry I couldn't eat a lot, but it's the best lamb stew I ever had," Leah said. "You have to give me the recipe. Is it complicated?"

"Easy as pie . . . ." Zuela began to explain the ingredients.

Laskey refolded his napkin and put it beside his plate. Thank goodness for Zuela and Jacob. Had it not been for them, they'd have been wallowing in gloom. Fritz and Leah sat at each end of the dining room table, he and Zuela on one side, and Jacob and Carlos on the other, a chair separating them since no one had bothered to remove the seat where Rebekah should have been. Carlos' arm rested on the chair's back. Both he and Jacob had their sleeves rolled up and the top button of their shirts unbuttoned. Carlos' dark hair was mussed, curling about his ears and flopping over his forehead as though he'd been running his hands through it all afternoon. Jacob's was combed and in place, a definite improvement over all the years he'd had to remind Jacob to comb his hair.

While Zuela described her crusade to find the right curry powder, Laskey leaned on his elbows studying Jacob. His godson had a healthy glow about him, and he'd maintained his athletic build, running, working-out, and slaving away on his new property. His blond hair was blonder and his blue-eyes seemed more blue as they looked out from a tanned face, thanks to the hours working in his yard. Why Jacob should be jealous of Carlos baffled him, yet there was something about Jacob's reaction that was niggling at him.

Zuela had moved on to naming the best grocery stores for baked goods. When there was an empty chair at the table what else could they do but talk about the quality of the curry, the best brand of poppy seed, and where to buy the freshest French bread? Jacob had described a wedding he attended in Rwanda where cows were given in exchange for the bride. Then he'd relived his trek in Rwanda to see the mountain gorillas made famous by Dian Fossey. Leah had responded to their chatter with nervous laughs and comments. Fritz, hiding behind a mask of deceptive attention, probably hadn't heard a word that was said. Nor was Carlos' attention real, Laskey guessed. Rebekah's fiance appeared to have an ear cocked to the conversation, but kept looking at the empty chair beside him.

Finally, Zuela stood up and began stacking plates. She handed the stack to Jacob who had also risen. "Carlos," she said, "Why don't you gather the utensils. You do know how to load a dishwasher, don't you. If not, then . . ."

Fritz's cellphone rang. A fire lit in his eyes as he grabbed the phone from the buffet.

"Hello," he said. . . . . . "Yes, this is Fritz Herschmann." . . . . "What? You have Rebekah?"

Laskey sprang up, slipped the phone from Fritz's hand, and hit the speaker button. Careful not to make any noise, he set the phone on the table.

". . . quite simple," a gritty bass voice was saying. "We'll send her back safe and sound. We just want a little something in return."

Leah gasped. Laskey's palm shot up, and he held the forefinger of his opposite hand to his lips, warning everyone to be quiet.

"You have a bunch of *bee-uuuuu-tee-ful* pictures hanging on your walls," the voice said, "and there are six of 'em that we want."

"Pictures?" Fritz croaked. He cleared his throat. "Pictures?"

"Deliver them, and you'll get your daughter back."

"You can have anything, just . . ."

"Get a paper and pen ready," the voice said. "I'll call back in five minutes. You won't call the police. You know what'll happen if you do." The connection went dead.

Laskey jotted down the number from the call log even though he knew it would be a throw-away phone and that the perpetrator would have a stack of untraceable SIM cards. When he looked up everyone had frozen. The silence was as dense as wood.

Finally, Leah sobbed. "She's alive; I was afraid . . . ."

Fritz let out a sound, something between a moan and the yowl of a wild animal, and covered his face.

Carlos looked stupefied; like he didn't believe what had just happened.

"Are you going to give Fritz a page from your notebook?" Zuela asked Laskey, her voice shaking. "Or should I go and look for something to write on?"

Relieved that someone other than himself still had an operative mind, he said, "Yes, find something. I'll make a second list here," he held up his notebook.

"I'll get paper from . . . ." Fritz headed toward the kitchen.

Jacob, still standing in the door between dining room and kitchen with a stack of dirty dishes, moved aside as Fritz grabbed pad and pen from the kitchen desk and then returned to the dining room. He handed them to Zuela. "I don't think I can write," he said.

Zuela took the pen and pad and then reached over to touch Leah on the arm. "It's going to be all right."

"Everyone sit down," Laskey said.

Jacob came back to the table, set the stack of dirty dishes at the place where he'd eaten, and slid into his chair.

Fritz moved restlessly about like an animal in a pen. "Someone has her. Why?" He held up his palms. "Who would . . . .? Why is he making us wait?"

"He'll want to limit his calls to a few seconds and knew you'd be in too much shock right now to get directions straight." Laskey saw that Carlos, too, was shaking. "It's going to be fine," Laskey said. "We just have to follow instructions."

Carlos looked puzzled. "Pictures? I can get money." His voice broke. "I can get money." He stood up, pushing his chair back violently so that it fell over. "Bloody bastards," he yelled and struck the air with his fist. Sucking in breaths and letting them out in huffs, he paced a few steps but then stopped to stand the chair back on its legs. "I'll call my father," he said. "He can wire money to HSBC bank in Philadelphia; we can . . ."

"Let's hear their demands first," Laskey said. "Sit down. When he calls back, we don't want him to know that a number of us are listening. You, too, Fritz. Sit down."

During the meal, Laskey had been seated to Fritz's left. After motioning for Zuela to take his place, he placed the phone on the table between her and Fritz. He stood a couple feet behind. His insides had turned to steel. Emotions, feelings, fear pushed aside, he was nevertheless aware of every movement, every sound, even the dripping faucet in the kitchen and the beating of moth wings against a window. The others – Zuela struggling to remain expressionless, Carlos looking like he had a bad case of food poisoning, Leah pressing her hands to her head like she'd been hit by a baseball bat, and Fritz overcome by an ice-cold-rigidity – kept checking their watches, measuring the passage of every half-second.

Only Jacob stared boldly back at him, his blue eyes narrowed, as though there was something he wanted to say, or something he *didn't* want to say but was trying to hold back.

The seconds ticked away. They'd asked for paintings, not money. Laskey searched for an answer to the anomaly, but the possible answers ricocheted off the sides of his brain like ping-pong balls. The phone – small, black, sinister – seemed alive, about to start breathing at any moment. He felt the same breathless anticipation swelling inside him he'd felt when standing on a cliff at Crater Lake years ago, about to plunge from a dizzying height into ice-cold water.

The phone rang, and everyone jumped.

"You have pen and paper?" The same gritty voice asked.

Fritz fisted his hands. "Let me speak to my daughter."

"After I give you the list, old man. Are you ready?"

Fritz drew in a quick breath and glanced at Zuela who nodded. "Yes. I'm ready," he said, his voice cracking.

"I want the two pastel studies by Kokoschka done in preparation for his painting, *Bride of the Wind*. . . ." The man sounded like he was reading from a list. ". . . and the two oil paintings by Kokoschka. I also want the two oils by Egon Shiele. One's a portrait, the other a landscape."

Laskey swallowed. The man had mispronounced *Kokoschka*, accenting the second syllable, Ko-KOSCH-ka, instead of giving all three syllables equal emphasis as a German speaker or someone knowledgeable of artists would have .

"You will wrap them in bubble wrap," the man continued, ". . . and pack them in a hard-sided suitcase. If you don't have one, you'll have to go out and buy one. I'll let you know . . ."

"Let me speak to Rebekah." Fritz had half-risen, one hand over his heart and the other flat on the table, propping himself up.

"Ten seconds," the man said after a pause.

The scraping of chair legs, a few breaths, and a sigh came from the phone. Then Rebekah, her voice shaky, said, "Dad?"

Leah's hands flew to her mouth.

"Rebekah, my darling girl," Fritz said, at the same time holding his hand out toward Leah even though he couldn't reach her at the other end of the table. "Tell me you're all right."

"The wind, Daddy. The wind. It's the . . . ."

"Yes, yes, I know. That and the two Schieles and the other two oils."

"But the *wind's* the one. The *Wind of the Bride*. Think . . ."

Then she made a little sound as though someone had shoved her aside.

"I'll be in touch tomorrow evening. Or the next day," the voice said.

The phone went dead.

"She's terrified." Fritz looked around at the others. "The *Wind of the Bride*, she said. She knows the name of the painting, but she got it backwards." Sweat flooded his face, oozing down his forehead, over his cheeks, down his neck.

"We have to involve law enforcement," Laskey said.

"No, no," Leah cried out. "You heard what they said."

Laskey looked at Fritz. "You know that's what we have to do."

Fritz shook his head. "Leah's right. We won't take that chance." His voice had risen. "Fuchs can have them all." He swept his arm around, indicating all the paintings that hung throughout his house. "It's him. Gustav Fuchs. He can have them all." He broke down in sobs.

Chapter Twelve

Laskey was examining the six works the kidnappers demanded when a squeaking from overhead drew his eyes to the ceiling. Fritz and Leah had gone upstairs. Zuela, who for some unknown reason kept a bottle of Ambien in her purse, had given each a tablet. Carlos had refused the sleeping pill when he escaped to the guest bedroom located above the living room, not to sleep apparently, but to pace.

Laskey hoped Fritz had taken the Ambien. His friend was in shock and needed a good sleep. "Gustav Fuchs can have them all," Fritz had said. Gustav Fuchs, Laskey knew, had been Joseph Herschmann's business partner in Vienna before the war. That Fritz's mind would go so far back in time to a man he'd never met, worried him. Until now, he'd never known Fritz to be anything other than logical, fore-sighted, and quick witted.

The two pastel studies for *Bride of the Wind* hung in a corner to the left of the archway between living room and foyer, placed there away from windows and direct sunlight to help preserve the colors. Laskey moved closer. When he was with the FBI, he'd been assigned to work with the Philadelphia Police Department when their property theft division asked for help. He'd taken an art history course at the Barnes Foundation in preparation for that roll. *Die Windsbraut,* sometimes translated as *The Tempest,* but more often as *Bride of the Wind,* was considered Kokoschka's masterpiece. The pastels in front of him were two of many practice sketches done before the artist rendered the final painting. The finished painting, which hung in The Kunsthaus Museum in Zurich, depicted a sleeping couple entwined in swirls of color. The couple in the painting represented Kokoschka himself and his infamous mistress, Alma Mahler, widow of Gustav Mahler, the composer.

He held up a forefinger to one of the studies and, without touching the piece, traced the swirls of color. The eddies of blue and green, according to art historians, represented Kokoschka's confusion and desperation over his relationship with Alma Mahler. By the time Kokoschka finished the painting, she'd lost interest in him, but he remained entranced by her and jealous of anyone else to whom she paid attention.

He tried to remember Rebekah's exact words. *The wind, Daddy. The wind. The wind's the one. The Wind of the Bride. Think . . ."* Had she been so frightened her brain was muddled when she tried to repeat the demands of the kidnappers? Or had she been trying to relay a message? Attempting to give them a clue to her location? The coils of color looked like a child's drawing of a tornado. His guess was that she wasn't too far away, but he couldn't relate the sworls in the drawings to a site where the wind was any different than any other place in southeastern Pennsylvania. *The wind. The wind's the one.* His instinct told him that, although frightened, she was thinking clearly and trying to convey a message.

He turned to examine the two paintings by Schiele hanging on the wall opposite the entry. In one, tortured trees stood at the top of a pyramid-shaped hill. The other portrayed a man with dark hair angling in all directions and head tilting forward to glare at the observer from beneath bushy black brows. A few years ago, the portrait had hung in the dining room. "I don't like that man," Rebekah said one evening when he'd been invited to dinner. "He looks like he's ready to cut someone's throat."

Both paintings were done mostly in cool colors: ultramarine,

Payne's gray, and Naple's yellow. There were also a few touches of what looked to be burnt umber. He was only guessing. He'd acquired a fair knowledge of artist's paints, but his identification of color was in no way on a par with that of an artist.

The two Kokoschka oils, one a landscape, the other a portrait, hung over the sofa he'd been sitting on earlier. The landscape pictured blue-green, jagged mountains thrusting into a swirly sky. Along with shades of orange, Kokoschka had used the same blue-green in both sky and mountains. The sun, at the half-way point, was surrounded by a corona of teal. Remembering one critic's assessment of Kokoschka's color palette, Laskey almost smiled but caught himself and pressed his lips together. Hopefully, he'd be able to smile another day, but not yet. The critic had accused Kokoschka of . . . *brewing up his paints from poisonous putrescence and the fermenting juices of disease.* The critic went on to say. . . *the artist smeared the paints on like salve, allowing them to crust scabiously.*

The second painting portrayed a white-faced man, his face distorted, and his body half-turned with an unnaturally large hand held in front of his chest. An example, Laskey knew, of how Kokoschka took liberties with physical likenesses in order to convey the suggestion of mood.

The distorted faces, the *scabious* paint, the tortured trees – these would be ridiculed by most people in Goose Bend. He'd venture to say many had never even been inside an art museum. But someone who knew the Herschmanns also knew the value of their collection.

The crime had to be a local production. The gritty-voiced man, with his drawn-out *bee-uuuu-tee-ful* dripping with sarcasm, had revealed that he didn't think the paintings beautiful at all, but rather ridiculous. He must either have seen them himself or knew someone who had. He'd also given himself away with his pronunciation. In most of the country, people pronounced the second syllable of beautiful as *uh*, while people in southeastern Pennsylvania pronounced it either *tee* or *dee*. *Buuu-dee-ful.*

A question had been bothering him ever since the phone call. The shock, the commotion, and the waiting for the second call had, at first, relegated the issue to the back of his mind . But now the puzzle hit him full force: Why bother with kidnapping when the paintings could so easily have been stolen?

Chapter Thirteen

Laskey left the outside lights on so he could find his way to his car, closed the Herschmann's front door behind him, and was about to descend the front steps when the sensor light on the roof flicked on to illuminate a man carring a battered suitcase coming up the walk. The man, who Laskey guessed to be in his thirties, stopped when he saw Laskey and stared at him for a few seconds and then came hesitantly toward him. Curious, Laskey waited. When the man came close, the smell of his rumpled clothes suggested he'd been wearing them a few hours too long. His reddish-blonde hair stuck up in tufts, and freckles covered a sunburned face blotched with the uneven tan of the fair-skinned. A birthmark approximately the size of a quarter and shaped vaguely like Australia, hovered above his left eyebrow.

"Yer not Fritz Hersc hmann, are ye?" the stranger asked.

Laskey, unable to place the accent because the man mumbled, descended the steps to stand beside him. "I'm Detective William Laskey."

"Ahhhh," the man breathed out a long sigh. "And where is Rebekah? Did she get home?"

"And you are . . . .?" Neither Fritz nor Leah had mentioned

anything about expecting company, yet here was a stranger with a suitcase, poised to walk into their house.

The stranger extended his hand. "I'm Dr. James MacNeish. I work with Rebekah."

"Ah, the infamous Dr. MacNeish." Laskey shook his hand.

"Infamous?" MacNeish raised his eyebrows.

"Fritz told me about his conversation with you yesterday."

MacNeish looked down at his shoes and shuffled his feet. "He caught me at a bad time. I'm sorry; I was rude." His face averted, he looked at Laskey from the corners of his eyes. "But you did'na answer my question. Is Rebekah home?"

Laskey shook his head and felt a bit of vindication when a frown worried itself across MacNeish's brow. "How is it that yesterday you were in Amman, Jordan, too busy reattaching limbs to give Fritz thirty seconds," Laskey asked, ". . . and today you're on this side of the Atlantic standing at his front door?"

"Got a call from the American Embassy." MacNeish was mumbling again and looking off into the night. He shifted his suitcase from one hand to the other. "They said there was some sort of problem with her not showing up when she was supposed to. I have to be in Atlanta for a meeting at the CDC in a couple days, so I bribed someone to cover for me in Amman and grabbed an earlier flight."

Something about the way MacNeish wouldn't look him directly in the eyes, bothered Laskey. Not to mention that after being rude to Fritz, he'd shown up at Fritz's front door, suitcase in hand and without so much as a *Maybe I'll drop by after flying in from half a world away*. "How did you get here?" His Sequoia and Carlos' rental car were the only vehicles parked in the driveway and there were no cars at the curb.

"Took a bus from the airport. Where *is* Rebekah?" MacNeish raised a palm.

"No idea." Laskey had his feet firmly planted and his hands dug into his pockets, waiting for MacNeish to vindicate himself for showing up unannounced at bedtime. To suddenly abandon a vital job to fly across an ocean to check up on one of your supervisees didn't strike him as normal behavior even using a meeting at the CDC as an excuse. "When did you last talk to her?"

MacNeish ran his hand over his neck. "I had'na talked to her much recently. I uh . . . . Well, I'll go in and say a few words to her parents. Then I'll find a hotel." He let out a long sigh. "I've probably slept all of ten hours in the past week. Could'na sleep on the plane. I'm afeerd my mind has shut down."

"Scots," Laskey said. "You're a Scot."

MacNeish nodded. "From Aberdeen. But I went to med school in Chicago. There *is* a hotel around here, isn't there?"

"Afraid not. And you can't go in now. They're getting ready for bed."

"No hotel?" MacNeish turned his head first one way and then the other as though he expected to find a Holiday Inn on the darkened streets of a residential neighborhood. "There must be . . . ."

"Afraid not." He was rather enjoying the vexed look on MacNeish's face.

"Then, I guess. . . . a bus back to the next town where there *is* a hotel."

"Don't think there's another bus tonight." He didn't have a clue when the buses ran but the man deserved a bit of tormenting. Then he relented; MacNeish looked exhausted and ready to cry. "I guess we have to figure out what to do with you."

"Who is it?" Fritz's voice came from the half open door. He wore a plaid housecoat and held a glass of water.

MacNeish walked up the steps and held out his hand. "I'm James MacNeish."

Fritz shot Laskey a look of puzzlement as he shook MacNeish's hand.

"I'm sorry, about our conversation the other day," MacNeish said. "So sorry. I din'na know what . . . . I was sort of . . . . Well, I'm on my way to Atlanta and thought I'd check up on things here. See if Rebekah's okay, and . . ." He shrugged.

"Please . . . come in." After throwing another look at Laskey, Fritz opened the door wider and stepped aside for the two to enter.

"What's going on?" Leah appeared, also wearing a housecoat and carrying a glass of water.

"This is Dr. James MacNeish." Fritz, who had been studying MacNeish from head to foot, lifted his hand toward their visitor.

"Didna' know I was going to be so late getting here, and I'm right sorry." MacNeish set his suitcase down. "I had in mind to check up on Rebekah and then find a hotel, I . . . ." He was doing something with his right hand, moving the fingers as though exercising or stretching them. "I understand she didna' come home." Still manipulating his fingers, he looked first at Leah and then at Fritz for an explanation.

"He needs a place to stay," Laskey interjected.

"He's welcome to stay here," Leah said, looking doubtfully at Fritz.

"Yes, yes, he's welcome." Fritz's voice lacked the ring of sincerity.

"I'm sure he's grateful for the offer," Laskey said, "but I'll take him to Jacob's.

Jacob won't mind offering his spare bedroom." He expected MacNeish to say that he was indeed grateful, but the only expressions the Scot revealed were of relief and exhaustion.

A stair squeaked and everyone turned to see Carlos half-way down the flight, gaping at MacNeish.

MacNeish froze. "Vientos," he said finally. "Good to see ye again."

From his tone, Laskey knew MacNeish meant the opposite.

"Well . . . , I'm surprised to see you here, Dr. MacNeish," Carlos said.

MacNeish explained that he was on his way to the Center for Disease Control in Atlanta.

"Really?" Sarcasm dripped from Carlos' mouth.

"Yes, really." MacNeish's reply was equally cynical.

"Good night, everyone," Laskey said quickly and then turned to MacNeish. "We need to get going. Jacob will be going to bed soon."

THEY RODE WITHOUT TALKING. In his peripheral vision, Laskey saw MacNeish occasionally nodding off but then jerking his head up, trying to stay awake.

"Let me guess," Laskey said, breaking the silence as he turned into the lane leading to Jacob's house, ". . . you and Carlos are not enamored of each other."

"Imagine having more medical emergencies to take care of than ye can ever begin to handle and a journalist getting in the way," he said after an interval. He clamped his mouth shut then and looked out the window into the dark.

There was no point in quizzing him now. After the Scotsman got a few hours' sleep, they'd talk. And the questions were mounting. For one, Fritz had said MacNeish was an orthopedic surgeon, so why was he attending a conference at the Center for Disease Control? And question two: it would have been to MacNeish's advantage, and that of Doctors without Borders, to have a journalist draw attention to the plight of the camps and the need for more personnel and more supplies, so why the antogonism? Mainly, why had MacNeish shown up here? Something about the disheveled Scotsmen lacked authenticity.

THE SNORING all but shook the rafters in the guest bedroom adjacent to his study where Jacob had been preparing for a meeting the following morning. MacNeish had taken a shower lengthy enough to be worthy of Guinness Record consideration, probably using up all the hot water. After showering, he'd walked straight from bathroom to bed, and without closing the door, dropped onto the bed. Jacob heard the *whummmp* of body hitting mattress and the squeak of bed springs as the Scotsman's body impacted. He was fairly sure MacNeish's snores started before his head hit the pillow.

Daisy Mae, blissfully indifferent to the seismic rumbles coming from the guest bedroom, lay curled up in a nearby chair.

"How you can sleep through that astounds me," Jacob said to the cat as he tiptoed over to close the door of the guest bedroom.

Then realizing that even a cement mixer probably wouldn't wake the man, he didn't bother muting his steps when he returned to his computer.

An hour ago, having an overnight guest had been the farthest thing from his mind. Busy finishing preparations for his meeting, the beam of headlights coming up his lane had brought his work to a halt. It wasn't surprising to have Laskey show up at a late hour, but when he went downstairs to meet him he'd been amazed to see Laskey escorting a freckled-faced, reddish-blonde-haired stranger to his backdoor. Laskey had made short shift of explaining the situation and then driven off leaving MacNeish drooping in the middle of the mudroom like the unwatered ficus on the kitchen counter.

The Scotsman needed watering of the soap and shower variety, Jacob noted as he took a whiff of clothes odorific from many hours traveling. After depositing MacNeish's suitcase in the spare room and showing him the shower, Jacob returned to his work.

He put the final touches on his report, but instead of logging off, he typed "Palestinian Refugee Camps" in the search line. A long list of sites came up. He clicked on an article called "If Americans Knew" which compared the camps to a medieval ghetto with no streets, sidewalks, gardens, patios, trees, flowers, plazas, or shops. Three generations of Palestinians, the writer claimed, had been born and lived in one or two bedroom houses so poorly constructed they had to lean against each other to keep from falling down. The walkways through the camps were nothing more than narrow alleys skirting open sewage ditches. Still, Jordan had provided a place for the refugees, taking on what the rest of the world wouldn't. The article went on to describe the medical issues in the camps where communicable diseases proliferated. And now refugees from Syria flooded field hospitals and emergency units adding more work than they could handle.

Jacob leaned back, clasping his hands behind his head. Laskey had shot MacNeish a hard look as he left. Tomorrow, the poor man was going to fall victim to a merciless interrogation with Laskey's dark eyes boring through his freckles right down to his soul. Jacob guessed the Scotsman had been too tired to notice, but Jacob knew that look well. It had been enough to keep *him* on the straight and narrow as a youth spending time with Laskey. It took one time – just one little embroidered fact about homework, or rather the lack of homework – for him to discover his godfather could go from teddy bear to grizzly in a flash.

There were two things Laskey didn't abide: one was rudeness and the other lying. He didn't kn ow if Laskey's intolerance for lying was the Quaker in him, or if it was just *him*. MacNeish had committed sin number one when Fritz called him; he was going to have to do some groveling on that account. Heaven help him if Laskey caught him committing sin number two.

Chapter Fourteen

F ritz slipped out the front door, closing it softly behind him. He
was in his pajamas, but they were mostly concealed by his raincoat. Leah had taken the Ambien and was out cold, but Carlos
might still be awake, and he didn't want Carlos chasing after him to
see that he was alright.

He moved quickly away from the front door lights and the
sensor light on the roof, but slowed when he came to the sidewalk.
Goose Bend's street lights were spaced far apart, so he could walk
shielded by semi-darkness. The stars twinkled as though nothing
had happened, and the errant moon floated overhead, callous in its
orbit when he'd been knocked from his.

Suddenly cold, but not knowing if it was the temperature or his
fear, he drew the lapels of his raincoat closer as he passed the Patter-
son's colonial next door. Laskey had given him a disbelieving look
when he spit out the name, *Gustav Fuchs,* and then grilled him, trying
to find a clue as to who else might have invented the horrific scheme
— A neighbor? Employee? A casual acquaintance? Fritz had
clamped his mouth shut and shaken his head in answer to his
friend's queries. Though paralyzed by shock, he'd known from the
beginning that the answer lay on another continent. Gustav Fuchs

was the one person who thought he had a right to the paintings; the one person who would arrange a fiendish plan to get them. But why now? Why not twenty years ago? Or thirty, or forty, or ten? Had what was happening in America spurred Gustav to act now? The white supremacist demonsrations? The swastikas painted on churches? Mosques vandalized? His father would be heart-broken to know about the hate that was being relived.

Fritz let the raincoat fall open. He was hot now. Maybe it was the walking. Or maybe it was anger at having to admit that Laskey was half right when he insisted that someone who knew them, someone nearby, was involved. Gustav Fuchs was responsible, he was sure of that, but, yes, Fuchs had recruited someone to carry out his vile plan. Someone who knew Rebekah's travel plans.

Without breaking his tempo, Fritz clasped his hands together, hard. His shoulders tightened and a pain shot up the back of his neck. He almost stumbled on an uneven slab of pavement, but caught himself in time. He needed to be careful and keep himself in one piece. Attention had to be focused on Rebekah's release, not on a broken arm or knocked out tooth.

Someone who knew them. It wouldn't be his neighbors. How could he, even for a minute, think one of them would align himself with the devil? Widow Greeley across the street? The Pattersons next door? The Meyers? The Smiths, whose red-shuttered house he was just passing? They all knew what he had on his walls, though he doubted they knew the value of the collection. It was absurd to even consider them.

At the end of the block, he stepped off the curb into a puddle, soaking the hems of his pajamas, but he crossed the intersection anyway, ignoring the cold, wet cotton clinging to his ankles.

It was equally absurd to suspect his employees. Yet Laskey had questioned him about them. Eli, Bay, Erika, and all the others.

Eli Fluck was his manager. Twenty-five years younger than Fritz, yet already bald, Eli started work in the factory as a mechanic taking care of the machines. Fritz had made him manager twelve years ago. A thin, rangy man with eyes like two pieces of dark chocolate, Eli had proven to be able, dependable, and hard-working. A strict

Mennonite, he declined wine when he and his wife were invited to gatherings Fritz and Leah hosted for the employees. Someday, the factory would belong to Eli. Fritz had already worked out a plan for him to purchase the business by having Eli remit a percentage of the profits to him over a fifteen year period.

Laskey had even questioned him about Erika Schwarzkopf, his accountant and business manager. She'd worked in the business for almost as long as Fritz. Like him, she was the child of Viennese refuges. Her father hadn't been guilty of the sin of being Jewish, but was rather an academic out of favor with the Nazi regime. Fritz gave a wry smile. Erika was what people classified as a "character." Gruff, sometimes plain-spoken to the point of being tactless, her work uniform consisted of a pair of khakis, a man's pin-striped shirt, and a dark, brown corduroy blazer. Or in the case of warm weather, no jacket, and the pin-striped sleeves rolled up to her elbows. She wore the same outfit to social gatherings and funerals. He imagined if Erika had been invited to the Vienna Opera Ball, she'd show up in khakis and corduroy blazer. The locals knew Erika to be the fond and indulgent grandmother of eight, otherwise they might have inferred from her bearing and mode of dress that she was of a different orientation.

Bay Hedge, the wiry, dark-haired chief candy maker, called *The Sultan of Sweet* by the employees, had been with him almost as long as Eli. Bay gave the impression that his main reason for living was making candy. Becoming involved in a kidnapping/art theft scheme would be the furthest thing from his mind. As it would be from the minds of any of his employees.

He'd come to the end of the second block. He didn't cross over, but stood for a few moments, heavy-footed, slump-shouldered, and adrenaline-drained. The thing to do now was to follow instructions. Deliver the pictures. Let Fuchs have the accursed things. Let Fuchs twist a knife in his back, punishing him for something that happened years ago that had nothing to do with either of them.

He turned around. He'd go back, take the Ambien, and hope for the blessing of a dreamless night.

Monday

October 22

Vienna, Austria

Gustav Fuchs pushed the chessmen to the center of the board, scrambling the opposing pieces on the black marble and green malachite squares. He took great pleasure in mixing up the chessmen and then arranging them back in their places, first lining up the yellow brass opponents and, after polishing them with a clean handkerchief, the black marble pieces. The blacks were his. If only humans could be arranged in their proper places as easily as chess pieces.

He lined up the yellows, saving the queen for last, and then took the handkerchief from his pocket, flapped it in the air to unfold it, and began polishing his blacks. He buffed the players that belonged in the back row, holding each piece up to the lamp to ascertain that fingerprints had been rubbed away, and that each chessman shimmered in the light. When the blacks had been set back in place, he rested his elbows on the armrests and admired the back-row pieces, the king and queen, the bishops, the castles, the knights – the main players. The ones that, in real life, pulled the strings, issued the orders, planned the battles.

This was the week of the pawns, however — his living pawns who would take back what was rightfully his. He didn't know each personally, but he'd chosen his pawn-in-charge well, trusting him to find the right players. He'd been assured there was enough greed and resentment among those chosen to guarantee success, and that the rewards were ample enough to insure that the plan worked. Lawmen might eventually catch and prosecute the pawns for theft, kidnapping, and murder. Let them be caught. They were only pawns, after all. But no one would be able to touch him.

His only regret was that he couldn't see the look on Joseph Hershmann's face. Like him, Joseph would be an old man now. Fuchs sighed. Unlike him, with his shaky hands and legs that no longer supported him, Joseph would be healthy and stalwart, as always. Fuchs grimaced. Joseph had been blessed with a charismatic personality and bestowed with physical and intellectual gifts denied to himself. Then, as though that weren't enough, in a quirk of fate Joseph had been elevated to partnership in the company while he had to stand aside. He'd raged at the unfairness.

He'd lost track of Joseph. By the time it dawned on him that a computer could be used for spying as well as for data retrieval and file storage, his hands had failed him. His nerve-impaired fingers pecking at the keyboard had the same result as a tornado striking a feather warehouse. His son Karl, in an unreasonable edict, had given his secretary/nurse/jailer instructions not to do research for him on the subject of his old partner, justifying his command with the claim that picking at old wounds was detrimental to his health.

Then the girl showed up. Annemarie Leitner. Daughter of one of the company's research consultants. He chuckled at his good fortune.

In spite of Karl's not wanting him to pick at old wounds, his son had arranged for the driver to take him to Pöchlarn tomorrow. He'd go back to where it all started and savor the contemplation of righting the past. The Jew needed to be put in his place.

Chapter Fifteen

Daisy Mae had mastered the art of untying one shoe while he tied the other so, leaving the cat imprisoned in the house, Jacob had sought refuge on his back steps to put on his running shoes. He finished, stood up, and stretched in preparation for his morning run. Gold-tinted ripples flickered on the pond. A half-dozen geese, their feathers burnished by the same rays, floated lazily near the shore. Normally, the site would have put a spring in his step, but this morning his feet dragged as he began his run, every step heavy with the weight of Rebekah's kidnapping.

Thirty minutes later he burst in from his run, sweaty and out-of-breath, to find MacNeish seated beside the cold fireplace. Jacob swiped the back of his hand across his brow to wipe away perspiration and went to join MacNeish. He'd neglected to sweep away the ashes from the past several fires so the smell of soot was strong.

The Scotsman rose and smiled shyly. Definitely more civilized looking, Jacob thought, propping his forearms on the back of a rocking chair to catch his breath. Clean shaven, body odor replaced with the smell of menthol, hair sleeked down so that it no longer sprang out like he'd walked in out of a hurricane, MacNeish wore clean khakis and a pin-striped dress shirt, though both could have benefitted from the use of an iron.

"Din'na know if I thanked ye properly afore, for havin' me here," MacNeish said, looking doubtfully at Jacob. "Probably should'na shown up at the Herschmann's like that, but I was right worried about Rebekah."

Jacob moved around and sat down, motioning for his visitor to do the same. "Glad to have you, MacNeish."

"Call me Jamie."

"All right, then. *Jamie.*" Reaching down to pick up Daisy Mae who had padded over to brush against his legs, Jacob realized how lonely he'd been with Kate in Italy. What happened yesterday had intensified the scourge of solitude. "Actually, I'm glad to have company," he said. "My girlfriend's away for six months. I'd gotten used to having someone around to talk to other than a kitten."

"Away?" MacNeish cocked his head.

"In Florence. Studying art. You're on your way to Atlanta, I understand?"

"Conference at the CDC. But I din'na feel much like going. Not with Rebekah . . ." He frowned down at the fireplace. "She was quite anxious to get home. I can'na imagine she'd of wandered off somewhere without telling anyone."

"I know you work for Doctors without Borders, but what kind of doctor are you?"

"Surgeon. Mostly, I patch and re-attach."

"I guess there's plenty of that to do over there." Why was a surgeon going to a conference at the Center for Disease Control? "Want coffee?" He set Daisy Mae on the floor.

"I'll be right glad for a big one. Thank you. Loaded with cream if you have it. Otherwise, . . . however." He shrugged.

A couple minutes later, Jacob handed a mug to MacNeish.

MacNeish took a few gulps and then wiped his mouth with the back of his hand. "Maybe Rebekah never left Amman. Although, I can'na imagine why."

"She arrived at the airport Thursday as she was supposed to. Laskey saw her on the security videos."

MacNeish stared at him. Then he propped his elbows on the chair arms and tilted forward, frowning into the cold fireplace.

Jacob sat down and sipped his coffee. MacNeish seemed different today. Last night, he'd been abrupt, disconnected. Due to exhaustion, no doubt, but Jacob guessed there was something else. Or maybe it was just a case of his imagination running wild.

"Sometimes Rebekah stops off in Vienna and stays with Annemarie for a couple days before traveling on," MacNeish said, still frowning at the fireplace. "But she would'na have this time. Not with Carlos coming." He looked up at Jacob. "Annemarie Leitner is from Vienna. She's an epidemiologist like Rebekah." He sighed and leaned back in his chair. "I wonder if ye could do me a favor. I, uh, . . . well, I'd like to rent a car. I won't bother the Herschmann's this morning, but thought I might go out for a drive."

Jacob supposed it was natural that MacNeish didn't want to be stuck alone in the country all day, but surely he didn't come here to *go out for a drive*. "I'll call Aunt Zuela. She doesn't have to be at work as early as I do. I'm sure she can drop you off at a rental agency on her way in to Philadelphia."

"Zuela? Don't think I've heard that name before."

"You haven't seen one like her before either."

MacNeish raised his eyebrows.

"She isn't really my aunt." Jacob rose and headed toward the kitchen where he'd left his phone. "She's my mother's best friend and a Shakespearean scholar. I'll let you discover the rest for yourself."

"A Shakespearean scholar? Shit. Bloody bastard fucked up my academic record first year at uni. I wish the English would keep the arse to themselves."

Jacob smiled. He hadn't particularly liked Shakespeare either. "You might want to keep your opinion of Shakespeare to yourself around Aunt Zuela."

He leaned against the counter, while he waited for her to answer her phone. Maybe he'd been around Aunt Zuela too long. He was getting as bad as she was about concealing worry beneath a barrage of banter. And MacNeish? He handled *his* by going out for a drive?

JACOB WAS ABOUT to climb into his Subaru when Aunt Zuela pulled in next to him. She lowered the window and leaned her head out. "Is he ready?"

"He's in there having a last cup of coffee."

"I told him I'd be here at seven sharp. My class is at nine, so I need to get going."

Jacob waved at the window where he knew MacNeish was watching and then walked over to the Beetle. "Laskey hinted at bad blood between MacNeish and Carlos," he said. "He wanted me to keep my ears open. Maybe you can do the same. You're good at that."

"Maybe Dr. Jamie MacNeish dislikes Carlos for the same reason you do."

"Which is?"

"How the hell should I know? You're the one who prickles around him. Must be jealousy over those sweltering, Latin good looks. Ahhh, here he is." She nodded at MacNeish coming down the backsteps. "Good morning, Dr. Jamie MacNeish," she called out.

"Prickle?" Jacob said, ignoring MacNeish's approach . "Don't be ridiculous. I don't prickle."

"You do. You need to calm that jealousy while you're off suing fracking companies this morning."

"You're suing fracking companies?" MacNeish had come even with them. "I din'na ken you were that kind of lawyer."

Jacob stepped back from the car window. "Not suing yet, but I will be."

"Are ye not taking your life in your hands when you tangle with those beasties?"

"He's a brave and fearless warrior," Aunt Zuela said. "Climb in MacBeth. Or MacDuff. Or MacNeish. Whoever you are. Those

Scots names all start to sound alike after a while. If you want to rent a car this morning we need to get going. Otherwise, you'll wind up having to sit through my Shakespeare class."

"As long as you na' teaching *MacBeth*. I hated it." He gave Jacob a sardonic grin and went around to the passenger side and climbed in.

Jacob stood aside to watch her barely miss his vehicle as she turned the Beetle around and then roared away with a screech of gears and a rattle of tires against gravel. Only Aunt Zuela could *roar away* in a Beetle.

What was Dr. Jamie MacNeish going to do with a rental car all day, he wondered. *Just tool around*, he claimed when Jacob asked where he planned to take a drive to. *Not exactly in the right frame of mind for sightseeing, but I have to keep busy. Can'na just sit here and wait.* How could he even afford a rental car? If what he'd read about the salaries of MSF doctors was true, a rental car ate up half a week's earnings. But maybe the good doctor had another source of income.

Chapter Sixteen

Laskey pushed through the swinging doors of the Doylestown Public Library, grateful that it opened at seven. He walked past the circulation desk, waved at Miss Berry, the librarian, and then headed for his special nook tucked away in a corner of non-fiction. When his thoughts blew in a hundred different directions, when the pounding of his pulse needed to be reined in, when fear had to be suppressed in favor of logic, the one place he could count on regaining equilibrium was in the quiet and order of the library. Surrounded by books and the smell of dusty shelves and old wood-work, his thoughts usually settled into clarity.

And he needed clarity this morning; he needed to separate what happened to Billy Thatcher from what had just happened to Rebekah. Billy had been the reason Laskey had defied his mother's and his grandfather's religion to join the FBI where he was required to take an oath and carry a gun. He no longer carried a gun; the one they'd issued him was locked in a safe. The teachings of the Quakers had reasserted themselves. But back in the beginning, he'd carried a gun.

As he passed through the 500's, he pulled a few books from the shelf, took them to what he had come to regard as *his* table, and placed them strategically to make it appear as though several people were using the table. He didn't want anyone joining him. He set the yellow legal pad he'd brought with him beside the books. The other thing he brought with him wasn't so easy to put down. Fritz, one of the most logical, methodical, and intelligent people he knew had attributed what had happened to an old man living on a different continent. There was a good chance Gustav Fuchs wasn't even alive. Fritz appeared to have been shocked into a momentary loss of reason, and that frightened Laskey.

He sat down, closed his eyes, and let his chin rest on his clavicle. *Silent waiting.* That's what Quaker worship was based on and, as an adult, *silent waiting* had provided him answers innumerable times. As a boy he'd detested it. Every week he'd gone with his family to the Friends Meeting House, and every week he hoped it would be the Sunday no one stood up to speak. The sooner they left the meeting house, the sooner they ate, which meant joining the baseball game down the street in time to be one of the captains who got to choose up sides. Or it meant not getting left behind when the others ran off to the woods beyond their street to explore a pretend jungle. Most Sundays, luck went against him and he had to endure five, six, seven, sometimes more speakers, while wriggling impatiently in his chair. At least until his mother ended the wriggling by pinching his arm. The pinch carried with it an unspoken threat: *be still, or spend the afternoon at home without friends,* and he knew the threat would be kept. His father was no help. His father had grown up as a Presbyterian but deferred to his mother in things religious.

Laskey never ceased to be surprised how as an adult he'd come to value what he hated as a child: sitting quietly. His grandfather had once marched him into the meeting house when he'd done something unacceptable, and demanded he sit there, *quietly,* and when, and *only* when, the Inward Light spoke to him about his wrong-doing, was he allowed to leave.

The Inward Light didn't put in an appearance that day. When he could no longer stand to sit on the hard seat of an old Windsor chair, kicking his legs back and forth, probably putting nicks in the chair legs, he went in search of his grandfather.

"The Inward Light has come to you. What do you plan to do?" His grandfather, a tall muscular man with a salt and pepper mustache and eyebrows to match, was leaning on the shovel he'd been using to turn the soil in the garden.

Laskey caught himself before replying, "Cease and desist." Instead, he said something along the lines of being misguided, and that he would never do it again. His grandfather was a fair man, hard-working, honest to a fault, and loving in his own way. It was at that moment that Laskey decided his grandfather's commitment to what was right had more influence on keeping him on the straight and narrow than sitting quietly while waiting for the Inner Light to show up.

He didn't expect an answer today, but maybe enlightenment as to what to do next. He'd dealt with kidnappings before, but this one was different. Not just because an unusual ransom had been demanded, but because he'd known Rebekah since she was little. Bright, inquisitive, and well-behaved to a fault, he'd thought her the ideal child, unlike Jacob who managed to stumble across trouble everywhere. Or maybe trouble itself chased him down. He loved Jacob, but damn, Jacob had given them all gray hairs and sleepless nights. At various times, he'd accidentally set the town on fire, crippled the district's school buses by stuffing potatoes in the tail pipes, and switched mail from box to box in his neighborhood incurring the wrath of the U.S. Postal Service. The list went on. But Jacob had turned out fine in the end.

In spite of Rebekah's being what he considered average looking, she'd won the affection of a handsome man. An author. A journalist. That Carlos appreciated and loved a woman for her character and intellect impressed the hell out of him. His Quaker upbringing had taught him that women were equal in every way, and that those who treated them merely as objects of desire were faulty and selfish. He had great difficulty understanding a culture that didn't believe the same. What the world needed right now, he decided, were more Quakers, an admission his grandfather would have loved to hear.

What *he* needed right now was to know who called Rebekah at the airport, along with the other question: If she'd lost her phone and bought a new one, why didn't she inform her parents and Carlos?

The professional calm he'd mastered as a requirement for his job had begun to crack. His head throbbed. His hands sweated and shook. People made mistakes when they were too closely involved, hence the reason for doctors not operating on their own families, but since Fritz and Leah refused the police's help, he was forced to make a choice. The first was to do nothing. That wasn't going to happen. The second was to ignore their wishes and involve the police anyway. He couldn't do that. He'd already sent Bump a text asking him to refrain from doing anything, promising to call later with an explanation.

Carlos had echoed Laskey's arguments and tried to convince the Herschmann's to involve law enforcement. "Please, please, let them help," Carlos kept saying. Finally, after giving Laskey a helpless look, he'd escaped to the dark of the back yard to puff on the Dunhill he'd been nervously fingering during the failed attempt at persuasion.

The third option was for Laskey to proceed as if this were a case he'd been assigned to, and try to do it without alarming Fritz. He understood Fritz and Leah's worry about not following the kidnappers' instructions. The police had messed up in the case of Billy Thatcher. That had been due to not thoroughly checking out their information source, something he would never do.

The choice, of course, had already been made. Last night, he'd left a message at headquarters saying he needed a few days off for a personal matter, and this morning, before setting out for the library, he left another with Janis, his assistant. "Taking time off to review a situation," he'd texted. "Will probably drop by office, but that's not for anyone else to know."

His toes curled inside his shoes. He'd been sixteen when they kidnapped Billy Thatcher. Billy was seven, his family a member of the same Fellowship of Friends as Laskey's. The culprits grabbed Billy on his way home from school and then demanded a million dollar ransom from his industrialist father. Billy's family insisted that law enforcement not be involved per the instructions of the kidnappers, but the police chief found out where Billy had been taken. Or so he thought. Ignoring the family's wishes, he had his officers surround the old farmhouse, only to find it empty. A few days later they found Billy's mutilated body stuffed in the trunk of an old Chrysler.

He heard footsteps and looked up to see a barrel-chested man with short, stocky legs emerge from between the stacks.

"Whoops, it looks like there's no room here." The man held three volumes in his hand. "Just wanted to . . . ." His voice trailed off as he changed direction and headed away to find another place to settle.

Laskey gathered the books he'd placed on the table. On the way out, he added them to the book cart at the end of one of the aisles and then headed for the exit, stopping to speak to Miss Berry who was staring at her computer screen.

"Surfing the internet during working hours, Miss Berry?"

She leaned back and crossed her arms. "Well, if it isn't our famous detective. You scoping out the activities of librarians now?"

He plunged his hands into his pockets. "I am, as a matter of fact. It has come to my attention that librarians are a dangerous bunch."

"Hmmm. I guess that goes along with *The pen is mightier than the sword*."

"Yes, ma'am, it does. So watch it. I'm keeping a close eye on you and your activities. See you later."

Amazing, he thought, as he exited the library, how you could hide what was going on inside with meaningless banter. He supposed everyone must be an actor of sorts. The thought sobered him. Fritz and Leah wouldn't acknowledge that there was a Judas in their midst, someone acting the part of congenial neighbor, affectionate friend, loyal employee.

Chapter Seventeen

The headquarters for The Troop M section of the State Police Criminal Investigation Section was headquartered in Bethlehem, but Laskey had his own office in an old house on Court Street. The two-way walk – office to library, library back to office – would do him good, he'd reasoned when he left his car in the courthouse lot which provided parking spaces for his annex.

The gloom and doom of yesterday had been replaced by sunny skies, and the temperature called for nothing more than a light jacket. It would probably be one of the last perfect days before winter struck. But feeling the sun on his back, stretching his legs, and breathing fresh air, did nothing for his headache.

As he passed Danny's Diner a few doors down from his office, a customer exited bringing with him with the smells of coffee and bacon grease. Laskey reversed course. Coffee would soothe the pounding in his head.

"Well, look who decided to show up ," a well-endowed redhead called to him from behind the counter. She was removing donuts from a bakery box and placing them in a glass case.

"Good morning, Hilda. I'll take whichever coffee you've got

that's strong enough to set me in orbit." He raised his hand in a weak salute and headed toward the empty booth in the back corner.

He sat facing the end wall, his back to the customers, his yellow pad in front of him. He tapped the table impatiently. Five minutes for coffee. Then a stab at trying to find answers. Somewhere there were answers, but right now the questions were piling up while the answers hid.

Fritz and Leah owned valuable paintings which the kidnappers had ignored. A Braque, more valuable than the Kokoschkas and Schieles, hung in their living room. They also owned a piece of Picasso's pottery as well as a painting by Margaret Keane. He couldn't imagine anyone coveting a portrait of one of Keane's bug-eyed children. Personally, he'd pay someone to burn the thing had it been given to him. He suspected *Bug-Eyes* was Leah's purchase and not Fritz's or his father's. Still, the Keane was worth something.

"You don't look so good this morning." Hilda set a mug of coffee in front of him, along with two donuts.

" I didn't order . . . ."

"I know. You didn't order donuts, but one look at that sad sack face tells me you need sugar. They're on the house."

"Thanks, Hilda. I'm not going to refuse. I'll give up sugar tomorrow. Or next week."

"You're never going to give up sugar, you old codger." She gave him a poke on the arm as she turned to walk away. "Enjoy," she called over her shoulder. "Next time you find your way back to our lowly establishment, if we're not so busy you can tell me about whatever horrific crime you're about to solve."

About to solve? He wished.

He gulped half the cup down in one go. The jolt helped. He pulled the yellow pad closer and took the pen from his pocket. With his other hand he grabbed the cinnamon donut. First cinnamon; then chocolate.

Lacking something specific to write, he scribbled − circles, zigzags, slashes. Most of the locals wouldn't know the value of the paintings or recognize the names of the artists. They'd simply view the works as *crazy modern art.* Outside Goose Bend, very few would even know about the collection. Fritz ventured into Doylestown once a month for the wine tasting club, where discussions about art didn't usually crop up. Otherwise, as far as Laskey knew, Fritz confined his activities to a few local events. He was a member of the Rotary Club. He and Leah put in an appearance at the yearly charity ball supporting the local hospital. At various times, Fritz had been asked to run for school board and city council, but declined. He appeared to be perfectly happy coming home from the factory to build model boats or to settle in his chair to listen to Mozart or Schubert, or his favorite symphony: Mahler's ninth.

Leah managed to get outside Goose Bend more often. Once a month, she headed over to the Main Line for a meeting of Hadassah. Fritz often invited him for a chess game on those evenings. There were also frequent social occasions among members of Hadassah – bridge games, teas, bridal showers for daughters and granddaughters. Sometimes Leah and Fritz were invited to parties in Bryn Mawr, Radnor, Lower Merion, or any of the other towns along the *line*. Occasionally, friends from there drove out to Goose Bend for dinner. Unlike the locals, many of the Main Line friends knew the names *Kokoschko* and *Schiele* and would recognize their work.

But his instinct told him this crime had nothing to do with their friends from elsewhere, but was of local origin. Regretably, his instinct wasn't infallible.

He finished the coffee and twisted around, hoping to get Hilda's attention. She was taking toast out of the toaster. When she glanced in his direction, he held up his empty cup, and she nodded.

His head was a smidgen better. A second cup, would help, and a chocolate donut provide further alleviation. Then finally, an aspirin. He'd be fit as a fiddle then.

"You're really bolting it down," Hilda said, refilling his cup. "Maybe I should leave the pot here."

"This should do it." He lifted the cup toward her as though making a toast.

"Well, let me know . . . ."

He drank the second cup more slowly, his pen hovering over the pad on which sprinkles of cinnamon had been added to the doodles, but no names of suspects.

The Kokoschkas and Schieles had been acquired by Fritz's grandfather, Joseph Herschmann I, who lived in a suburb of Vienna during the same time period as the artists. His son, Joseph II, who was Fritz's father, escaped Austria at the age of twenty-one after smuggling the paintings out with the help of an American acquaintance.

Fritz's father, the epitome of old world charm, had died five years ago. But charm and old-world manners aside, Joseph II had been full of spunk. Not as tall as Fritz, Joseph II had a round face, a mustache and a permanent twinkle in his eyes. He adored Rebekah, certain that she was the most magnificent child ever to grace the planet.

Laskey picked up the chocolate donut and took a bite. Fritz's father was a world-class raconteur, however, it was Fritz who first shared with him the tale of how the paintings had been smuggled out of Austria.

Fritz's grandfather, Joseph Herschmann, I and Otto Fuchs had founded a pharmaceutical firm and then had sons two years apart. Joseph II was only twenty years old when his father died. Although young, he assumed his father's position as partner. Otto's son Gustav demanded that he, too, be elevated to the position of partner instead of having to wait for his father's death. Otto declined. When the Nazi government called Otto to Berlin for a consultation regarding troop medical supplies, he stepped into the path of a speeding lorry. He never recovered from his injuries, and Gustav, at the age of eighteen, became a partner in the firm.

Shortly after that, the Nazis set out to steal the wealth, position, and happiness of the Jews, along with whatever else they had to steal. Joseph II had to hand over his share of the business to the eighteen-year-old Gustav. Gustav promised to remit the usual share of profits to Fritz's father, a promise which lasted exactly one month. Not only did Gustav keep all the company's earnings for himself, but he demanded that Joseph II hand over the paintings collected by Fritz's grandfather, claiming they had been bought with company profits and thus belonged to the company. According to Fritz, who always told the story with dancing eyes, his father had had the temerity to challenge Gustav. The works, Joseph II claimed, had been purchased with his father's private income, and he wasn't about to hand them over. Nastier, and nastier, the wind blew, until Joseph II realized that sooner or later Gustav would bring in goonies to rip the collection from his walls, and there was nothing he could do to stop a bunch of bullies sporting armbands emblazoned with swastikas.

"You can get them on Friday," he said to Gustav on a Tuesday .

"I'll take them today."

"I'm afraid you can't get at them today." Laskey imagined Joseph II faking an apologetic look. "We're painting the apartment; I put them in storage for safe-keeping. Sorry, I should have thought of this before we packed them up, but, oh well . . . . I didn't. The paintings will be brought back on Friday, already in crates. You can send someone to pick them up in the afternoon."

Retelling the story to Laskey as his father had told it to him, Fritz always burst out laughing at this point, wiping tears of merriment from his eyes. "My father had *stored* them in the possession of a Jewish-American banker who had decided it was high time to leave Austria. The banker shipped them to the United States along with his own possessions. When Gustav went to my father's place to get the paintings, all he found was an apartment with drop cloths over the furniture, rolled up carpets, and a few unopened cans of paint in the middle of the floor. My father must have put the paint cans there for effect. Neither the paintings nor my father were anywhere to be found. I think he'd reached Portugal by then and was about to board a ship for the United States."

A thought struck Laskey. It was far-fetched. Or maybe not. Could the person behind this crime be someone associated with the banker? If Fritz and his father enjoyed telling the tale, the banker probably enjoyed telling it, too.

Chapter Eighteen

Fritz arrived at the candy factory at seven-thirty sharp, his usual time. He unlocked the doors, flicked on the hall light, and picked up the mail that had fallen through the mail slot onto the floor. The fragrances of Pomegranate liqueur and Orange Curacao blew through the building like olfactory hurricanes. And chocolate. Always chocolate. Lately, too, the scent of coffee flavored rum spiced the air. Bay had already chosen a name for the new candy product he was experimenting with: *Kava-Rhumbar.*

Still in an Ambien-induced fog, Fritz dragged himself to his office, his feet more like concrete blocks than appendages. The sleeping pill, however, hadn't numbed him so much that he didn't feel the nakedness of being watched and of someone knowing his daughter's plans and what hung on his walls. He found himself looking over his shoulder even though no one was around.

He set the mail down on the corner of his desk and checked his messages without actually hearing them and then shuffled through the correspondence without being aware of what he was looking at while Rebekah's voice played and replayed in his head. *It's the wind, Daddy; the bride of the wind.* Like a needle stuck in the rut of an old phonograph record, the phrase repeated over and over. *The wind, the wind, the wind. The wind of the bride.*

Setting the correspondence aside, he covered his mouth and nose with one hand. His desk faced a half-glass wall which looked out over the enrober room where the candies were coated with chocolate. In spite of the wall, the unrelenting aroma of chocolate, sugar, and vanilla seeped from every crack and crevice, sickening him.

The lights in the enrober room flicked on, and Eli walked in, wrench in hand, his bald head reflecting the lights as he bent over to examine the machine they called the chocolate car wash. Fritz sat down and watched Eli. Soon, *he'd* have to go out there. Adopting the habit of his father, Fritz appeared on the factory floor between eight-thirty and nine to make the rounds of the various stations, speaking or nodding to each worker. They greeted him with, "Good morning, Mr. Fritz," except for the new employees who called him "Mr. Herschmann" until they learned better. Occasionally he stepped in to do a job when a worker was out sick. Last week, he'd helped Bay measure ingredients. The week before that, he'd spent part of one day running a mixer.

His stomach clenched. How could he go out there today and look with interest at what they were doing and pretend to care how the candy turned out? "How's Rebekah?" they'd ask. "Aren't you glad to see her Mr. Fritz? She's going to come over and say 'Hi' while she's here, isn't she? How long will she be home?"

He'd practiced the story he'd give to those who asked: *Two doctors at her camp came down with food poisoning, so Rebekah can't come home until next week. And if I don't appear quite normal, it's because I'm getting a cold. Which will be better by the time Rebekah arrives. So things have turned out well since I prefer she not come home to a sick father. Not with all she has to deal with over there.*

Later in the day, he made the rounds a second time, stopping to examine the work. He praised when he could. If something wasn't up to par, he stared at it for a few seconds and did something with his mouth that he wasn't aware of doing until Erika had pointed it out. When he moved on, he did it without saying anything. No reprimands. No threats. The next time he passed the worker, workmanship had risen to acceptable standards. Only twice had he been forced to fire someone.

Each day after his first round, he made the five minute trip back home to make coffee for Leah and bring her the paper in bed. He'd sit down and they'd chat while she scanned the news which she had no interest in reading in great detail. Then he'd go back to the factory, leaving her to study the bridge column which she did read in great detail.

He'd been the one to see Rebekah off to school every morning, something he missed greatly in the fourteen years since she left home. Leah had taken care of the night time duties, seeing that Rebekah got to bed on time; checking that she'd done her homework, not that it had ever occurred to Rebekah to *not* do her homework.

Rebekah and Leah were his only family. His father was dead, and he could barely remember his mother's face. She died of breast cancer when he was ten, a disease she fought during his entire memory of her. Mostly what he remembered were her long, thin fingers laying against the pink coverlet where she lay in bed. Rebekah had her fingers.

Rebekah was his and Leah's future. The other *futures* in their families had been worked to death or gassed at Bergen-Belson, Dachau, and Mauthausen-Gusen. Cousins, uncles, aunts. For Leah, three brothers. He'd known his relatives only through his father's stories, yet he felt their loss keenly.

Eli had finished with the chocolate car wash and was doing something at one of the cutting stations. Fritz watched him until he finished with whatever he was doing, left the floor and disappeared through the door into the hall that led up to the office. Fritz pulled the stack of orders close, grabbed a pen, and let it hover over the papers as though ready to make corrections or notes.

"Good morning," Eli said, sticking his head through the door. "Do you know yet which day the new distributor plans to ship? Also,

Watson is on vacation and his assistant has the flu, so I'll call Peterman to fix the plumbing in the women's toilet unless there's someone else you'd rather me call."

"Peterman is fine. I'll check on delivery dates."

Eli narrowed his eyes. "Is something wrong?"

Fritz sat back, affecting nonchalance. "I should have told you, but I have one of those infernal check-ups with the doctor this morning so I have to leave in a few minutes. Sorry, I didn't say something before."

Eli frowned. "Everything okay?"

"I'm fine," Fritz lied. "It's just a routine check-up, but I hate wasting a morning sitting around in a paper cover-up with artificial lights glaring at me just to be told I'm fine."

"Yeah, I don't imagine it's any fun. But don't worry about here. I'll get Peterman to take care of the problem in the women's room and, other than a loose bolt on a mixer which I fixed, we're problem-free at the moment. Go enjoy exposing your legs to all those nurses."

"Right." Fritz faked a smile. "I imagine my legs give them a lot to talk about."

"I need to call the plumber before he takes off on another job." Eli gave a cursory wave and left.

When Fritz looked back out at the floor, he saw Bay pulling a wagon loaded with chocolate from the storage area toward the grinding machines. As soon as Bay had his ingredients lined up for the morning, he'd walk up to the office to say hello and ask about Rebekah. Bay always asked about Rebekah. Then Fritz realized that Eli hadn't asked.

The Ambien was wearing off, and he felt a rush of adrenaline. He knew that people thought he was easy-going, non-confrontational, caring. What they didn't know, and what he hadn't known about himself before, was that when pushed he'd turn into a beast. For now, he'd pretend patience. Go home. Wait for the phone call giving directions for delivering the ransom. But the moment he hung up from that call, he'd find the gun his father had brought with him from Austria and learn to shoot. If anyone, *anyone,* harmed one hair of Rebekah's head . . . He fisted both hands until nails cut into palms and hissed, "I swear on the incinerated ashes of all my family, I will kill that person."

Chapter Nineteen

"Got any Tylenol, Aspirin, Bufferin or relatives thereof?" Laskey asked Janis, as he swept into his office.

"Well, good morning to you, too."

"Maybe I didn't say *good morning* because it's *not* a good morning which you might have deduced from my request for something to kill a headache."

Janis, a fortyish, sharp-featured brunette, who preferred wearing all shades of green to any other color, had been his assistant long enough to reply in kind to his brashness, and he rather enjoyed her lack of restraint.

"So the great detective is in a shitty mood this morning." She sat back, letting her arms

slide off the desk to rest on the chair arms. "Were you successful in *reviewing a situation*? If you were, you did it awfully fast. But judging by your wonderfully friendly tone, I'm guessing you didn't solve crap."

"You're right; I didn't." He flopped down in one of the chairs meant for visitors. "I'd love to share, but I'm afraid this is a burden I have to bear alone, and it's given me a hell of a headache."

She opened a drawer, pulled out a bottle of Tylenol, and tossed it to him. "Take two, drink lots of liquids, and get plenty of rest."

"Right. Any calls?"

"Nope, all's quiet on the western front."

"Good. I'm taking a few days off to pursue a private matter, but I expect to drop into the office occasionally. I'm not here to anyone other than you; I need you to run interference for me."

"I'll try, boss."

"I have a job for you."

"Which is?"

"Check auction catalogs and make a list of collectors interested in Austrian artists from the first half of the twentieth century. Kokoschka and Schiele, in particular."

She raised her eyebrows.

He shuffled to his feet. "I'm sorry, Janis, I can't tell you. Eventually, you'll know."

She nodded. "I'll get on it."

He went in his office, closed the door, and tapped out the number for Dr. Annemarie Leitner. In Vienna, it was two o'clock in the afternoon. When she didn't answer, he rang again, hoping the reason for her not answering the first time had something to do with her being too busy to get to the phone before the answering machine cut in. The second time, he left a message instructing her that it was imperative to return his call.

Still clutching the phone, he opened the blinds and stood in the stripes of sunlight.

The wind, Daddy. The wind. It's the . . . .

"Yes, yes, I know. And the four oils."

But the wind's the one. The Wind of the Bride. Think . . .

Was she being held in a place where there was unusual wind? The top of a hill? A silo or tall building? Maybe somewhere near the Delaware where the wind funneled along the river's course?

He chose a number from his list of contacts and pressed the "call" button. A voice even deeper than his own answered on the second ring.

"Well, if it isn't the great man, himself," the deeper voice rumbled.

"Good morning Thunder. I need your help."

"Again?"

"Yes, again." He and Thunder had worked together in the FBI. Thunder still worked as an agent and had, on occasion, done favors for Laskey.

"Good God," Thunder said when Laskey finished telling him about the kidnapping and the demand for paintings. "Wouldn't it have been easier just to steal them? Why add kidnapping to the mix?"

"Exactly. But it might take more time than we have to figure that out. What I need is . . . .." He explained to Thunder what he wanted.

"Consider it done," Thunder said.

After he hung up, Laskey booted up his computer and typed *Fuchs and Herschmann Pharmaceuticals, Vienna* in the search line. Several sites popped up, a number of them in German. He chose the Wikipedia entry. . . . *a pharmaceutical company established in 1907 by Joseph Herschmann I and Otto Fuchs. After developing an antibiotic, originally called* Freiheit, *Herschmann, a pharmacologist, forged a partnership with Fuchs who financed the company. The company's initial line consisted of the antibiotic,* Eierheilen, *a medication for eye inflammation, and* Keinhusten, *a cough suppressant. In the beginning, the products were marketed mainly in the local area, but when the company's product line grew to include other medications, sales spread to encompass not only Austria, but markets in Hungary, Italy, Germany, and Czechoslovakia. In 1935, after a fatal heart attack, Joseph Herschmann's share in the business was passed down to his son, Joseph Herschmann II. Otto Fuchs was killed in an accident shortly afterwards, and his partnership was transferred to his son, Gustav. Joseph Herschmann II signed over his shares to Gustav Fuchs in 1937, conforming to the laws of the Nazi Regime. In 1980 Fuchs and Herschmann was bought out by Seltzer. Gustav Fuchs remained with Seltzer until his retirement in 1985. Fuchs' son, Karl, joined Seltzer that same year as counsel.*

Laskey waved his hand dismissively. To think the old man had waited this many years to seek revenge was absurd, and he wasn't going to waste time pursuing it. He needed to get out to Goose

Bend and inform Bump of what had happened and then look for plausible answers.

———————

BUMP STARED at Laskey in disbelief. Laskey had asked the police chief to meet him at the Goose Bend Library in case the kidnappers had a spy watching what went on at the police station. He'd found Bump seated at one of the tables, a newspaper in front of him.

"Both Carlos and I tried to persuade Fritz and Leah that the police should be involved," Laskey said. "We might as well have been trying to stuff a sausage through a straw."

"And I'm supposed to sit around and pretend I don't know? What should I tell the force?" He raised his hands in frustration. "They know Rebekah didn't come home, and they're on edge over what could have happened. A couple of them were in school with her. Crap, I had one of my officers down at the airport helping me look for someone who might have seen her. They and their wives and their children and their neighbors and their . . . . Hell, by now probably half the town knows she was on the flight and didn't show up."

Laskey shifted from foot to foot. "Tell them it's been a long time since I've seen her, and that I made a mistake when I identified her on the videos. When I looked a second time I realized it wasn't her." He hated lying any time, but especially when it made him look like a bumbling idiot. "Tell your staff they were short staffed in Amman, and she couldn't get away as planned, but she'll arrive home this coming weekend."

This coming weekend. That should give them enough time, he thought. By then, everything should be resolved, paintings delivered, Rebekah back home, everyone relieved and happy. And *that* was the way it was going to turn out: everyone relieved and happy. No harm done.

"I find it hard to imagine that either Fritz or his father had enemies," Laskey said. "But is there something I don't know?"

Bump shook his head. "Never heard a bad word about either of them."

Laskey pulled out a chair and sat down opposite Bump. "There *is* something you can do. We'll just keep it between us."

"Anything."

"I asked Fritz if he'd ever fired anyone. He'd sort of zoned out at that point and wouldn't answer. It's hard to imagine even an easygoing employer like Fritz not having the occasional problem. Can you find out? Without people wondering why you're asking?"

"Ah." Bump smiled broadly. "As it happens, I can find that out quite easily. Up until a couple months ago, my Aunt Sarah pushed a cart around the factory, distributing supplies. She talked to everyone, and if anyone knows the dirt, it would be her." He pushed back his chair and stood up. "I'll pay her a visit right now."

Chapter Twenty

S hreya Karthikeyan was a bird of a different color. Actually, she was a bird of multiple colors, Jacob mused as he heard his secretary enter the outer office. She half-hummed, half-sang *Come together, yeah; Come together, yeah; Come together, yeah*, while the ballet-style-shoes she always wore brushed across the floor in time to the beat. The musical entrance was followed by the thud of a water bottle being set down.

Jacob knew the routine and settled back to wait. First, she'd fling her purse on the chair near the window. Sometimes she missed, and the purse thudded to the floor, forcing her to go over and pick it up along with her scattered belongings, an undertaking always accompanied by a *shit* or two. This morning her aim was true. Jacob heard the whomp of oversize purse hitting chair seat. Due to Shreya's ongoing dispute with the custodial staff over furniture arrangement, the next order of business was to reposition the visitors chairs, scraping their legs across the tiled floor in a screech that made him want to cover his ears. That task completed to her liking, she'd call out to Jacob, "I'm here." As though he didn't know.

Grinning, he waited for her announcement. In short order, it came.

"I'm here."

"Good morning, Shreya," he called back.

"Shall I come in, or are you coming out?"

"I'll come out."

Shreya had become his secretary by default. The person he should have had was on maternity leave, so the agency saddled him with the regular's sub, a perky, spike-haired and tattooed cousin of someone high up the chain of command. Her looks had obviously put off the others who thought a proper assistant should dress in *office-traditional* clothes, hide the frogs inked onto upper arms, and style her hair, including the color, within the parameters of acceptability.

He shuffled through the file folders on his desk, found the two he needed, and headed for the outer office. Mostly, Shreya wore leggings and short, belted tunics, and her hair color was . . . He paused in the door between inner and outer office . . . Purple! Last week it had been green. The week before that . . . . He couldn't remember. Maybe that was the striped week. What those who'd pushed her off on him didn't know was that she was bright, efficient, industrious, and had an imagination equal to his own. Imagination always helped when there were problems to solve, and the problems with fracking were rising as high as the Himalayas, only much faster.

"I need more information on these upcoming court cases." He handed her the files. "I've made notations as to exactly what I want."

"And you want it yesterday?" Her ready smile was missing this morning.

"Indeed I do."

She gave him a salute and sat down. "I'm on it." She opened the top file and ran her finger down the page. "Hmmmm. Hmmmm, hmmmm. Easy as pie. Why don't you give me something challenging?" She raised her eyebrows at him. Still, no smile.

"I'll work on that. Do you have the data I asked for yesterday?"

She twisted her chair around and picked up a stack of charts and documents from the ell of her desk. "A history of water sample tests from Susquehanna, Tioga, Lycoming, and Bradford counties. I put them in your electronic files yesterday."

"Thanks." He opened the top one and glanced down the page. He liked having paper files in addition to the electronic ones since it was easier to spread out the paper ones for comparisons. "Good work."

"Anything else?" She picked up her water, unscrewed the lid, and took a long drink.

"There's a lot *else*, but I'll dole it out as the day progresses."

He started to leave, but stopped. "What's wrong?" There was no glimmer of pleasantness, friendliness, or compatability about her this morning.

"They're shooting Indians."

"Who's shooting Indians?"

"You didn't see the news this morning?"

"No." He'd been too busy playing host to Dr. James MacNeish.

"A man in Ohio shot an Indian woman after screaming at her to go back to her country."

"Shit." He sat down on the corner of the desk.

"An Indian man in Colorado had his house egged and smeared with dog feces, and then somebody wrote racist slurs all over it. A Sikh got shot in Kentucky for no reason other than being a Sikh. *Towel Head,* is what they call Sikhs. He was washing his car. Minding his own business, and then . . ." She shaped her hand into a gun. "Bang!" She took a deep breath and blew it out in a huff. "I bet you didn't know there's a video going around announcing that Indians have ravished the Midwest."

"You're kidding?"

"No, I'm not kidding. It's like hate bubbling away in people's magma chambers, getting hotter and hotter, until it starts oozing its way up the vent toward the crater." Little by little, she raised her hands, wiggling her fingers in imitation of boiling lava. "And then it comes spewing out like lava from a volcano." She splayed her hands and hissed when her imaginary lava reached the imaginary crater. "Speeeewwwww."

She lowered her hands. "And they're picking on Jews again.

Yesterday, someone started a fire in a temple up in Wilkes Barre. What's happened to the country of *give me your tired and hungry and your huddled masses*, or however that poem goes?" She gave him a plaintive look.

He shook his head. He didn't understand it either.

"Well, I'm American, too," she said, ". . . and they're not going to run me off just because my father was born in Delhi."

"They aren't going to run you off because I need you here. If they try, I'll dole out the same punishment to them as the frackers are going to get."

She smiled. "Can I go to court with you when you bust those polluting, fucking, fracking bastards and send them off to rot in jail?"

"I'll definitely have you there with me, Shreya, only you'll have to cover up that hair with a barrister's wig."

"Don't you like my hair?

"I liked it better when it was orange."

"You're kidding?"

"Yes, I'm kidding." He started toward his office.

"Hey, boss."

He looked around. "Yes?"

"I'm not the only one in a funk this morning. What's wrong with you?"

"What do you mean *what's wrong?*"

"You're not your usual perky Monday morning self."

She was like a bloody barometer, sensing his moods when he thought he'd done a decent job concealing them. "I have a friend who has a problem, and it's sort of weighing on me." He shrugged. "I'll forget about it as soon as I get busy."

He wouldn't forget, of course. Not by a long shot. He partially closed the door and then threw the files down on the glass top desk they'd furnished him with instead of the standard wooden one with drawers he'd have preferred. In a beige office, no less, when his brain fed on color. They'd promised a paint job, but there'd been no move in that direction. Maybe he had to win a few court cases and, like Shreya said, *bust all those polluting, fucking, fracking bastards and send them off to rot in jail* before they sent up a painter with a few cans of blue or green. Even gray would have sufficed. Anything was better than beige. Especially when you weren't your *usual perky Monday morning self.*

He opened the window. A breeze carrying the scent of dead leaves blew in to replace the Monday morning smell of must and dust. His office overlooked the parking lot where sun glinted off vehicles. The WARPA building and its parking lot were smaller than the others in the industrial park. "About right," he mumbled. "Another example of David and Goliath. *Water and Air Resources Protection Agency* against the industrial complex." He hoped what he was doing would have more impact than Rebekah's protests against the pharmaceutical industry. The pharmaceutical Goliath, powerful enough to control the U.S. congress, as well as legislative bodies in other countries, would never be concerned about a few protestors. That would be like a T-Rex battling a worm. But sometimes you had to make a stand even if it accomplished nothing, so he understood why she did it.

What he didn't understand about Rebekah was Totsy. For the life of him, he couldn't figure out the attraction between a scatter-brained, wanna-be actress, and a brilliant, responsible woman like Rebekah. Nor did he understand her attraction to Carlos.

He sat down, tapped the return bar on his computer, bringing the screen to life, and

typed *Carlos Vientos* in the search line. He had a lot to do, but preparing suits against oil companies that were polluting drinking water could wait ten minutes. After all, in the next ten minutes only a piddling several thousand people in the state would be consuming water laced with 2-Butoxyethanol and natural gas. Let them wait.

He chose the *Wikipedia* article. *Wikipedia* was often the quickest and easiest route to basic information, although the veracity of that information might be in doubt more often than the site managers wanted to admit.

The picture that came up with the article showed a scruffier Carlos − longer hair, the beginnings of a beard, a rumpled dress-shirt with rolled up sleeves. Jacob smiled. Carlos had cleaned himself up a bit, but he knew how that went. Meeting your girl's family *did* require greater attention to hygiene and haircuts. Carlos Vientos was a journalist and author from Mendoza, Argentina, the article said. He did free lance work for two newspapers, *Diario Democracia* and *El Cronista*, as well as *Television Publica Argentina*. His book, *Living in Space*, was a bestseller in Argentina. After listing several major magazine articles authored or co-authored by Vientos, and a couple documentaries to his credit, there was a brief mention of his family's vineyards.

Jacob exited the site. An impressive biography. He still didn't like the man, but he supposed the one he should worry about was Dr. James MacNeish. Why was he here, tooling around in a rental car, enjoying the fall sunshine, when he was supposed to be a few hundred miles south at a medical conference? *Concerned about Rebekah,* MacNeish had said. If the Scotsman was so *concerned about Rebekah* why had he been rude to Fritz? Why was he out sightseeing this morning?

He pulled the stack of files toward him. He needed to tackle the issues on his plate, or rather on his desk, and leave the saving of Rebekah to Laskey. He opened the top file which dealt with the refusal of the Pennsylvania Department of Environmental Protection to make information on fracking complaints available to the media. He'd lead the charge when they went to court, and he intended to win. If that meant taking on the Pennsylvania Department of Environmental Protection, then so be it.

Halfway through reading the first paragraph, he stopped. *The saving of Rebekah?* Where had that come from? It was just a matter of turning over the six pieces of art and then waiting for the culprits to release her, wasn't it?

Chapter Twenty-One

An index card taped to the door of the house where Totsy Love lived with her mother informed Laskey that the doorbell wasn't working. He knocked, waited, and then leaned his forehead against the door. He heard no approaching footsteps, no turning down of the television, no scraping of chair legs as someone got up to see who was at the door. It had been almost seventy-two hours since Rebekah was supposed to arrive, yet Totsy had neither called to welcome Rebekah home nor had she returned anyone's calls. He would have thought she'd be curious about Rebekah's fiancé and want to meet him ASAP. Instead, it was as though she, too, had disappeared.

He let out a huff. He'd already had two failed contact attempts this morning: Annemarie Leitner hadn't answered her phone, and MacNeish hadn't come to Jacob's door even after Laskey pounded on it for several minutes.

He knocked on Totsy's door again and then turned to examine the neighborhood. Bungalows, small ranches, and Cape Cods lined the street. Like the Love's bungalow, most had chipping paint, missing shutters, or broken roof tiles. Garbage cans stood beside the curbs along with piles of leaves raked into the road to await the street vacuum. Moss grew in the cracks of sidewalks and driveways were mainly rutted hardground. Next door, a dark haired man in jeans and orange tee was getting ready to trundle his garbage cans out to the road.

The third time Laskey knocked, he rattled the door in its frame. A few seconds later, Totsy, sporting bed hair and wearing a pink velour housecoat loosely held together to reveal a generous cleavage, opened the door. Except for the aggravated expression on her face, she looked exactly as Fritz had described her: caramel-colored skin, full lips, eyes the shape and color of almonds. A Barbie doll.

"If you're selling something, we don't want any." she said through the screen door.

"Good morning, Totsy." Laskey was aware of the deep resonance of his own voice

compared to her high, musical one.

"You are . . .?"

"Detective William Laskey." He held out his ID.

"Detective? . . . What are you doing here?" Her hand flew to her throat.

"May I come in?"

"What do you want?"

"Haven't you checked your messages?"

"Why? Did you leave a message? I was away for the weekend and not paying any attention to my phone."

"Rebekah is missing."

"What do you mean she's missing?" She pulled the lapels of her housecoat closer as though she were cold even though it was shirt-sleeve weather. "Didn't she come home Thursday?"

He studied her for a few moments. "We can talk out here if you're more comfortable on the porch," he said finally.

She gave a huff, threw open the screen door slamming it against the side of the house, and headed for the end of the porch where there were two rattan chairs. A swing hung at the other end. "Rebekah's been delayed before, so what's the big deal?" she asked without looking back. Then she did an abrupt about face. "Shit. Let's go inside."

Laskey looked over and saw the orange-shirted neighbor standing beside his garbage cans leering at Totsy.

"Good idea," he said and followed her into the house.

Jarred by the colors and the cacophony of smells — bacon, beer, onions, glue, air freshener — he stopped a couple feet beyond the threshold and looked around while Totsy went toward a door to the left which opened into a hallway.

"Give me thirty seconds," she said. "I want to jump into some clothes." She slipped away before he could respond.

The color scheme screamed at him. Three walls of the living room were painted a lemon yellow, the fourth red. The adjoining room was also yellow. Cheap curtains, upholstery, and throw pillows contained the same vivid colors worked into checks, plaids, and florals. An arch separated the living room from an even smaller dining room, or what would normally have been a dining room had it not been converted into some sort of crafts room. Most of the space was taken up by two long, folding tables cluttered with containers. Jars, cookie tins, an Easter basket, flower pots, and plastic storage boxes were filled with bits and pieces of broken tiles. Bottles of mastic, several artist's paint brushes, and a pile of pictures torn from magazines filled the spaces between containers. A stack of thin plywood occupied the far end of one table.

"My mom's decided she's an artist." Totsy had slipped up beside him. Barefooted, she wore a pair of jeans and a tee shirt, but no bra. "She makes pictures out of broken tiles." She picked up one of the plywood pieces and held it up for Laskey to see. It was an unfinished mountain-scape mosaic.

"It's . . . uh . . . interesting. I see she's hung a few." He went over to study one of the creations hanging on the wall nearest him, standing for a few moments as he pretended to enjoy the piece. "I'll have to take a better look some other time," he said finally and turned to face her. "Why haven't you returned calls? I've been calling you. Fritz Herschmann has been calling you."

"He called, too?"

"Do you not check your phone?" Pretty much everyone, including people as old as Methuselah, checked phones with unfailing regularity these days. That a young woman wouldn't was inconceivable.

"Where the fook *is* my bloody phone." She went into the living room and pushed aside stacks of magazines, looked underneath sofa cushions, picked up a jacket and felt inside the pockets. "You know, you have Al Pacino's eyes," she said, looking up as she threw the jacket over the back of a chair. "But a little darker than Pacino's, I think. Anyone ever tell you that?" She lifted up the chair cushion, searched beneath, and then let the cushion fall back in place.

"No." He realized he'd been abrupt, but impatience pricked at him like ants crawling beneath his skin. He'd been trying to get Totsy for two days; Fritz had been trying for three. Jacob had also tried. Yet she didn't even seem curious.

"And you favor Kevin Kline a little bit, the way he looked in *Beauty and the Beast.* He made one hell of a good-looking older man in that movie. Jesus Christ, where is my . . ." She propped hands on hips, swept her gaze around the room, and then went toward the cabinet supporting the TV.

Laskey's forebearance had reached its limit. "Sit down, Totsy." He pointed to a chair. Straight-armed. Forefinger extended. A gesture of authority.

Totsy ignored him.

"Just let me look onnnnnne more place." She pushed aside a stack of *People* magazines on the TV cabinet. "Aha," she said, and triumphantly held up the phone. "Shit," she said lowering it. "I forgot and left it on 'mute'." She toggled the sound button to *on* and then studied the call log. "I was at an acting workshop at Penn State since Friday morning. We were so busy in our workshops I think we all forgot we had phones, and I got back really late last night. I was too tired to talk to anyone, so I didn't look at messages." She lifted her eyebrows. "Soooo, I see you called a bunch of times, and Mr. Herschmann called a bunch of times, and . . . Jacob Gillis? Why was he calling me?" She furrowed her brow.

"Jacob was helping me out. Sit down, Totsy."

She sank into a chair and set the phone on the cushion beside her. "Why don't you start at the beginning," she said and shrugged.

"Rebekah didn't come home when she was supposed to. It's happened before. She missed her plane, or got bumped, or had to stay a little longer over there." she waved her hand in the air, indicating *over there*, "Maybe she couldn't get off work when she thought she could. So why are you all worried now?" She drew her feet onto the seat and wrapped her arms around her legs. Both her fingernails and toenails were a bright blue.

"When was the last time you talked to Rebekah?"

Totsy shrugged and studied her fingernails. "A week ago, maybe. No, it was longer than that. Jeez, I don't know. Oh, no, I'm wrong, I forgot, we Skyped on Tuesday evening. She told me Carlos was meeting her here." Her eyes widened. "You don't really think something happened to her?"

He had the impression he was being played to. The widened eyes. The theatrical voice — breathy, modulated, just the right amount of suspense. Leah had called her *wifty*, but he didn't think that was the right word. It looked more like a case of life being one big stage for Totsy. She was an actress through and through. "When you Skyped, what . . ."

A door slammed in the back of the house.

"Someone's here, Mom," Totsy called out.

"Let me guess," a raspy voice answered, coming from what Laskey guessed was the kitchen. "Miss High and Mighty has returned."

A few seconds later, Totsy's mother, wearing old jeans, a black knit shirt with a plunging neckline, and large, hoop earrings, appeared at the door between kitchen and craft room. Her dark blonde hair was pulled back in a ponytail. Rubbing the back of her neck, she squeezed past the craft tables and then stopped short when she looked up and saw Laskey. "You aren't Rebekah."

Laskey rose.

"He's a detective," Totsy said. "Detective William Laskey. This is my mom, Delores."

"Glad to meet you." He extended his hand.

Throwing a puzzled glance at her daughter, Delores shook his hand.

"Rebekah was supposed to come home Thursday, but she didn't," Totsy explained.

"Why not?"

"That's what I'm trying to find out," Laskey said.

Delores raised her eyebrows. "So they've hired a private detective? Some people can afford anything, can't they?"

Exasperation spasmed through him. "I'm not a private detective. I work with . . ."

"So what happened to Miss Perfect that she didn't come home?" She fiddled with one of her earrings.

"Mom . . ." Totsy raised her palms toward her mother in a gesture of frustration. "She isn't always like this," she said to Laskey, but with eyes still fastened on her mother.

"No, I'm not always like this." Delores flung herself into a chair. "But some of us have to work long hours just to eat and have a shelter over our heads." She flitted her hand at the ceiling. "While others have furs, and paintings, and big cars. What kind of car is it they have?" She arrowed her eyes at Totsy.

"Mom's tired." Totsy rolled her eyes. "She had to work late last night. Forgive her."

"No, don't forgive me. There's nothing I need to be forgiven me for."

"I have a couple questions for Totsy," Laskey said. "Maybe we can talk on the front porch. He rose and started for the door. Totsy followed.

"Your mom has something against the Herschmanns?" he asked when they were outside and the door closed behind them.

Crossing her arms, Totsy leaned against one of the porch pillars and let out a sigh. "She's embarrassed. Every now and then she gripes about me having a friend with loads of money when we have next to nothing. I never know if she's blaming me or Rebekah. Mom's afraid I'll fault her because I never had expensive clothes like Rebekah and because we don't live in a nice house with all that crazy art work. Mostly she's embarrassed because . . . ." She clamped her mouth shut.

Laskey stuck his hands in his pockets. "Because?"

Totsy took a deep breath, her shoulders rising and then dropping, as she blew the air out in a rush. "Mr. Herschmann paid our mortgage once. Actually, he paid it for three months. We weren't supposed to know. Mom was about to declare bankruptcy because she missed work a couple months with pneumonia. Then the bank told us somebody made the mortgage payments but the person wished to remain anonymous. Mom knew some young guy from the loan department who spent time at Billy's Bronco Bar where she works. She wheedled it out of him. She was really angry at Rebekah's dad. Sometimes Mom isn't very reasonable." She shrugged. "She never said anything to Mr. Herschmann though. Because she was embarrassed, you know."

"I understand. Did Rebekah have plans to see anyone while she was home? Maybe meet an acquaintance at the airport?"

Totsy looked at him like she thought he was crazy. "Why would she meet someone at the airport?"

"Maybe an old college friend passing through at the same time?"

She shrugged. "How would I know. I didn't know her college friends. When they came to visit, I wasn't invited over."

He tried another tack. "Sometimes you picked her up at the airport or at the train station in Lansdale?"

A pout formed on her lips. "I told her I'd pick her up this time, but she didn't want me to. She said we'd get together later in the week." She looked down to pick at a piece of lint stuck to her jeans. She removed the lint, rolled it back and forth between thumb and forefinger, and then threw it aside. "I really don't see why you're so concerned. Like I said, she's been held up over there before." She went over to one of the rattan chairs, brushed a leaf off the seat, and sat down.

He pulled a card from his pocket and handed it to her. "If you remember something you think might be helpful, give me a call." If she couldn't keep track of her phone, he expected she'd lose his card in less than thirty seconds.

Chapter Twenty-Two

Fritz set his phone on the kitchen desk and, beside it, the tape measure he'd used to measure the paintings. He sat down and, while Carlos waited a few feet away, added up the lengths, heights, and depths of the four paintings and two drawings, and then wrote down the aggregate measurements on a sheet torn from Leah's grocery list pad.

The hairs on the back of his neck bristled. Every action during the past few minutes – finding the tape measure, measuring the paintings, doing the math, writing down the numbers – had been done with a spectral gun held to his head, and he knew who held the gun. Hatred didn't die. Hatred was like fabric bleached by Clorox – a permanent mark, not a stain to be washed away.

"Are you finished?" Carlos asked.

Fritz nodded but still held onto the piece of paper. He appreciated his future son-in-law's sensitive reticence and wished the wedding were tomorrow. He wanted Leah to be in a frenzy, dashing around, opening the refrigerator, checking the pantry, calling the caterer for the umpteenth time. Normally, he'd slip away to escape that kind of tumult, but today he'd welcome it.

Rebekah was never in a frenzy. She'd beg Leah to stop fretting about the wedding. *Stop worrying, Mom. Everything's going to be okay. All that counts is that the Rabbi and you and Dad are here for me and Carlos. Everything else is icing on the cake.* She'd say that. Or something like that. Though it wouldn't do one bit of good. Leah would still be as nervous and fussy as an old hen.

He'd almost forgotten Carlos was waiting. He handed him the measurements. "You remember how to get there?"

"Yes. I have directions here." Carlos touched his shirt pocket and then stuck the second piece of paper, the one with the measurements, in the same pocket.

"Make sure the interior of the suitcase extends four or five inches beyond the size of the paintings to make room for the bubble wrap."

Carlos nodded.

"I think they have hard-sided suitcases that large?" He looked at Carlos for confirmation.

"If not, I buy two. As soon as Laskey gets here I'll . . . ."

"You don't have to wait." Fritz picked up the phone and frowned at the black screen as though it were hiding something from him. He hit the "on" button to make sure he hadn't missed a call even though the phone had been his constant companion from the time he woke up.

"Laskey was very clear about not leaving you alone in case they call," Carlos said. "He want to make sure no mistakes with instructions."

A clumk on the floor above them drew their eyes to the ceiling. "The cleaning woman cleans Rebekah's room every week whether Rebekah is here or not," Fritz said, "But I suppose Martha might have missed two dust particles."

Carlos's lips formed a half-smile. "My mother same way. Mostly, when she's angry. She whacks at furniture with a duster, drives vacuum around like a tank, and then goes on rampage throwing out old clothes, especially comfortable ones I want to keep."

"You don't have household help?"

"We do. But she claims cleaning is terapeutic. . . . thhherapeutic."

"Maybe we should learn a lesson from the women." Fritz looked at his watch. "Laskey should be here soon. Shall we go sit in the living room?"

He led the way, his eyes avoiding the six unframed pictures on the dining room table. The empty frames leaned against the far wall. Illogical thoughts clung to him like leeches: his perspiration would coat the phone so it wouldn't respond to his touch when they called; the phone would crash; the kidnappers had lost his number, and Rebekah would be too upset to remember; cell phone towers would cease to work because . . . . A storm? An airplane crashing into a tower? Interference from Russian hackers? Logic told him none of those things was going to happen, but his reason had crashed and burned.

He sat down and absently moved one of the mahogany pawns on his father's chess set. Then he swept his palm across the board, brushing the chessmen to the center of the board, toppling a couple. Never had he even imagined he could take another life, but now he knew he could. Without reserve. Without compunction. Without guilt. He'd send Eli out to buy ammunition. His explanation would be that everyone else had guns, so he might as well be prepared, too, in the event someone broke in in the middle of the night. Eli was a deer hunter; he could teach him to shoot.

He set the chess pieces upright, absently nudged them back to their proper positions, and then let his eyes rest on Grandfather clock where the hands now took an hour to travel a minute's distance.

Across the room, Carlos sat with his elbows propped on thighs, face resting in hands – a face that told the tale of not having slept. "I'm sorry," Fritz said. "I haven't asked after your family. I'd like to hear about them." Something to pass time, he thought.

Carlos sat back, draping an arm loosely over the back of the sofa. "I have one brother and two sisters, although I think Rebekah might already told you that. My father is self-made man. He began with mountain of debt, but he worked hard. Now he own most successful vineyard in the area. My mother . . . Well, she cleans for therapy. Not that she needs much therapy. They play bridge in

South America, too. She reads a lot. I got my temperament from her, not my father. The work I prefer is with the head, not the body." He nodded to his novel on the coffee table. "I like physical activity when it's connected to fun. Mountain climbing. Biking. Surfing whenever I happen upon a wave, which hasn't been in awhile." The muscles in his face tightened. "I finding it very hard right now to contain myself. Fear and anger are getting best of me. Maybe I should pick up a boxing bag along with the suitcase."

"I could use that, too." Fritz had gotten accustomed to Carlos' accent, barely noticing his struggle to pronounce "th" and his confusion of "e's" with "i's".

Someone tapped on the front door. He went to let Laskey in. As Laskey stepped inside, Carlos went out. Fritz saw them nod to each other. They looked like they were passing the torch in a relay. Zuela would come to do her lap later, sitting with him and the phone.

"Coffee?" Fritz asked when the door closed behind Carlos.

"Please."

In the dining room, Laskey stopped and frowned at the six pieces of art laid across the dining room table.

"You know about these, don't you?" Fritz gestured to the *Bride of the Wind* pastels.

"A tribute to a mistress who lost interest in him after a couple years," Laskey said. "Or maybe wishful thinking that the mistress would come back. I'm sure Kokoschka had a hard time accepting that he was nothing more than a passing fancy to Alma Mahler."

"Kokoschka wasn't the only man she left with a broken heart. Alma Mahler left a whole row of spurned men in her wake." Then he said softly, "Sometimes spurned men immortalize their lovers in paintings; and sometimes they seek revenge or teach their sons to."

LASKEY SAT down at the island while Fritz knocked and banged about, opening and closing a cabinet and then a drawer, setting out cups, clinking spoons down on saucers. A cloud of sweetness rose from the vase of pink roses sitting on the island. Laskey touched one, and a petal fell off. He picked it up, held it above the arrangement and let go, watching it fall to settle on another rose before drifting down onto the island.

"Carlos ordered the roses for Leah," Fritz said.

The scratch-scratch of a rake drew Laskey's attention to the wall of French doors. The yardman raking around the edges of the patio wore baggy khakis and a plaid flannel shirt rolled up to his elbows. He raked with a vengeance, straining against the piles of leaves, wet and heavy from rain. Laskey rose and walked to the window just as the yardman moved on to the backyard, leaving a couple piles to be picked up later.

"Are your neighbors interested in art?" he asked, glimpsing over his shoulder at Fritz.

Fritz had taken a bag of sugar from the pantry and was refilling the sugar bowl. "My neighbors would never . . . ."

"That isn't the point." Laskey turned around to face him. "A friend next door, or an acquaintance down the street might have inadvertently told the wrong person what you have. Did any of them know Rebekah's travel plans?"

"Maybe not her exact schedule, but they knew she was coming home." His face taut, Fritz rolled the top of the sugar bag to close it and then set it back in the pantry.

Laskey drew in a deep breath. He was suddenly suspicious of everyone – the yardman, the cleaning woman, the Herschmann's friends, Fritz's employees at the factory, Rebekah's acquaintances. Had one of them turned traitor? And how much time did he have to figure it out? A few hours? Two days?

"MacNeish said Rebekah bought Totsy a ticket so she could visit her in Amman," Laskey said.

Fritz gave a hint of a smile. "That was more a case of *Daddy* buying Totsy a ticket. Rebekah barely makes enough to buy a new pair of shoes. We didn't tell Totsy who paid for the ticket." He took a carton of cream from the refrigerator, set it down, and then folded his arms and leaned against the counter as he waited for the coffee to filter into the carafe. "I don't think you believed me when I said this before, but Gustav Fuchs is behind this." Fritz's face was dark.

"You can't be serious?"

"I am serious." Fritz's gaze met his, hard, as though he dared Laskey to contradict him.

"Chances are, Gustav Fuchs isn't even alive. He'd be . . . . how old?"

"Nearly a hundred."

Laskey winced. If Fritz seriously thought a man who was almost a hundred years old would suddenly decide to take what he could have had years ago by hiring a pair of second-rate thieves, then Fritz was losing his reason. "Gustav Fuchs couldn't have known about Rebekah's travel plans," Laskey said, walking back over to the island and sitting down.

"He hired someone to know."

"Why now? He could have hired someone to steal them at any time during the last six decades."

"I don't know why he waited until now." Fritz looked off to the side and, for a few seconds, Laskey thought he was going to cry. "Maybe because once again it's alright to despise anyone who isn't a WASP. Although I guess the Protestant part doesn't apply to Gustav Fuchs since Austria is the most Catholic country in Europe. People are setting fire to synogoguges and burning mosques. They're defiling homes of Indians. Refusing services to gays. Shooting black people in their churches."

Laskey frowned. Recent news proved his friend to be correct. Hate for minorities oozed from cracks and crevices from sea to shining sea. Still, he refused to believe that after so many years, Fuchs would retaliate for something that happened during the Nazi era.

"You know what hate is like?" Fritz asked. He narrowed his eyes.

"A few minutes ago, you said it was like a Clorox stain."

"It is, but I have another metaphor I like even better. Hate is like a buoy tied to the bottom of a lake. Eventually, the ropes rot, and the buoy shoots to the surface where it bobs around until someone manages to tie it down again. Lately, the ropes have rotted."

Laskey acknowledged the truth of this with a barely perceptible nod. Had Rebekah fallen victim to rotting ropes?

He knew what Fritz's father had been through. The Nazi era had been a time of powerful feelings, of intense hatred, of unforgivable crimes when too many people acted on their most base instincts. Maybe they'd been born without a conscience in the same way some people were born without an arm or ear. He'd always believed hatred was nutured, not passed on in DNA, but lately he'd begun to wonder if he was wrong. After forty years in his profession, he'd seen the worst of humanity; he'd tracked them down, arrested them, offered them up for prosecution. He wanted to believe that deep inside even the worst person there was a conscience, and he'd looked for evidence of that, but in too many cases he'd failed to find it. Still, he hoped.

But all that aside, Gustav Fuchs was too old and too far away. He closed his eyes and listened to the sputters and hisses of the coffee maker.

"Did I ever tell you that my grandfather knew Alma Mahler?" Fritz asked.

"No." Laskey opened his eyes. "You told me he knew Kokoschka, but nothing about him knowing Kokoschka's mistress."

The buzzer sounded, indicating the coffee was ready. Fritz held up a finger delaying an explanation while he poured. He set a cup down in front of Laskey, and then brought over his own, along with the ever-present phone, and sat down. "Let me tell you a story."

Chapter Twenty-Three

"M y grandfather's family lived in Pöchlarn, on the western edge of Vienna," Fritz began. "It's a beautiful walled village in the Danube Valley, not far from the Melk Monastery. Some people call the town Die Nibelungenstadt, or The City of Nibelung, because it's featured in *Song of the Nibelungs*, an epic written in the 12th century when the Huns invaded Europe.

"Pöchlarn is also the town where Kokoschka grew up and lived with his parents for many years even after he became an adult. My grandfather's Cousin Felix lived next door to the Kokoschkas."

Fritz propped his elbows on the counter. "I grew up on stories, and the ones about Felix are among the best, although some of those might best be left untold." He picked up a spoon and stirred his coffee, swirling it round and round, like a child playing with food. "Stories are what I have in place of family. Except for my parents, and Leah, and Rebekah, I've never had kin that I could see or touch or smell except through my father's memories. There are no family photos or mementos like a grandmother's china, or a great aunt's hand-embroidered handkerchief, or an uncle's gold watch. There aren't even any graves to visit. Yet, in a way, I *do* know my relatives because of the stories." A dream-like look came into his eyes as though he were savoring the memories of those he'd never known. "There was an aunt who was obsessed with removing warts. She invented remedies that never worked, but undeterred, kept at it. It's funny that someone should be remembered by posterity for their wart-removal efforts. One of my father's cousins was a poet, another a rogue. An uncle got rich by convincing a well-known courtesan to pose in ads for the ladies' night gowns he manufactured."

Laskey smiled. "I'm guessing it was the husbands who purchased the gowns for their wives?"

"I believe that might have been the case. But I'm digressing. Felix had dark, curly hair, long legs, and, except for a crooked nose, was considered to be one of the better-looking members of the family. He was also the one most likely to get in trouble. Once, he threw books from the window of the library at Karl-Franzens-Universität in Graz. Felix had a major paper due on Monday, but the library was closed on Sundays. On Saturday, he gathered the references he needed, lugged them down to the first floor of the library, and tossed them out a rear window to a friend. A groundsman pruning shrubbery saw them. The university was about to expel both Felix and his friend, but the professors came to their rescue, claiming students should be able to access the library on Sundays if they had papers due on Mondays.

"The near miss didn't teach him a thing. He continued to get in trouble one way or another. But you wanted to hear about Kokoschka. When Felix introduced my grandfather to Kokoschka, my grandfather wormed his way into Kokoschka's circle of painter friends. That's how he came to buy many of the works he collected. Most of the artists in the group didn't become as famous as Kokoschka and Schiele, of course."

"And so your grandfather got to know Kokoschka's mistress. Did he know her husband, Gustav Mahler?"

"I don't believe he ever met Mahler, but he saw him conduct the Vienna Court Opera plenty of times. They say Mahler treated his musicians like a lion tamer treats his lions. He was Jewish, you know?"

Laskey shook his head. He knew Mahler's music but very little about the man.

"But I'm digressing again."

Laskey smiled. "Your digressions are fascinating so I don't mind."

"Mahler died in 1911. It was during the two or three years after his death, that Alma had an affair with Kokoschka, and that's when my grandfather met her. His partner, Otto Fuchs, wrangled an introduction to Alma through him." Fritz gave a little snort.

"What was the snort about?"

"Apparently, my grandfather didn't get to know Alma nearly as well as his partner did."

Laskey raised his brows. "Your grandfather's partner had a liaison with Alma Mahler?"

"Who knows?" Fritz shrugged, drank a few sips of coffee, and then set the cup down.

"Whether or not he actually did, Otto wanted people to believe he had. Otto Fuch's one fault was womanizing. Otherwise, he and my grandfather were not only partners, but good friends despite my grandfather being Jewish and Otto being Catholic.

"I believe the seeds of what happened were planted when Otto's parents arranged for him to marry a third cousin. She had inherited a fortune, but was neither attractive nor especially intelligent. Her main interest in life was embroidering handkerchiefs and nagging everyone to *sit straight, shoulders back, chin tucked in.* Rumors were that she was frigid." He shrugged. "People talk. She may have been frigid, or maybe not, but that she and Otto had a miserable marriage is a fact."

Laskey swallowed the last of his coffee, rose, and took his cup over to the carafe. "You?" he motioned to Fritz's cup.

"No thanks."

Laskey refilled his cup, came back over, and sat down.

"Alma was a serial flirt," Fritz said. "She had a gift for making men feel like they were special. What the men didn't know was that Alma had a hearing problem and would lean toward them to hear what they were saying. When a beautiful woman leans toward you, opens her eyes wide, and keeps her gaze riveted to your face, it's easy to take that as attraction."

A clunk on the floor above them caused Laskey to look up.

"It's Leah. She's in a cleaning frenzy, and for once I'm glad. It's good for her to keep busy. By the time she's finished, Rebekah's room will be as antiseptic as an operating room." He ran a finger around the rim of the cup.

"Go on with your story," Laskey said. "I'm fascinated."

Rubbing his throat, Fritz looked up at some distant point on the ceiling. "Several people were at Kokoschka's studio one day, drinking and celebrating because *Bride of the Wind* was finished. They must have sensed the painting was going to win accolades. In between celebratory drinks and whatever else was going on, my grandfather nosed about, looking to see if there was anything he could rescue from the slush pile. Several of the paintings and drawings out there . . ." Fritz waved toward the door leading into the dining room ". . . my grandfather got by sifting around messy studios. He had an eye for what was good. Hence a collection we couldn't afford today."

Laskey's gaze had followed Fritz's gesture. A slice of dining room wall was visible along with a couple oils hanging there.

"My grandfather found the pastel studies for *Bride of the Wind* on a table among a bunch of other sketches surrounded by paint and charcoal and pens and brushes. He pulled the pastels from the muddle and walked around with them for a while, wine glass in one hand, drawings in the other. When Kokoschka asked him what he was doing with the drawings, my grandfather asked what *he* meant to do with them. Kokoshka replied he had no plans for them, except maybe the trash heap. My grandfather asked if he could buy them. Kokoshka, although a little crazy because Alma had left him, was nevertheless happy with the way *The Bride of the Wind* had turned out and was in a generous mood. He said my grandfather could have the two pastels for the payment of a kiss on Otto Fuchs' cheek. A *Judas kiss*, he called it, although I'm not quite sure the allusion was correct. As a Jew, I doubt that Kokoschka ever read the New Testament. No matter." He waved his hand in dismissal. "Kokoschka had grown weary of Otto's persistent attention to Alma, and assigned blame anywhere he could for Alma's desertion.

"It wasn't a good time in Otto Fuchs' life. His marriage had reached new depths of misery and his behavior showed it. He had run-ins with people at work, with friends, with family. Even Kokoschka's friends were pissed with him, so when Kokoschka made his proposal they laughed and pushed my grandfather to pay the price.

"Someone rang up Fuchs and told him they were having an impromptu party and to Schieb mal deinen Hintern hier rüber! When Otto arrived, already a bit inebriated, my grandfather kissed him on the cheek. Otto didn't like being touched by another man; he liked it even less when everyone laughed. He knew something was up and demanded to know what it was. At first, no one told him. 'Just a bet,' they kept saying.

"My grandfather put the the two drawings on top of a bureau where Kokoschka kept supplies and laid his jacket over them. When it was time to go, he grabbed his jacket and the drawings, said his goodbyes, and was headed toward the door when Otto stopped him and asked what was in his hand. My grandfather showed him.

'Are you stealing them?' Otto asked.

'I bought them,' my grandfather replied.

'You're not allowed to buy them.'

'Why not?' my grandfather asked.

'Because they were supposed to be mine. Alma promised I could have any studies Kokoschka didn't have plans for."

'They weren't hers to give away,' my grandfather retorted. 'Not then, and especially not now when she's abandoned him.'

"Kokoschka, who had overheard the exchange, stepped in and told Otto that my grandfather had payed for the pastels.

'I'll pay twice as much,' Otto offered.

'Then you'll have to kiss yourself twice,' Kokoschka said.

Fritz stopped. The muscles in his face, which had relaxed somewhat in the telling, suddenly became taut again. His mouth hung open, and the color drained from his face like water when the plug is pulled from a tub.

Laskey jumped up and put his hand on Fritz's arm. "Are you okay?"

"It isn't my heart," Fritz whispered. His splayed fingers pressed into the counter. "I can't . . .." He swallowed. ". . . I can't tell you the rest right now."

Chapter Twenty-Four

F ritz picked up *Art Treasures of the Vatican* from the coffee table and sat down. Hands shaking, he opened it, and pretended to look at the picture of the *Pieta* on the first page. Zuela sat across from him on the sofa. She'd arrived to take her turn sitting with him and the phone just as he finished telling Laskey the first part of the story.

"Forgive me," he said. "If I look at pictures of the Vatican, a few minutes will pass and I'll be closer to when . . . ." He tried to hold his hands steady so she wouldn't see how they shook.

She wiggled her fingers in dismissal. "You don't have to entertain me; I have papers to grade. I'd go upstairs and help Leah, but Laskey made it clear I'm to stay close to the phone." She pulled a stack from her brief case. "If you change your mind later and want to talk, I'll gladly procrastinate. Grading student essays on symbolism in *King Lear* isn't exactly uplifting."

He liked plain-spoken people, and Dr. Zuela Hay was nothing if not plain-spoken. It made it easier for him to say *Thank you, Zuela, I just don't feel like talking right now.*

Even his knees shook as he ran his finger erratically over the outline of the Pieta. How could he have forgotten something so vital? Gustav Fuchs *knew. He* would never forget something like that. Leah didn't know. He hadn't even thought of telling her. Not because it was a secret, but because it never crossed his mind. Now, thanks to his silence, his daughter's life was in danger. Leah would collapse if she knew. His mind raced, trying to find a solution.

"Fritz, are you all right?" Leah stood in the archway. She was in her stocking feet so they hadn't heard her coming. "Your face is covered with sweat."

"It isn't my heart." That was becoming a refrain. *It isn't my heart. It isn't my heart.* He forced away the blackness that threatened to engulf him and willed the room to stop spinning.

Zuela, red pen poised in mid-air, stared at him.

Leah took a step forward. "I'm going to call the doctor."

He struggled to his feet. "I'm okay, Leah."

"No, you're not. I'm calling Dr. Donalson." She came over to where he was and put her palm on his forehead .

"All I need is a glass of water. I've forgotten to drink, and I'm dehydrated." He pulled her to him and hugged her tight.

"It's going to be all right," Leah said into his shoulder. She drew back and looked at Zuela. "Tell him it's going to be all right."

"It will be," Zuela said. "It's simple. Deliver the paintings; they'll let her go."

He shivered. They wouldn't let her go when they saw the paintings. *It's the wind, Daddy, the wind of the bride.*

Chapter Twenty-Five

The wind whistled around the top of the tower, while MacNeish stood at the bottom leaning against the entrance door, his stomach in turmoil. He was used to the rhythmic beeping of monitors in the operating room, not the erratic, soughing, shrieking sound of wind. The wind blowing the trees back and forth, back and forth made him seasick. Or windsick. Or just sick. His belly seethed as if a rumbus of squirming rattlesnakes nested there.

His mind was in even worse shape. If only he hadn't done what he'd done. Or maybe, if he'd done what he *should* have done. Or maybe, he was wrong about everything. He wanted to lash out at something or somebody and end the agony, but there wasn't anything or anyone around to hit at other than the stone tower in front of him, and he would'na be lashing at that unless he wanted a broken hand.

Except for his rented Prius, the parking lot stood empty. Other than the tower, there was nothing around except maples, oaks, pines and whatever other trees he'd forgotten the names of after spending a ten-year eternity in a place where there weren't so many varieties.

Nor did the trees they *did* have in Jordan grow close together like this. He was standing in the middle of a bloody jungle, tree tops swaying and swishing in the wind, making him dizzy, closing him in. His nose prickled. He'd forgotten how it was to inhale so many outdoor scents at one time, dead leaves, pollen, sap, pine needles, bird droppings, bark.

He rattled the sign on the door of Bowman's Tower for the third time, or maybe it was the fourth, checking to see that it was securely fastened. *Tower Closed for Repairs*, it said. The sign was screwed firmly into the door, so there wasn't much chance of anyone knocking the sign off and then climbing the stairs or taking the elevator to the top of the 125 foot structure. They'd have to come back another time for a bird's eye view of the countryside surrounding Washington Crossing State Park.

Satisfied that no one could enter, he considered what to do next. It would take forty minutes or so to get from here to the place they were going to meet at one o'clock. If he set out around noon that would give him a twenty minute leeway in case he got lost. It was only eleven, so he still had an hour to waste.

He climbed into the Prius, drove the short distance to the Washington Crossing Visitors' Center, and parked. When he'd gone in earlier for a map so he could find Bowman's Tower, the woman had also handed him a brochure. He opened it and saw there were several things at the park to keep him busy until twelve.

Inside the visitors' center was a replica of *Washington Crossing the Delaware*, an event most people outside the United States hadn't heard of. Hell, most hadn't heard of George Washington, period. A big surprise to the natives. Thanks to going to med school in Chicago, he knew a few bits and pieces. Like George Washington being the father of the country and the accompanying joke: *George Washington slept here!*

The Crossing the Delaware painting was pictured on the front of the brochure. There he stood, the father of the country, ill-advisedly standing up in a boat crossing an icy river. If the boat overturned the freezing water would flood those oversized boots of his, drag him down into the mud, and he who had slept in so many places would probably have his last sleep at the bottom of the Delaware.

MacNeish turned the brochure over and looked at the back. When he tired of viewing an unrealistic painting, there was the park village to visit which, according to the text, consisted of several historical houses, an old inn, and a blacksmith shop. That's what the brochure said, *old*. They didn't know what *old* meant, these Americans. He could also visit the Thompson-Neely House which served as a temporary regimental army hospital during Washington's winter campaign of 1776-1777. . . . *a fine example of vernacular 18th-century architecture.*

Bloody hell. He did'na want to look at a *fine example of vernacular 18th century architecture.* He wanted things to be over. "But dear God," he moaned aloud, head jammed back on the head rest, "does it have to end this way?" How stupid he'd been. If he'd acted differently, spoken up when he had his chance, would things have come to a different ending?

Their first meeting had wound up in a yelling match. The day she reported for duty, he'd been busy, more than busy, having to slink past patients who weren't going to make it in order to take care of those who had a chance. He felt like a criminal for abandoning them. When he finished — except they were never finished; it was more accurate to say *when he stopped.* So, when he *stopped*, leaving an overcrowded ward of people still to be mended — he was dead on his feet, while *she'd* been engaged in a sit-in protesting the cost of vaccines. As if that would do any good. Newly arrived, and protesting.

"And what did you accomplish?" he asked when introduced, he, still wearing bloody scrubs, and she, a pair of jeans dusty on the butt from *sitting.*

"Attention to some of the greed in the world."

"You think a few paltry scunners are going to change the pharmaceutical companies' greed for profits?"

"No, but at least I'm . . . ." She stopped short, her head doing a little jerk. "Scunners?"

"*Whiners* in that language you speak in America." Then he'd suggested taking care of a few hundred people lined up to be treated for hepatitis, cholera, malaria, and a long list of other ills might have been more productive than sitting on her bum all day. That was when he first noticed that Rebekah acquired a special kind of beauty when her eyes fired up like she was about to shoot off projectiles from those lovely green-brown orbs. There'd been times when he thought those eyes looked like they wanted to leave her body behind and go out dancing on their own.

In the end, after they'd calmed down, Rebekah expressed regret at not having gone straight to work examining, inoculating, and dispensing those all-too-expensive drugs even though her official starting date wasn't until the following day. "But still . . .," she added, "... fighting the high cost of meds is important, too."

She'd continued the fight, while he turned his back metaphorically and refrained from repeating that she did'na stand a chance in bat's hell getting the companies to lower their prices. Months later, she told him about her grandfather's and great grandfather's company in Vienna, and about their giving free medications to those who couldn't afford it. He checked out the company and discovered what she said was true. Fuchs and Herschmann gave away free drugs in the value of three percent of their profits. That was before the Anschluss. He also discovered that before the outbreak of World War II, the company dropped *Herschmann* from its title and became simply *Fuchs, Inc.* A few years later, Seltzer Pharmaceuticals bought out the company. Karl Fuchs, third generation of the family, still worked for Seltzer.

MacNeish groaned. Telling him about the family business was something Rebekah shouldn't have done.

He wadded up the brochure and threw it on the floor. He wished he'd never heard of Fuchs and Herschmann. Or was it Herschmann and Fuchs? Enlightenment had turned him into a blithering idiot and a scabby, meddling bastard. And that arsehole Carlos had turned up in Jordan at exactly the wrong time. Not that any time would have been the right time for Carlos Vientos to put in an appearance

He got out, slammed the car door, and stormed toward the visitor center. "Get yourself together," he muttered between clenched teeth. "Go and look at the father of the country standing in a fooking boat, and then get your arse over to the restaurant and have your little meeting with Totsy."

Chapter Twenty-Six

Laskey unlocked Zuela's front door and entered the darkness of a living room with drawn drapes, and the quiet of a house located on a street with little traffic. The house smelled strongly of sawdust, and a light rain peppered the roof.

He flipped on the lights. The carpenters had finished building the shelves; all they had left to do was paint and clean up the mess. He waded through the wood shavings and sawdust in the dining room, trailing footprints onto the clean tile of the kitchen. Thanks to four bossy, but loveable, older sisters, he knew how to wield a broom and mop; he'd take care of his mess before he left.

He set his IPad down on the dinette table. Zuela had arrived at the Herschmann's to take over the watch exactly when she said she would, and after a whispered conversation in the entry, she'd handed him the key to her house. There'd been no reason for them to whisper except he didn't want Fritz hovering over him, questioning every thing he did, or warning him off. He could have gone to the office in the police station, but he didn't want the officers to wonder why he was there. *Has something happened? Are you working on a crime in the area? Why aren't the local police involved?* He hoped they would accept Bump's explanation that Rebekah was still at work in Jordan and wouldn't arrive until the end of the week.

He sat down and whipped out his phone. "Got anything for me, Janis?" he asked when his assistant answered.

"A list of collectors of early twentieth century Austrian, slash, Viennese art, and a shorter list of people interested primarily in Kokoschka."

"Read them off to me." Then he remembered the IPad. "Can you email them?"

"I can. Hold on . . . ."

While he waited, he opened the IPad, put the tip of his forefinger on the sensor, and watched the screen come to life.

"Okay, it's sent," Janis said. "Do you want to see if you got it, before we hang up?"

He checked his email and found it. "Got it," he said. "Thanks. There's something else I need."

"Yes, boss?"

"See if you can find an obituary for Gustav Fuchs, a resident of Vienna, or articles relating to his death. Get back to me right away if you find anything."

After hanging up, he checked the list of collectors for Gustav Fuch's name. It wasn't there. He began googling the names of the collectors from Janis' list and discovered they were located primarily in the United States and Europe, Austria in particular. Several lived in Norway and France; a few were scattered among the other European countries. One was from Dubai and another from South Africa. None raised an alarm. Nor should they have. Had they been dishonest, they would simply have paid for someone to steal the paintings.

He grabbed a napkin from a napkin holder and wiped his palms. Urgency drove him. His adrenaline was pumping, sweat glands doing double time, and muscles tightening like knots on a noose. He rose and paced while he tried calling MacNeish. No answer. He must still be asleep. He'd get him later. The Scotsman wasn't going anywhere unless he was prepared to walk the two miles from Jacob's into town.

Zuela had invited him to help himself to whatever was in her refrigerator, so he put together a roast beef sandwich. He ate it standing up, torn between going back to stay with Fritz, delving into the identity of the Judas in their midst, or trying to discover Rebekah's place of concealment. *The wind, Daddy; it's the wind.* He was certain she'd been trying to tell them something.

He sat down and typed "wind farms in PA" in the search line. Several sites came up, one showing a list of twenty-five wind farms but they were all in the northern or western part of the state. Maybe she was in a tower of some sort?

He finished his sandwich, wiped a mustard stain from the counter, and then typed "James MacNeish" in the search line. He didn't suspect Doctor James MacNeish was anyone other than who he said he was, yet he still felt a pang of disappointment when MacNeish's picture and bio popped up verifying his identity. Native of Aberdeen, Scotland. Graduate of University of Chicago Medical School, first in his class. Employed by Medecin Sans Frontiere in Amman, Jordan.

No suspicions, yet he was annoyed with MacNeish. Irrationally, he knew. It was evident that MacNeish had been too exhausted yesterday evening to give him much, or any, relevant information. And this morning, Laskey couldn't rouse him from bed. Or from whatever he was doing. Maybe he was sitting on Jacob's back door steps counting geese. Laskey slouched back in the chair, letting his arms fall limply to his sides. He wanted *something* to sink his teeth into. MacNeish's boarding pass had fallen out of his pocket and onto the seat of the Sequoia when he drove him to Jacob's the previous evening. Laskey had found it this morning. According to the boarding pass, MacNeish had arrived when he said he had.

Even if he allowed himself to believe what Fritz believed, that Gustav Fuchs was responsible, there had to be others involved. Someone local.

He closed the IPad with a snap. Totsy might be wifty, but there was something else, something he couldn't quite put his finger on, about Rebekah's friend that had questions reverberating in his head. He pushed his chair back abruptly, grabbed his IPad, and started for the door. He also wanted to encourage Totsy's and her mother's belief that Rebekah had been held up in Amman.

LASKEY KNOCKED on Totsy's front door, and then paced a few steps before knocking again. The Chevy Volt was still parked in the driveway. Unless it belonged to her mother, Totsy hadn't gone anywhere.

Two houses away, the street vacuum roared, sucking up leaves while the two men in charge shouted at each other. "You left a pile." "Get out of the way." "You drive like a woman."

Finally, the door opened.

"You again?" Delores Love crossed her arms and glared at him through the screen door.

"Yes, it's me." He glared back. "I'd like to see Totsy."

"You already saw her."

"I want to see her again."

"She isn't here."

"Where is she?"

Delores's lips twitched. "At work."

"Then I'll talk to you."

"I have nothing to tell you." The crossed arms tightened. "If Rebekah Herschmann didn't show up yet, it ain't got nothing to do with Totsy."

He brought out his ID and tapped it on the palm of his other hand.

She gave him a searing look, then opened the screen door and let him enter.

"You were working?" He motioned to the table in the dining room. Judging by the smell of glue and the white ooze that lined her cuticles, he guessed she'd been occupied in the creation of one her masterpieces.

"Yes, I was working. You interrupted me."

He walked the few feet into the next room and saw that she'd glued a mirror onto a piece of plywood. In the four-inch margin between the mirror and the edge of the plywood, she was creating a frame by gluing on tile shards of different colors and shapes.

"It's for our bathroom," she said coming up beside him.

He tried to look interested. "Very nice. Do you sell them?"

"I'm going to start taking them to craft fairs. I don't have much time after working fifty hours a week, but Totsy might help me. Or maybe not." She shrugged. "Totsy manages to be busy when I need her. But maybe if I share the profits . . . . She's always trying to get money."

Laskey raised his eyebrows.

"She wants to go to Hollywood and get a job in the movies."

"She's quite beautiful."

Delores seemed to swell a bit. "I wasn't so pretty myself. I was okay, I guess, but not what you'd call beautiful like Totsy. Maybe she really can be in the movies. Who knows? She tried her luck on Broadway and got a couple jobs, but not enough to live on."

"I hear it's hard to get started in show business."

"A man in New York promised to introduce her to people in Hollywood."

"That sounds promising. I hope it works out for her." How old was that line? *I know someone who can get you into the movies.*

Feigning calmness, he wandered over to the wall where one of the shard compositions hung. He ran his finger over a tree that looked like it had been created from depression glass. "I guess you must have seen the Herschmann's paintings?"

"Them ugly things? Yeah, I got invited to one of Rebekah's birthday parties once. They invited all her friends and their parents. There were graduation parties, too. High school, college, and med school. They say some of them pictures are worth a lot."

He turned around. "Who says?"

She shrugged. "I don't know. Everybody, I guess. This is a small town. Everybody knows pretty much everything. "What did you want to ask Totsy?"

"I had some questions about Rebekah's college friends. The

ones Totsy met when they visited Goose Bend. And I hoped Totsy could give me names and where the friends lived. Maybe you can."

"Fritz can't do that?" Delores looked puzzled.

"You probably know he had a heart attack a few months ago. He's having some routine tests, and Leah's with him."

"Why do you need to know about Rebekah's college friends? You think that has something to do with her not coming home?"

"Ahhh, I guess I forgot to tell you." Laskey tried to look contrite. "It's exactly as you and Totsy said: Rebekah has been held up in Jordan. She'll be home in a few days. This is about something else."

She stared at him, waiting for an explanation.

"There was an attempted robbery a few months back," he said. "Fritz thinks someone was after his paintings and is afraid they might try again. It's possible one of Rebekah's friends inadvertently told someone about the collection."

Delores rubbed her chin, thinking. "Maybe Totsy did mention a few names and where they were from, but I wasn't real interested in Rebekah Herschmann's college friends so I didn't listen."

"I guess Totsy met them on several occasions."

Delores nodded.

He'd grown up with four older sisters and knew how they were when one was pissed off at another. Totsy's lie about not knowing Rebekah's college friends probably had more to do with a slight than with a kidnapping. A tiff? Jealousy over an engagement? A feeling of rejection because Rebekah didn't want Totsy picking her up at the airport?

He moved over to another shard picture, this one of . . . . Actually, he wasn't sure. A barn with a lake in the background? Or was it Noah's ark floating on the flood? "Are you familiar with any of the artists in the Herschmann's collection?" he asked.

"What does that have to do with the price of tea in China?"

"Did you ever discuss the Herschmann's art collection with your customers at the Bronco?"

She narrowed her eyes at him. "The first time you showed up, it was about Rebekah not coming home, now you're talking about someone trying to steal their pictures."

"I guess that does seem rather odd." He tried to smile. "You know how it is. Sometimes you're focusing on one thing when another pops up. Like starting to take out the garbage but realizing the floor is a mess, so you stop to sweep." She looked puzzled, and he wasn't sure the metaphor fit, but he pushed on. "Did you talk to anyone about the Herschmann's collection?" Attempting another smile, he softened his tone and said, "Don't take offence. I'm asking a number of people the same thing."

She rubbed the front of one hand with the palm of the other. "Maybe I did talk about their pictures. I don't remember." She shrugged. "It's something to talk about, isn't it? A rich Jewish family living in our little dump of a town with stuff the rest of us don't have."

"Fritz is very concerned." A feeling of hopelessness washed over him. By the time he tracked down everyone who had been in the Herschmann's house and checked out their connections, Rebekah Herschmann would be long home or . . . .

"Thank you for your time," he said and started for the door, but then stopped and turned back to Delores. "When did you say Totsy will be home?"

"I didn't. I don't keep up with my daughter's work schedule."

LASKEY CRAWLED INTO HIS SEQUOIA, checked his phone, and saw a message from Bump: *Call Me.* He hit the recall button.

"I saw your vehicle in front of the Love's," Bump said by way of answering. "You still in the house?"

"Just left, I was about to crank up. Are you tailing me?" He tried to fasten his seatbelt one-handed.

"We always tail suspicious looking characters from out of town. Do you have five minutes? I just paid Aunt Sarah a visit."

Laskey gave up with the seatbelt. "Where can I meet you?"

"I'm down by the river. If you park in the lot at River Point Café and walk down the path though the woods behind the restaurant, you'll find me. There's usually no one around this time of day so we can talk in private."

"Be there in five."

River Point was a small restaurant on the banks of the Pumqua. He'd passed it numerous times, but nothing about the low-roofed, gray shingled place had ever enticed him inside. He pulled into its half-full parking lot, got out, and found the path. He walked through a stand of spruces, ash, and maples to where Bump sat on a bench beside the bike trail that hugged the banks of the Pumqua.

Bump slid over and patted the space beside him. "How are Fritz and Leah holding up?" he asked.

Laskey sat down. "They're trying to keep from falling apart, and they're working hard to believe that if they follow the kidnappers' directions everything will end up okay. I hope they're right."

"So do I," Bump said. "How much did they demand?"

Laskey stared at the river lapping at the bank and at the geese waddling about on the shore or paddling in the water. He both wanted and didn't want to tell Bump they'd demanded paintings instead of money. His experience with Bump in a murder case several months ago had shown Bump to be fair-minded and cooperative, unlike some he'd worked with who had as much interest in getting the credit as in solving the crime. But the demand for paintings was unusual enough he feared Bump would inadvertently let it out. He couldn't risk that.

"Fritz is able to give them what they asked for," he said, hoping Bump wouldn't press further. "Carlos also offered to get money from his parents if necessary." He kicked at a stone that lay near his feet.

Bump took a pipe from his jacket pocket, knocked it on his knee a couple times, and then let it rest there. "Aunt Sarah told me Fritz fired two people in the last couple years. My aunt has a memory like a steel trap. I'll bet she could even tell me what kind of clothes the two were wearing the day they got fired." He stuck the pipe in his pocket, leaned back, and draped his arms over the back of the bench. "Two years back, Fritz fired a young man named Freddie Haynes. Freddie kept showing up late for work even after several warnings. One day he messed up a batch of chocolate by dropping a cigarette in the mixer. Smoking isn't allowed anywhere near the building. Imagine a chocolate bar tasting like cigarette smoke. Fritz shafted him on the spot. Freddie made a big fuss about going and had to be escorted out. Turns out, he had a drinking problem."

"Where's Freddie now?"

"Haven't seen him around in awhile.

"And the other person Fritz fired?"

Bump frowned, removed his arms from the back of the bench and repositioned his body. "James bloody Eakins."

"Sounds like there's no love lost there."

"James Eakins was, and probably still is, one of the greatest assholes of the century. Well . . . , there *is* someone who beats him, but we won't talk politics now."

Laskey studied Bump. Assholes, by virtue of being assholes, often got blamed for things they didn't do simply because they *were* assholes. A surly attitude toward a police chief and a few ill-considered responses could put a person like that in the limelight and sometimes in the lineup.

"Is he still around?"

"Insofar as I know, he left town a while back and hasn't returned."

"Why was he fired?"

"Theft. Caught red-handed. He was an obnoxious little shithead."

"Little?" It was the first time Laskey had seen Bump express contempt and loathing for someone.

Bump's face turned red. "He's short; not little. A weight lifter, so he's muscular. But his arrogance exceeds both his musculinity and his masculinity."

"I'm guessing there must have been a run-in or two between you."

Bump shrugged and gave a sniff of a laugh. "Just small town stuff. Car parked in wrong place. Nasty comments to the receptionist when he came in the station once. Stuff like that."

"And where is this obnoxious little shithead now?"

"James Eakins is Totsy Love's uncle. Her mother's half-brother."

Zing! Laskey's brain churned. "Where did you say he is?" He tried to keep his voice calm.

"He used to live in an apartment building where Seventh intersects Vine, but I haven't seen him in ages. He must have left town."

Laskey had seen the building, a run-down, three-story affair. "Think you can find out where he is?"

"I'll run a search. On the off chance he has something to do with this, I won't ask Totsy or Delores straight out.

"Text me when you find out something," Laskey said, rising. "I have one more thing to do, and then I'm going to stand vigil with Fritz."

"I'm putting everyone on duty between now and . . . . whenever," Bump said. "I'll think of some excuse. Like the Martians are about to land, or ISIS plans to fly planes into the Pennston Hotel. We'll be standing by for whatever you need us for."

"Thanks, Bump."

LASKEY, about to back out of his parking place, jammed on his brakes. Totsy and MacNeish were walking out of the restaurant, heads together in conversation. They stopped for a few seconds to finish up whatever they were talking about and then went to separate cars, Totsy to a Honda Civic and MacNeish to a silver Prius. Totsy climbed in and drove away.

MacNeish opened his car door, but instead of getting in, stopped to look down at something. He stood in the triangle between door and driver's seat so Laskey couldn't see what he was looking at. His phone? After a few seconds, MacNeish got into the Prius and set out in the opposite direction from Totsy.

Laskey tapped out Bump's number. "Where are you?" he asked when Bump answered.

"Parked on the opposite side of the restaurant from you."

"Do me a favor?" Laskey was backing out as he talked.

"Name it."

"Totsy just left the restaurant. She turned right. Can you follow and see where she goes?"

"Totsy? . . . . . Sure."

Laskey hung up, pulled out of the lot, and shot off after MacNeish.

Chapter Twenty-Seven

Fritz stared at the three masted schooner he'd been working on last week. Bits and pieces of balsa and string lay scattered beside the vise. He stuck the ship back in the foam cradle from which he'd removed it a minute ago, and would undoubtedly remove it again in another minute. He unstacked the beeswax bars he used on his models, restacked them, and pushed them to the edge of the table. Then he pulled them back toward him and unstacked and restacked them again.

Leah was still in Rebekah's room wearing herself out dusting, polishing, and windexing. Zuela had gone home shortly after Carlos arrived. He heard Carlos opening and closing drawers and cabinets in the kitchen, and wondered what he was doing. His future son-in-law had come back from the mall with the requisite hard-sided suitcase and, after Fritz examined it, left the piece of grey Samsonite in the dining room.

Fritz guessed Carlos hadn't eaten lunch and was looking for food. He should be a good host and go and help him, but he hadn't the energy. He ran his forefinger aimlessly along the schooner's port and starboard. A few seconds later, or maybe it was minutes – his sense of time had warped – the shuffle of shoes drew his eyes to the door where Carlos stood with three stems of wine.

"You need to de-stress if that's possible, so I got a good Rombauer while I was out." He walked over and handed a glass to Fritz. He set the other two on the coffee table. "I go try and lure Leah down."

When Carlos had gone, Fritz swirled the wine, observing the legs from habit, and then he held it to his nose, also from habit, and inhaled the floral aroma. Habits, like hate, hung on. He took a sip, and then another. It was a good wine. Smooth and dry. He was glad for the drink. In his agony over what to do about his dilemma, he'd forgotten to drink anything. Now he realized how thirsty he was.

He heard Carlos coming down the stairs alone.

"I can pack the pictures for you," Carlos said walking in. He sat down on the sofa, picked up a glass of wine, and took a sip.

"Not just yet." Fritz sank back in his chair – one of two he'd been living in since Thursday evening; this one and the chair in the living room. Even though he'd been over to the factory, taken a short walk on Sunday evening, and gone back and forth to the kitchen several times and upstairs to check on Leah's frenetic cleaning, he *felt* like he was permanently glued to the accursed chairs. When this was over, he'd throw them out. He wanted no reminders of his wretched vigil.

"Is there anything else I can do?" Carlos asked.

Fritz squeezed his eyes shut. This was his daughter's fiancé, yet he didn't want to talk to him. Not that he had anything against him; he rather liked Carlos as a matter of fact, but he didn't want to make conversation with anyone right now. Not even Leah. He'd burrowed so deep inside himself that to climb out and attend to someone's chatter required superhuman effort when he needed every power he possessed to work out a solution..

Leah trudged into the room, her clothes mussed from cleaning and her mouth drooping. "Have either of you eaten today?" She looked from one to the other.

"We're fine," Fritz said, even though they weren't. "Carlos poured you a glass of wine. Sit down and join us."

She shook her head and pressed her lips together.

Fritz saw she was trying to keep from crying. "Then go and relax," he said. You're tired. Have a long soak in the bathtub. When you're ready, we'll have an early dinner."

"I haven't put anything out to thaw."

"Don't worry, dear. We'll figure it out. Go take a rest."

"I think I'll do that. You'll get me if . . . ." She nodded to the phone.

"Of course."

Aware of Carlos' eyes following him, Fritz went to stand at the window. How much longer could he stand upright? Everything had become an effort. Standing, eating, sleeping. His heart beat erratically, furiously at times, skipping and racing toward a rendezvous he didn't want to think about. If he could only bring his daughter home, he didn't care what happened to himself after that. His time was written in the sands, and what was to be, would be. At least for him. But Rebekah's fate was in his hands.

Then the solution came to him. Of course. Had he not been so addle-brained with worry, he'd have known immediately what he had to do. It might not work. But it also *might* work.

Chapter Twenty-Eight

L askey trailed MacNeish through town, then when MacNeish turned right onto Blushing Road, followed by a left onto Third, Laskey guessed he was returning to Jacob's.

Five minutes later, MacNeish turned into Jacob's lane. Lasked followed, drove around to the back of the house, and parked beside the Prius.

MacNeish was standing at the edge of the yard, looking down at the pond, but turned around as the Sequoia rattled to a stop. Laskey got out, slammed his door, and headed toward MacNeish.

"Where were you this morning?" Laskey demanded when he was within hearing distance.

"Driving around." MacNeish lifted his shoulders in a question. "Why?"

"You had lunch with Totsy Love."

"Yer spying on me?"

Laskey was fighting to control his anger. "You must have figured out by now we're a little desperate here, trying to figure out who knew about both Rebekah's travel plans and the Herschmann's art collection. So if you're belly-aching about my spying on you, which I wouldn't have been doing had I been able to reach you this morning, then, tough." He stopped to take a breath. "How do you know Totsy?" He glared at MacNeish. "Why were you having lunch with her?"

MacNeish crossed his arms and glared back. "I know Totsy because she visited Rebekah in Amman. Rebekah bought her a ticket, and Totsy came for a week."

Laskey was momentarily silenced. Fritz had told him that, but he'd forgotten.

"As for lunch, we're both worried about Rebekah. We were trying to figure out what might have happened."

"Did you?"

"Sorry, I can'na help ye out. We have no answers."

Eyes narrowed, Laskey studied MacNeish. MacNeish wasn't telling him something. He knew that as surely as he knew the sun would come up tomorrow morning. "Why are you going to the Center for Disease Control when you're an orthopedic surgeon?"

"Sometimes they have conferences that ha' nothing to do with communicable diseases. But obviously I'm not going now." He gave Laskey a hard look.

"You were one of the last to see Rebekah, you and Annemarie. Forgive me if I'm off track, but I think you're holding something back."

MacNeish looked away. "I don't know what yer talking about." He turned abruptly and headed for the back door.

Chapter Twenty-Nine

J acob knew it was probably just another one of his crazy ideas as he pulled up in front of Aunt Zuela's. Maybe the idea even fell into the category of ludicrous, but if he didn't follow through, and if it turned out he was right when it was too late, he'd never forgive himself.

"I have to consult with a geologist at The University of Pennsylvania," he'd told Shreya when he left work early. Two Saturday's before, he'd spent the afternoon with Dr. Rosenhall who cleared up several questions dealing with the geology of areas in western Pennsylvania where fracking had created problems with the water supply. He had another question related to the same issue, and he also needed to return the maps Dr. Rosenhall had loaned him. Running down to the campus, returning the maps, and asking his question had taken no more than ninety minutes. Now, unless he chickened out, he was going to have a go at wheedling Aunt Zuela to help him with his ridiculous idea. He got out of the car and headed toward her front door.

A workman wearing off-white coveralls and wielding a paint brush, looked up as Jacob walked in without knocking. A gallon can of white paint stood on a drop cloth below the half-painted shelves.

The sawdust had been mostly swept up. There was only a small pile near the kitchen door.

"Don't let me disturb you," Jacob said.

"Are you a thief, or are you looking for Dr. Hay?" The painter, a beefy man with wide shoulders and huge hands, had stopped mid-stroke, brush poised in its swipe across shelf.

"The latter."

"Back there, then." The painter jerked his thumb in the direction of the hallway that ran from the dining room to the rear of the house. Skirting the paint can and a step ladder, Jacob made his way to her office and found her scowling at the computer.

"Good heavens, what has Jezebel done to deserve that look?" he asked. She always named her computers.

She huffed. "It isn't Jezebel that's causing the look. I was trying to work on a paper, but all I can think about is Fritz and Leah." She clicked *save* and swiveled her chair around to face him. "I just got home from the Herschmann's."

"They didn't call?" *They*, spoken in a certain tone, had come to mean one thing, and one thing only: the kidnappers.

She shook her head. "Come have a cup of tea with me." She stood up and led the way to the kitchen. "I guess you don't really want tea?" she asked when they got there.

"A coke's fine."

She put the kettle on to boil and then handed him a coke from the refrigerator. "You can get your own glass and ice. Isn't it a little early for you to be home from work?"

"It is." He tore the tab off the coke and dropped it in the trash can beneath the sink. "I have a favor to ask."

"You left work early to beg a favor?" She leaned against the stove, arms crossed. Behind her, the stove eye was turning red. "I can hardly wait to hear. The last time I let you talk me into something, I wound up in New York City freezing my butt off. I'm not up for that again. Although I do have to admit that adventure came to quite an interesting conclusion."

He gave a brief smile at her reference to an event a few months ago when he'd inadvertently gotten mixed up in a murder investigation and persuaded her to go to Queens in search of information. "Nothing as drastic as that, and it doesn't involve exposure to the elements. All you have to do is go over to the Herschmann's this evening and follow a few simple instructions. I'd do it myself, only they'd notice."

"Why would they notice you and not me?"

"Because of the nature of what I want you to do."

"Which is?"

"Don't you have something to go with this?" He held up the coke. "Peanut butter cookies or something?"

"Do you think I run a bakery?" She fumbled in the pantry, pulled out a package of Oreos, and handed them to him. "Go sit down before you get crumbs all over my floor, and tell me what it is you want. I'm not promising anything, but you can try me."

He straddled a chair and opened the Oreos. She sat down opposite him. He bit into an Oreo, took another bite, and another, while she thumped her fingers on the table impatiently. He knew she was one of the most curious creatures on the face of the earth, and that it had to be truly painful to wait for him to reveal his plan, but he was a little hesitant. The idea was ridiculous. Finally, he brushed the crumbs from his lips and explained what he wanted.

"You're kidding," she said when he finished. She sat back, letting her arms fall limply to her sides. "You're kidding," she repeated.

"Maybe, I'm wrong, but. . . ."

"Of course, you're wrong. Good lord, what an absurd idea."

"What if I'm right?" He raised his eyebrows at her. "No one will realize what you're doing, so if I'm wrong I won't come across as a complete idiot to anyone except you."

She narrowed her eyes. "If you're not wrong, what's the motive?"

He shrugged. "Money?"

When she sat up straight, her eyes sparking with devilment, he knew she was in.

"What excuse do I give for showing up at the Herschmann's again?" she asked. "I've already been there once today. They might prefer to be alone."

"Bring food. Tell them you're just going to leave it and go away, but if they ever want you, you're there for them."

"But I won't be leaving if I do what you want."

"Just take a long time leaving. I'll bring MacNeish over at the same time. He'll want to pay a visit to Rebekah's parents. We'll take a long time leaving, too. There'll be enough people and activity that no one is going to notice what you're up too."

"I hope you're right about this." Her forehead creased. "Actually, I hope you're *not* right. Either way, right or wrong, things aren't good. Does Laskey know what you're up to?"

"No."

"That was a rather abrupt *no*."

"It was. What we're doing can't do any harm, so there's no point telling him."

Chapter Thirty

F ritz slipped into the mudroom and closed the kitchen door behind him. Carlos and Leah were in the den staring blankly at the news, the volume turned down so low no one could hear what was being said. He'd excused himself saying he needed a glass of water. He moved to the far end of the mudroom and turned his back to the kitchen door just in case one of them walked into the kitchen and could hear through the closed door. Without asking, he'd taken Leah's phone, not daring to use his own, which was in his pocket, in case *they* called.

He tapped out Eli's number.

"Is everything under control over there?" Fritz asked, keeping his voice down.

"Absolutely. Your medical check up went okay?"

"I'm good. I need a favor. Leave Bay or Erika in charge and go out to Fopple's Guns and buy ammunition for the pistol my father locked in the safe. You can bring the gun and bullets over after work. And I'd appreciate it if you didn't say anything about this."

There was silence on the other end. "The pistol?" Eli finally asked. "And you want me to buy ammo? You haven't had any . . ."

"No, no intruders, but there've been break-ins around town."

There *had* been break-ins. One or two in the past fifteen years. "Can you take care of it today?"

"Uh . . ., sure."

Laskey hung up before Eli could ask more questions and before someone came into the kitchen and heard him. He left the mudroom, went to the sink, and poured a glass of water. His father had brought the gun with him from Austria. Until now, there'd been no reason to take the pistol out of the safe.

Chapter Thirty-One

L askey knocked on Zuela's door. "I wonder if I could impose on you again," he said when she opened it. "I need a quiet place to make a couple phone calls. If I go to the police station they'll wonder what's going on. If I go back to my office in Doylestown, it'll take too much time, and I want to get back over to the Herschmann's ASAP.

Zuela motioned toward her study at the back of the house. "Be my guest. I'll send out rent bills next week."

"Thanks. I appreciate it."

"If you need anything, holler."

Laskey headed toward the rear of the house, nodding at the man painting shelves as he passed. "Looks good."

"It's the second coat. I'll be finished in another hour and out of everyone's hair." The painter pushed back his cap with the back of his hand.

Laskey sat down at Zuela's desk and called Janis. "Any luck finding an obituary for Gustav Fuchs?"

"Nothing," she replied. "I found some old references to him regarding his former position at Seltzer Pharmaceuticals, and quite a few on his son, Karl, who still works for Seltzer. But no obits. Sorry. Or maybe that's good. Did you want him dead or alive?"

"I'm not sure."

"Anything else, Boss?"

"See what you can dig up on a James Eakins. He was, and maybe still is, a resident of Goose Bend. If I think of something else, I'll get in touch."

He stuck the phone back in his pocket. His reason told him that even if Gustav Fuchs were still alive, he'd be too old to be responsible for Rebekah's kidnapping. Viscerally, he wasn't so sure. Fuchs would have had to rely on someone who knew the details of the Herschmann's lives. It was possible that both Freddie Haynes and James Eakins carried grudges against Fritz for firing them, and James would be in a position to know about Rebekah's plans through Totsy, but he'd bet the possibility of either man knowing anything about Kokoschka or Schiele was almost nonexistent. In the unlikely event Gustav Fuchs was responsible, and if either Haynes or Eakins was involved, there had to be yet another person connecting them. Totsy? Could a young woman as wifty as Totsy appeared to be organize a kidnapping?

Laskey propped his elbows on the desk and leaned his chin on clasped hands. Other than Fuchs being the unlikely culprit, he didn't have many theories to explore. Many? He didn't have *any* to explore other than this one in which there was an ocean between a possible culprit and the scene of the crime, and several decades separating motivation from action.

So what did he do now? The strain of having to rely on the kidnappers keeping their word ate at him like worms devouring rotten meat. He couldn't put a tracer on the suitcase. They'd find it. If they were smart they'd switch the paintings to a different suitcase. He couldn't put a tracer on the paintings themselves. Not that it would do any good. Whoever received the paintings when Fritz delivered them would hand them over to an appraiser. It was possible that the person receiving them wouldn't know where Rebekah was being held. Once the authenticity of the pieces was established, the paintings would be sent to the person responsible for this nightmare, and then the culprits would either keep their word and let her go, or they wouldn't.

Or they wouldn't. A coldness cut Laskey to the core. Rebekah almost certainly knew her abductor. She wouldn't have taken a call at the airport, left the terminal, and crawled into someone's car without knowing the person. He was, of course, assuming she crawled into someone's car. Regardless, the abductor wouldn't want to risk Rebekah's being able to identify him or her.

He tried to banish the images of Billy Hatcher's tormented body that kept flashing through his head. The images were of his own invention. The newspapers hadn't shown pictures of the dead boy, but on TV they'd shown EMTs carrying a covered body on a stretcher. His imagination had filled in the rest.

His phone rang.

"Totsy went straight home after lunch," Bump said. "I'm at the station now, doing a search on James Eakins. I'll let you know as soon as I find out something." He hung up.

Laskey hit the "recall" button for Annemarie Leitner's number. She answered on the fourth ring.

"Ja?"

Caught off guard that she'd actually answered her phone, he sat up straight. "This is Detective William Laskey calling from The United States."

"Was sagen Sie? Villem. . . .? Scheiss. It's midnight."

"I said this is Detective William Laskey, I've tried contacting you several times, but midnight seems to be the only time you answer your phone."

There were a few moments of silence, then, "I was in Mayrhofen, mountain climbing. What do you want?"

"To ask about your friend, Rebekah Herschmann."

"What the fuck? Excuse my language, but you're calling at midnight to ask about my friend?"

"She's disappeared."

"What do you mean, *she's disappeared?*"

Laskey frowned. First there was Totsy who didn't read her messages, and now Annemarie who didn't listen to her voicemail.

"She didn't arrive home on Thursday. I believe you were the last person to see her."

"We went to the airport together."

"She got as far as Philadelphia and then disappeared."

"She couldn't just disappear; Carlos was coming."

"Well, she did. I know Vienna's population is edging up toward two million, but you don't happen to know Gustav Fuchs, do you? Or Karl Fuchs, his son?"

He heard her breath catch. "I've met both." She hesitated, and then said, "I met them at a party my parents were invited to eight or ten months ago. My father does consulting work with the company. Karl Fuchs was the host, but the old man was there. I was home on leave and asked to tag along because I thought he might be the same Fuchs Rebekah told me about. Her grandfather's business partner."

"And he was?"

"Yes. Strangely enough, the old man didn't act surprised when I told him I worked with Rebekah. He kept asking questions about her."

"Did he ask when she was going home on leave?"

"Yes. I told him she sometimes stopped off in Vienna for a visit on her way home to America. He asked about the next time she planned to come because he wouldn't mind meeting her. I said we were both on leave in October, but I thought she was going straight home."

Laskey had gone cold. "Could you find out if either or both of the Fuchs are in Vienna at the present time and let me know right away?"

"Why?"

"Fritz Herschmann is sure the old man is involved."

After a period of silence, she said, "I can try."

He gave her his number and hung up. Could it really be that an old man, nearly a hundred years old, had engineered Rebekah's kidnapping?

Chapter Thirty-Two

Annemarie swung herself around to sit on the edge of the bed, bare feet resting on the cold floor. Scheiss. What had she done? What had MacNeish done? She should have taken him seriously instead of brushing his ranting aside as . . . . well, as *ranting.* Damn him. And that idiot, Totsy? Had she fallen in with MacNeish? Scheiss, Scheiss, Scheiss.

She switched on the table lamp and fumbled for her phone in the bedding where she'd set it after the detective's call. Jamie MacNeish, possessor of a brilliant mind and extremely talented as a surgeon, was as stupid as a turtle when it came to human relations. Or maybe she was the one who was stupid. She hadn't believed for one minute he'd carry through. She'd chalked up his threats to letting off steam. She should have warned Rebekah. Like MacNeish, Rebekah was brilliant, yet sometimes failed to see what was right under her nose.

Jamie's number, where was it? Her glasses were in the kitchen and the floor between bed and kitchen counter was cold, so she took a stab at remembering, but hit "end" before the phone rang on the other end. Verdammt, what *was* his number? It had a zero; a couple nines. Giving in, she traipsed across to the kitchen, put on her glasses, and found MacNeish's number. Somehow, she knew he wouldn't answer.

Chapter Thirty-Three

Zuela was a maven at taking charge, Laskey noted. While she stirred barbecue pork in the crockpot, she had him setting out plates, napkins, and utensils on the island in the Herschmann's kitchen. She'd directed Fritz to unload the dishwasher and ordered Leah to *sit down and take it easy.* Jacob was supposed to be putting ice in glasses for tea, but so far all he'd done was pull seven glasses from a cabinet and set them on the counter next to the refrigerator.

"Jamie MacNeish, you can dress the salad," Zuela said over the clink and clank of spoon hitting the inside of the crockpot.

"Dress?" MacNeish had picked up one of the 'Bekah Bars from the candy dish and was examining the picture on the wrapper.

"Don't you dress salads in Scotland?" Zuela raised her eyebrows. "Or do you just douse them?"

"Ah . . . , yes. My thoughts were off somewhere else." He put the 'Bekah Bar back in the dish and moved over to where the salad awaited his *dressing.*

Fritz opened a drawer, handed MacNeish salad tongs, and then retreated into his shell as he removed plates from the dishwasher.

Laskey shot MacNeish a quick glance and then focused on

setting out the flatware. MacNeish was avoiding him, but he'd pull the Scotsman aside when they finished eating and demand to know what he was hiding, although he was starting to have an inkling of what that might be. A sniff of a smile twitched at his lips.

He noticed that Zuela had ignored Carlos when giving out orders. Carlos sat at the island, elbows propped on counter, and head resting in hands as though he had a headache, but casting occasional surreptitious glances at MacNeish.

Testosterone overload, Laskey decided as he began folding napkins and placing them next to forks — three young men in the same room, all looking like they had an ax to grind. MacNeish's antipathy to Carlos revealed itself everytime he swiped a glance at the Argentinian. Ditto for Carlos regarding MacNeish. Jacob, meanwhile, showed every sign of being up to something. He'd known the boy long enough to know the look. Forgetting that he was supposed to be filling glasses with ice, Jacob leaned against the refrigerator darting his eyes around, sometimes throwing Laskey a brief look, sometimes snatching a glance at Carlos, sometimes not looking at anything in particular. Every few seconds, he smiled down at the floor. The warning signs were there, but what could Jacob possibly be up to?

"A couple more minutes and the buns will be warm," Zuela said coming over to the island. She had her phone in her hand. "I guess I should turn this off. She touched the screen as she sat down beside Carlos. "You haven't told me much about yourself, Carlos. You come from a large family?"

While Zuela engaged Carlos in conversation, Fritz and Leah made a pretense at listening, and MacNeish, having finished with the salad, strolled over to the French doors and looked out. Laskey went over and bumped shoulders with Jacob, nudging him aside. Then putting his hand on his godson's arm, he guided him out of the kitchen and into the foyer.

Jacob raised his eyebrows in a question.

"You keep giving me this look," Laskey said. "Something's on your mind. Spit it out."

"I've been wondering . . . ." Jacob let out a stream of air and looked off to the side as though reluctant to speak.

"Yes?"

"Do we really know Rebekah? We have this picture in our minds of a woman who's bright, responsible, empathetic, and in possession of a few dozen other excellent traits. But are we overlooking something?"

"Like what?"

"How can you be sure she doesn't have a dark side?"

"Why the hell would you think that?" Laskey felt his ire rising.

"I didn't say I thought that." Jacob backed off a step. "I'm just pointing out that everyone has a public side and a private side, and that sometimes a person's private side has secrets they don't want known. Can you honestly say you know everything about her, and that she doesn't have an ignoble habit or two?"

Laskey felt insulted on Rebekah's behalf. "Maybe *you* can explain her private side."

Jacob held his palms toward Laskey. "Don't get mad with me. I'm just pointing out that there are things about her we don't know. If someone hadn't told you, would you have thought she'd be a protester? Which, in my opinion, is a good thing. I just wouldn't have imagined her doing it. Or that she'd want to spend time in Vienna when both her parents and her grandfather refused to set foot in the country after the war? Or that someone as smart and responsible as Rebekah would have a ditzy, irresponsible friend like Totsy? Or that she'd fall for a hot-bloodied Argentinian?"

"Ahhh, so that's it. Carlos. You're still jealous." Laskey knew his smirk would annoy Jacob, but the boy deserved a little taunting. He wiped the smirk away when Jacob's face turned red.

"You always said when you were too close to something, you couldn't see the details." Jacob's voice had cooled considerably. "You're too close. There's something about Carlos and Rebekah that doesn't fit, and you're not seeing it. Or else, you just refuse to admit it." He turned and walked back into the kitchen to join the others.

Laskey felt a pang. Damn it, sometimes Jacob let his penchant for excitement and adventure warp his good sense. What possible *dark side* could Rebekah have? As for Carlos, both he and Jacob were alpha-males, to use a trite expression, and in his experience, alpha-males tended to be either buddies or enemies, and nothing in between.

He was about to rejoin the others when MacNeish wandered into the dining room. MacNeish, unaware of Laskey standing in the foyer, studied the paintings and drawings on the walls. The five works demanded as ransom lay in the middle of the dining room table. Laskey wondered why Fritz hadn't packed them up. The hard sided suitcase sat next to the archway, empty.

When the Scotsman finished examining the works on the walls, he looked down at the six on the dining room table, twisting his head first to one side and then the other, as he leaned over to study them closely. Suddenly he straightened and, blushing, looked into the foyer where Laskey was watching him.

"Rebekah told me her family was interested in art," MacNeish said. "But she did'na mention the extent of their collection."

"Yes, Laskey said. "They have quite a collection." He moved into the dining room. "I tried calling you several times before I finally tracked you down. Why didn't you answer?"

He shrugged. "Did'na feel like talking."

"What were you up to this morning?"

"I told you earlier. I drove around. Did'na know what else to do." He pointed to the works on the table. "I'm assuming those are the ones the kidnappers want?"

Zuela stuck her head through the door. "Food's ready. Come and eat."

Laskey, who had stiffened, ignored the summons to eat. "How did you know the kidnappers wanted paintings?"

MacNeish looked at him in surprise. "I heard you and Jacob talking about it after you delivered me to his house last night."

Laskey thought back. Had they talked about the ransom in MacNeish's presence? He remembered having a few words with Jacob while they were standing in Jacob's kitchen, but he thought MacNeish had already gone upstairs at that point.

MacNeish turned abruptly and headed for the kitchen. Laskey started to follow, but stopped. Had Jacob been right about his being too close? About him being in danger of missing details because of his personal involvement with the family, and had he made a stupid error in talking about the details of the ransom in the presence of someone who shouldn't have heard?

Chapter Thirty-Four

L eah stretched out on the sofa, the back of her hand covering her eyes. Zuela sat in a nearby chair. A few feet away, Grandfather Clock ticked on as though nothing had happened. "I'm so tired," Leah said. "So, so tired. I'm not sure I can even make it upstairs to the bedroom."

"I'm sorry for what you're going through."

"Why haven't they called?" Leah removed her hand from her eyes and looked at Zuela. "Shouldn't they have called by now and let us know where to deliver the pictures?"

"I don't think they'll call until they know you're ready, and when they do call, they'll expect Fritz to go without delay. At night, it would be too easy for an unmarked police car to leave off his lights and follow Fritz."

Leah wasn't sure Zuela knew how kidnappers would act, yet her explanation sounded reasonable. "Did you ever have someone close to you die, Zuela?"

"My parents."

"And were you exhausted when it happened?"

"Yes. Very."

Leah heard the clangs and knocks of the men cleaning up the

kitchen, but the buzz of conversation was conspicuously absent. Fritz had been rendered to near silence with worry, as had Carlos, while Laskey walked around with a frown. The poor man wanted to help but didn't know how. MacNeish hadn't had much to say since he first showed up; mostly he just glowered. Thank goodness for Jacob and Zuela. They made things half-way bearable.

"It's strange that Totsy hasn't called," Leah said, removing her hand from her eyes and frowning at the ceiling. "When Rebekah comes, Totsy usually shows up the first day. There've even been times when she's rushed over to sit in our living room to wait for her arrival." Leah rubbed her eyes. "I suppose it's because of Carlos that she hasn't come this time. She probably thinks she shouldn't intrude, but it's been four full days, and she hasn't called once." She looked at Zuela. "Do you find that strange?"

"I'm sure it's like you said; she doesn't want to intrude."

"Totsy met Carlos before we did. Rebekah flew her over to Amman a few months ago and Totsy met everyone. I guess she met MacNeish, too."

"Have you and Fritz been to Amman?"

"No. We took a trip to Israel two years ago, and Rebekah joined us there." Leah closed her eyes. The light bothered her, like when she was getting a fever. "I still think it's strange that Totsy hasn't called."

LASKEY WAS WIPING down the counters, Carlos and Leah were upstairs, and the others had gone home, when Eli knocked on the backdoor. Fritz had gone out and taken the package from Eli, then pretending a nonchalance he didn't possess, Fritz strolled in from the mudroom and went to the kitchen desk. He opened the bottom drawer, shoved the package beneath a stack of newspaper articles they'd saved for Rebekah's later perusal, and then closed the drawer with a click.

He ignored Laskey who had stopped to watch him, and went to the sink. He turned on the faucet, squirted soap on his hands, and stuck them under the water. The gun had been wrapped in a cloth and then stuck in a paper bag, but its cold steel brazened through the fabric and paper to make his hands feel dirty. Laskey's unspoken ˙questions burned a hole in his back as he rubbed his hands in the gush of cold water. Sometimes Laskey's silence said more than his words. Fritz dried his hands on a paper towel and turned around.

"Samples," he said, finally meeting his friend's eyes and motioning to the drawer. "From other candy manufacturers. We get them every now and then to see what the competition is up to. Eli thought we might like to have them for dessert. That's why he called me to the back door just now. We'll try them tomorrow." Every word of the lie made him shrivel inside.

"I'm staying over," Laskey said after an interval. "Invited or not. I don't expect a call this late, and certainly not in the middle of the night, but I'm not leaving again until it comes. You're stuck with me."

Chapter Thirty-Five

Zuela flipped on the lights in her living room, set her phone down on the table next to the sofa, and then sat down. Jacob and MacNeish, who had followed her from the Herschmann's sat down across from the sofa.

"Don't Scots like barbecued pork?" Jacob asked MacNeish. "You didn't eat much."

"Leave him alone," Zuela said. "At least he ate. Carlos didn't even touch it." She picked up her phone, looked at it, and then set it down again. "I'm sure barbecued pork can't compete with haggis," she said to MacNeish. "Or do you just pretend haggis is the greatest thing since lollipops for the sake of tourists?"

MacNeish's lips curled in a smile. "The game is up. Ye guessed it. Most of us can't stand the stuff. We bring it out once a year for Bobbie Burn's birthday. The cook displays the haggis on a platter and parades around behind a bagpiper, then some ba-heid spouts off." He lowered his voice, and declaimed, *"Fair fa' your honest, sonsie face, Great chieftain o' the puddin-race! Aboon them a' ye tak your place, Painch, tripe, or thairm: Weel are ye wordy of a grace As lang's my arm."*

Jacob laughed. "What language was that?"

"Bobby Burns lived south of Glasgow, and those buggers down

there ha' their own talk for sartain. Sometimes I can't half under-stand them meself."

"*Sonsie* face?" Feeling one tiny coil of stress unwind, Zuela propped her bare feet on the coffee table. MacNeish had been as tight as a bungie cord all evening, but as soon as he walked through her door he'd changed tone, tempo, and face. "Our Scottish friend here rattles off Burns as though everybody understands a tenth of it," she said to Jacob. "Yet he has the nerve to complain about Shakespeare."

MacNeish grinned. "How went *The Scottish play* this morning?"

"My students like it about as much as you do. Among other things, they fail to see the humor." She quoted in a deep voice, "*Drink, sir, is a great provoker of three things. Macduff: What three things does drink especially provoke? Porter: Marry, sir, nose-painting, sleep, and urine. Lechery, sir, it provokes, and unprovokes; it provokes the desire, but it takes away the performance.* Comic relief." Jacob and MacNeish were studying her much like her students did when they had nothing to contribute.

"You know who Jerry Lewis was?" she asked. From the way they looked at her, she knew they didn't. "He's from the dark ages as far as you're concerned. He was a comedian. One of those silly, slap-stick actors. Then someone invited him to be a guest in a TV episode. He played the role of a doctor who makes jokes about everything and engages in slapstick, in the operating room, in the intensive care unit, everywhere. The other hospital employees upbraided him for being inappropriate. When he finally took their words to heart and stopped finding things to laugh at or about, he fell apart. Turns out the only way he could handle the tragedy and sadness of a hospital was by being funny. That was the only time I ever liked Jerry Lewis."

At first neither MacNeish nor Jacob spoke. "I understand what you mean," Jacob said finally, a note of despair in his voice.

"The Herschmann's don't have the luxury of comic relief right now," she said. She sighed and, directing her attention to MacNeish, asked in a lighter voice, "What did *you* do today? I've pretty much nailed down everyone else's activities, but you haven't shared."

"Felt a great need to unwind. I drove around and looked at the trees changing color. We don't see much of that in Jordan."

"Washington Crossing Park is a good place for experiencing autumn. You should go over there one day." She raised her eyebrows at him. "At least, if you're here long enough and still feel the need to unwind."

"I'll be off as soon as Rebekah's safe and sound at home."

She wondered about the thing that fluttered like the beat of moth's wing in MacNeish's eyes and then disappeared. .

Jacob stretched out one leg, leaving the other tucked close to the chair. "I always wondered, do Scotsmen only drink Scotch, or do they imbibe other spirits? Hard liquor, that is. I know you like beer."

"We're no' a race to decline a drink o' any sort," MacNeish said. "And I thank ye for getting what we're called right. *Scotch* is a drink; the people are Scots."

"Shit," Zuela said, "I'm not being a good hostess. Would you two like something to drink? There's been enough stress in the past couple days to turn taffy to steel."

"Aunt *Zuela* . . . ." Jacob widened his eyes at her. A false sense of decorum. "Your language."

"Oh, don't go getting self-righteous on me, Jacob Gillis. If you can say *shit*, then so can I." She rose. "I'm going to have a stiff drink, or two, and go to bed assuming that tomorrow everything will be sorted out and we'll be celebrating. Jacob, you're allowed only one since you're driving. MacNeish, you can match me drink for drink, however many that is."

"I'll help you fix drinks." Jacob stood up quickly. "You have Jamison, I think." He looked at MacNeish. "Want to try that?"

"Like the sound of it." On the verge of falling asleep, MacNeish sank back in his chair and blinked his eyes.

"Jet lag. Ten to one, he'll be snoring in thirty seconds," Zuela said when she and Jacob were in the kitchen. "And you're giving me that look. *Did Aunt Zuela remember my instructions?*" She gave him a dismissive wave. "Stop worrying. As technology-unsavvy as I am, at least I know how to operate an app." She reached for glasses while Jacob opened the cupboard in search of Jamison. "The

Herschmann's kitchen was too echoey for a good recording, I think. My living room is better."

"I wasn't giving you any kind of look." He shoved aside bottles of gin and rum, looking for the whiskey.

"Of course you were giving me a look. But I'm thankful for one thing. . ." She clunked three glasses down on the counter. "No one else will know about us making fools of ourselves in case you're wrong. As you probably are."

He pulled the Jamison from the back of the cupboard, filled the glasses half-way, and then dropped a couple ice cubes in each glass. "I don't know whether to wish I'm right, or to wish I'm wrong. How soon can you get part two done?"

"I'm meeting my friend in his office first thing in the morning. It shouldn't take long. At least I don't think it will. I don't have experience with this sort of thing."

She carried two glasses to the living room; Jacob followed with his own drink. MacNeish woke with a start when she touched his shoulder. "Not allowed to sleep yet," she said and set the drink on the table beside him. When she straightened, she saw Jacob looking down at her phone, the *Voice Memos* app as obvious as an elephant in a tutu, but she didn't think anyone else had noticed, and what if they had? Didn't everyone have an app on their phone for recording voices?

LASKEY SLIPPED out the front door. Fritz, Leah, and Carlos were involved in prolonged *good*-nights so no one saw him leave. Had they, he simply would have replied that he meant to take a quick walk before going to bed.

He shivered. The temperature had dipped, and he'd come without a jacket. A few hundred feet away from the corona of streetlights, he saw the flash of a lighter and walked towards the man who had been his partner in the FBI. He smelled the cigar from twenty feet away.

"It's taken care of," Thunder said when Laskey came within a few feet.

What he'd asked Thunder to do might not help, but at least it was *something.* "I owe you," Laskey said.

"And here are these." Thunder reached into his coat pocket, retrieved two devices, and handed them to Laskey.

Laskey stuck them in his pants pocket. "Thanks. Didn't have time to get back to my office and grab some."

"Is the person really a suspect?" Thunder asked, "Or are you just working all angles?"

"I'm grabbing at straws."

"You have a pretty good record of getting them right. The hunches, I mean." Thunder took a puff, dispersing the smell of Arturo Fuente into the night.

"I'd better do what I have to do and then get back inside before someone sees me. Thanks, buddy." He fisted Thunder's arm lightly and then walked away.

Five minutes later, Laskey returned to the house. His phone rang as he reached out to open the door.

"James Eakins hasn't been seen around town for quite a while," Bump said. "I checked all the sources I could and can't find out a thing about him. Do you want me to find out what Delores Love knows?"

Laskey considered. "No," he said with reluctance. "We're getting too close to the countdown. If James is involved Delores might scare him into doing something foolish; if he isn't involved, it won't matter anyway."

Chapter Thirty-Six

A round lunchtime, Laskey had realized he'd be spending the night
with Fritz, but the minutes had passed, and then the hours, and
before he knew it he no longer had time to run home to grab pajamas
and a toothbrush. He wasn't even sure where his pajamas were. One of
his sisters had given him a pair a couple Christmases ago, and he'd
stuck them in a drawer. Or maybe he'd given them to Good Will.

He buttoned, and then unbuttoned, the pajama top Fritz had
lent him. The top was at least one size too small, probably two.
Even though they were friends of long standing, Laskey felt funny
about crawling under the covers with nothing on but his boxers. He
pictured Fritz as belonging to that breed of men who never considered going to bed half naked.

Fritz nodded at the pajamas as he walked in. "Are they okay?"

"Perfect," Laskey lied.

Fritz set two glasses of water down on the nightstand, took his
phone from his pajama pocket, and placed it between the glasses.
Then, barely missing a beat, he removed the two glasses and set
them on the floor beside each bed. "Just in case one of us accidentally knocks over a glass and kills the phone."

They crawled into bed, and Fritz turned off the lamp. He'd left the door ajar, so Laskey smelled the Murphy's oil soap, lemon polish, and floor wax drifting from Rebekah's room. An overhead light was still on at the end of the hall where Leah and Carlos were talking in hushed tones. After a few minutes their voices stopped, two sets of footsteps went in different directions, and the light went out.

"Fritz, try not to worry," Laskey said into the darkness. "I know. . . telling you not to worry is like ordering water to run uphill. But it'll turn out okay. By the weekend, everything will be back to normal. I know it will be a long time before you *feel* normal, but at least this will be behind you."

"You're right. Tomorrow, or the day after at the latest, Rebekah will be home."

Fritz didn't sound convinced, and the fear that Rebekah might never be home again sent a shiver through Laskey. Someone wanted *more* than just six paintings. The question was: would the *someone* content himself with imposing a temporary nightmare on his adversary, or did he intend to carry through to a horrible, irreversible end?

An insect beat against a window. A fly trying to get out? A moth aiming for the faint glow of the street light in the alley behind? Laskey heard Fritz's irregular breaths, the creaking of the mattress as he shifted positions, a sigh.

"You never told me much about your family," Fritz said. "I know you have four sisters, and that your parents were school teachers. One sister lives in Pittsburgh, I think you said, one in Lancaster, and one in Washington D.C. And the other . . . .let's see if I can remember. . . . Louisiana?"

"You get an A+ for memory," Laskey said. Fritz was trying hard to distract his thoughts from the pit of hell that gaped before him. " Do you remember their names?"

"One is Mary."

"She lives in Pittsburgh. She's an accountant and is married to an accountant."

"And Agnes. She's the one in Washington D.C. I think you told me she worked for the Department of Education."

"Right again." Interlacing his fingers, Laskey propped his hands beneath his head.

"Judith lives in Louisiana, but I've forgotten what she does."

"She goes to luncheons and board meetings, plays bunco, and takes a yoga class. And she does a lot of entertaining, I think."

"Fancy is your youngest sister. The one in Lancaster. Where did that name come from: *Fancy?*"

"Francine. I couldn't pronounce it when I was learning to talk and called her *Fancy.* It stuck." Laskey was not a man that cried. Not that there was anything wrong with it. He just didn't. He expressed his emotions in other ways – not always in good ways, but he wasn't perfect, was he? He could pretty much count the number of times on one hand when he'd shed a few tears. When his best friend, Jacob's father, had died he cried. And there were a couple other occasions. But the one thing that always dampened his eyes was Fancy. The greatest wish in his life was to cure her somehow, but other than palliative care, no one knew how to help her at this point.

"How is her MS progressing?" Fritz asked.

"She won't be with us much longer."

"I'm sorry."

Laskey rolled over on his side, his back to Fritz, but after an interval, rolled back again. "How is it that you can remember everyone's names and everything about them?"

"I don't by any means remember everyone's names and everything about them."

"Well, you're a damn sight better than the rest of us."

FRITZ LAY ON HIS BACK, hands folded over his stomach, comforted by Laskey's light, rhythmic snoring. Laskey had no idea how much consolation he gave him and Leah just by being here. The others, too. Even MacNeish. They'd become like family, the hum of their conversation and their concern helping to ease the pain. By a hair.

He wondered at what point Laskey's sleep would be deep enough for him to get up without waking him. Laskey professed to be a heavy sleeper, so . . . in twenty minutes? An hour? Fritz broke out in a sweat. What if he failed to control his trembling hands and messed up, ruining everything?

Suddenly, he gasped. His stomach had clenched so tight that pain ripped through it and down into his groin. After a few seconds the pain eased. At least, it wasn't his heart. While the others ate, and talked, and cleaned up, he'd been aware of his too-rapid heartbeat but had tried to hide it. Leah was too worried to notice. But Laskey noticed. All evening Laskey's dark eyes had studied him, the left eye narrowed slightly, his lips tightened.

Fritz pulled the covers up around his ears and glanced over at the form of his snoring friend. Laskey stirred, gave a snort, and then fell back asleep.

"No, Laskey," Fritz whispered into the darkness. "Remembering names isn't a talent; it's a survival mechanism." He'd acquired the ability from parents who evaded hell. They'd come separately to the United States and met after the war, but they had similar stories. "During the evil times, we learned to read every nuance on a person's face," his father told him. "Learning names became easy when you were trying to figure out which person might turn against you. To your face. To your back. Always, there was this twitching in your stomach, while trying to read what lay beneath peoples' masks and wondering who had sold themselves to the devil." Mostly, his father avoided talking about that part of his past, but sometimes it erupted.

His father had failed to read the nuance's on his partner's face. "I knew I had to sign the company over to Gustav Fuchs; it was the new law," he told Fritz. "But when he demanded everything of value that I owned, it was like being hit by a truck. I didn't expect that of him. Our fathers had been friends." A look of pain and disbelief had shadowed his father's face each time he spoke of his former partner. "But there was nothing to be done. The Nazis ruled."

Whisking away the paintings from the greedy hands of Gustav Fuchs had been a symbolic victory. One battle won. In the end, his father wouldn't win that battle after all. Fuchs had reached his long arm across the ocean to collect what he considered his, and while Fuchs might want the four oils, it was really the *Bride of the Wind* drawings he coveted most. In his confused, self-centered mind, Fuchs thought his father had actually had a liaison with Alma Mahler.

Laskey appeared to be in a deep sleep. In measured movements to prevent the mattress creaking, Fritz sat up and eased back the covers. The nippy air of autumn cooled his body. He swung his feet to the floor and felt for his slippers. He found them, but remained sitting. He knew what he had to do, yet he hesitated. It would be safer to wait until morning when he wasn't so tired. He might mess up by attempting the job now. But he couldn't wait. Leah had taken another Ambien and would sleep late and, so far, Carlos had slept late every morning. But Laskey was an early riser.

Besides, there was the matter of drying. Glancing at Laskey to check that he slept soundly, he eased himself off the bed.

Downstairs, he carried the two *Bride* studies into the kitchen and placed them side by side on the island. The truth should have been shared with his family years ago, and had he thought it important he would have told them. That something bad could come from the decision his father made never crossed his mind.

Chapter Thirty-Seven

L askey's eyes sprang open, and he glanced at the twin bed next to him. Where the dark mound of Fritz's body should have been, there was nothing. He sat up and turned on the lamp. Both Fritz and his phone were gone. The clock on the bedside table showed one-thirty.

He slipped out of bed. Carrying his shoes in his hands so as not to awaken the others, he crept down the hall and then down the stairs. He stopped short in the doorway to the kitchen. Fritz sat at the island, a glass of wine in front of him, an open bottle of Merlot beside the glass.

Fritz, unaware of Laskey standing in the doorway, dipped a cloth napkin into the glass of wine. Laskey stood transfixed, an invisible hand clutching at his heart when he saw what else was on the counter in front of his friend. One of the *Bride of the Wind* studies lay inches away from the napkin dripping with wine. The other lay a couple feet away. Laskey held his breath as he watched the hand that held the wine-sodden napkin move toward the drawing. Then Fritz seemed to reconsider. His hand sank to rest on the counter.

"Fritz?" Laskey stepped into the kitchen.

Fritz jerked around. He let out a long, tormented breath, as he pushed the napkin away from the drawing.

"What are you doing?" Laskey came closer. Then realizing he'd spoken too loudly, he asked again in a hushed tone, "What are you doing?"

"They'll have them authenticated, you know." Fritz motioned to the two drawings.

"Yes." Laskey sat down next to Fritz.

"We're in trouble." Fritz let go of the napkin and pressed the fingers of both hands into his forehead.

Laskey's heart clunked to his feet. "They're copies?"

"The four paintings are authentic, but the *Bride of the Wind* studies are copies. My father knew the candy factory would never be more than a mom and pop operation unless he invested heavily, so he sold the originals." He swallowed. "Before he sold them, he had copies made. It didn't matter to me whether the drawings were authentic or just good copies, so I never told Leah. It wasn't that I was trying to keep a secret; I just didn't think of saying anything. We were young and concerned about other things. Until now, I can honestly say I never gave it another thought. What mattered to me was my father's victory in getting them out of Austria in the first place. Small victories were rare in those days."

"What were you going to do?" Laskey nodded at the napkin which lay in a puddle of red wine.

"I didn't tell you the whole story earlier." Fritz pushed the wet napkin further away. "When Kokoschka told Fuchs he'd have to kiss my grandfather twice, Fuchs, who was angry and humiliated, demanded an explanation. My grandfather turned to go, thinking it was best to leave him to sober up before pursuing the conversation. Fuchs, who still had a glass of wine in his hand, grabbed my grandfather's arm. When he did, his wine sloshed onto the corner of one of the drawings. That seemed to bring him to his senses, and he backed off.

"Fuchs apologized a few days later. When he was done apologizing, he begged my grandfather to sell him the pastels. My grandfather refused. For a few weeks, the matter was dropped. Then my grandparents threw a dinner party for Otto Fuchs on his birthday, inviting a few friends. Otto's wife wasn't around then. Pretending ill health, or maybe she really did suffer from ill health, she'd gone to a spa in Germany. Her ill health, or pretense at ill health because she didn't want to sleep with her husband, probably sounds like it has nothing to do with the story, but maybe it has *everything* to do with the story."

Fritz reached over and touched a corner of the closest pastel and then dropped his hand in his lap.

"You were talking about the birthday party," Laskey reminded him.

"My grandfather was embarrassed at his behavior, the kiss, the arguing, so he had the two pastels framed. He wrapped them and presented them as a birthday gift to Otto. The matting hid most of the wine stain. Two weeks later, Otto returned them and apologized for being such an asshole."

"That's an unexpected end to the story."

"Maybe the incident with the pastels is what woke Otto up. He began divorce proceedings, became a much happier man, and, a year or so later, married someone else.

"How does this relate to what's going on now?" Laskey asked.

"The second generation partners didn't get along so well. I won't go into all the issues my father had with Otto's son Gustav. Suffice it to say that Gustav Fuchs despised my father who was endowed with all the talent, intelligence, and good looks that Gustav lacked. Gustav was the son of the first wife, and it sounds like he must have inherited some of her undesirable traits. When the Nazis rose to power, Gustav finally had something over my father: he was a member of the master race and my father a lowly Jew. *The Bride of the Wind* painting was well known by then, and so Gustav demanded that my father return the *Bride* studies right after Otto stepped in front of the lorry. They rightfully belonged to him, he claimed, and he accused my grandfather of stealing them. You can imagine how angry he must have been when Dad smuggled them out of the country."

Laskey wasn't sure when it happened, but at some point he'd

begun to believe in the possibility of Gustav Fuchs being the master-mind behind the kidnapping, and Gustav would know about the wine-stained corner. "You were going to smear wine on the drawing to make it look authentic?"

Fritz nodded and then let out a low moan. "But I can't remember which drawing it was."

TUESDAY

October 23

Vienna, Austria

Gustav Fuchs barely glanced at the Benedictine Monastery when Karl's driver pointed to where it rose from the banks on the other side of the Danube. Sensing that his son had given the driver instructions to treat this as a scenic outing instead of what it really was, he grunted in reply. He'd seen Melk a few thousand times, but if he cooperated the drive might be prolonged.

The familiar white steeple rising from the center of Pöchlarn came into view a few minutes later. Fuchs leaned toward the window as they entered the town, drove along the main street, and then slowed to a crawl when they passed Bahnhofstrasse. The two and three story Baroque Bürgerhäuse of the Altstadt, painted a variety of colors, crowded both sides of the street. Gustav gave a little snort. Kokoschka had invented a story that this had all burned down, and that he, his older brother, and his mother had been rescued from the conflagration and taken to safety in the back of a hay wagon.

They crept past Rüdigerstrasse and then Oskar Kokoschka Strasse, turning finally onto Nibelungenstrasse where the driver resumed the role of tour guide as he expounded on the village's role in the Nibelungenlied. Fuchs clenched his fist and gave a little sniff. Once, he'd been the one in charge. Now he'd been reduced to a crippled old man, his power and his right to make choices gone, while his son carried on, even to the point of instructing his driver how to proceed on an outing.

They came to the end of the scenic part of the Nibelungen-strasse. "Turn back," Fuchs barked.

The driver looked at him from the rear view mirror, hesitated, but then pulled over to the curb. "Where to?"

"Rüdigerstrasse."

"There isn't much to see on that street now," the driver said. "A bit run-down, I believe."

Gustav glared at him. "Rüdigerstrasse," he repeated.

The driver nodded. He waited for an Opel and a Citroen to pass, and then did a u-turn and headed back toward the main street. He turned left, and two blocks further, turned left again onto Rüdiger. He pulled up in front of a two-story building and double parked. The old building had been painted an unidentifiable shade of green, and one of the second-story shutters hung loose.

The resentment was always there, but now Gustav felt it burn through him. Joseph Herschmann I and his father had leased this building as their first place of business, locating the main office and laboratory on the first floor and the manufacturing facilities for their limited line of pharmaceuticals on the second. From here they'd launched a business that had blossomed into a gold mine but, in the end, Joseph hadn't been able to mine much of the gold. Gustav gave a satisfied chuckle. The chuckle was followed by a frown. Joseph, the Jew, had been made a partner at an early age due to the death of his father. He, Gustav, had gone to his own father, still alive and healthy and not likely to kick off any time soon, and demanded that he, too, be made a partner. It was only fair, he claimed. If Joseph were to play a major role in the company, then he should also. His father refused. The refusal still ate at him like acid. Even after the unfortunate incident in Berlin when his father was hit by a truck, it was always Joseph who got to make decisions, because they, the employees, ignored him, going to Joseph behind his back.

"Take me to the museum," he said to the driver.

"Herr Karl thought . . ." the driver began.

"Verdammt. Take me to the museum."

The driver turned the car toward Oscar Kokoschka Strasse. The traffic had increased. They crawled along behind a red lorry with Beiersdorf printed in large black letters on the side, until they came back to the main street where the truck turned in the opposite direction.

Gustav swiveled his head back and forth, taking in both sides of the street. There'd never been a major fire on the main street, and certainly not the conflagration invented by Kokoschka. The man was crazy. After Alma Mahler left him, Kokoschka had a life-size doll made in her image. The artist described to the craftswoman the details of Alma Mahler's naked body, explaining that he wanted to dress and undress the doll. He'd already bought clothes in Vienna. He also insisted that the doll had to have a tongue. Unlike Alma, the doll would yield to his every whim.

As they turned onto Kokoschka Strasse, Gustav gave another snort. He'd seen photographs of the doll. The face looked like a mask. Nevertheless, the artist made paintings of it, took it for drives in a carriage, and to the theater where the doll had its own seat. In restaurants, he demanded a place be set for his inanimate companion. He even hired a maid to engage in private charades he designed for himself and his doll.

As though the resentment he'd harbored for almost eighty years had come to take its toll, tiredness swept through Gustav as they pulled up in front of the cadmium-red museum that was touted as the birthplace of the artist. "You're letting the Jew show you up?" An acquaintance asked when Joseph had once again gotten his way on an issue. It was shortly after his father stepped in front of the lorry. Had history not intervened, and if he'd had the opportunity to grow a bit older before Joseph slipped away in the night taking the paintings with him, there was no doubt as to which one of them would have been the stronger. But the Jew slunk away, making off with what should have been his..

"Are you going in?" the driver asked.

"No." He saw the puzzled look the driver shot him in the rearview mirror.

"I want to sit here for a moment, that's all." The special exhibition was set to open in three weeks — A Kokosckha Retrospective — Kokoschka paintings borrowed from around the world. Yesterday he'd informed the committee of his contribution: two pastel studies done in preparation for Bride of the Wind along with two oils. The members of the committee had practically shat in their pants, they were so excited. They were sending someone to interview him on Friday and had promised a big article about his contribution. He'd tell the reporter about his father's friendship with Kokoschka and his affair with Alma Mahler, and then he'd show the pastels and suggest that the reporter might want to take his picture standing beside them. He'd relate how the wine stain came to be on the corner of the one when Joseph I tried to steal them from his father.

In a few hours the pastels would be delivered to him along with the four paintings. The eighth pawn was standing by, airline ticket in hand, ready to receive them. He smiled. Tomorrow was going to be a good day. And the girl? Let them do with her as they liked.

Chapter Thirty-Eight

Jacob paced back and forth between the fireplace and the far end of the kitchen. Occasionally, he stopped to look out the window above the sink. MacNeish was down at the pond tossing rocks, sticks, and whatever else he could get his hands on. He'd been out there when Jacob came downstairs ready to go to work. At least the Scotsman avoided aiming in the direction of the geese although his show of anger, or whatever it was, clearly made them nervous enough to congregate on the other side of the pond as far away from the Scotsman as they could.

He understood that MacNeish was feeling some of the same things he was. The wish to hurdle over hours or days, for one — whatever it took to have everything behind them. The frustration at not being able to do anything was the worst. The recording he'd convinced Aunt Zuela to make didn't count because he knew how that was going to turn out: just another of Jacob Gillis' crazy escapades.

He paused a few moments at the window. MacNeish had stopped his angry tossing. Probably because he'd scooped up everything he could launch as a missile, every stick and stone on that side of the pond. He'd have to move to the other side for more ammo. Jacob looked at his watch. It was time to go, yet he hesitated. For the first time since beginning his job, he found it impossible to focus, so the temptation to not go to his office was strong. Much of what he planned to do today, except for finishing up a report, could be put off until tomorrow, and he could work all weekend to recover the time he lost if he called in sick.

During the next circuit from kitchen to fireplace, he saw MacNeish headed back toward the house, his powerful legs moving fast in spite of kicking sticks and stones out of his pathway. A few seconds later, the backdoor slammed and MacNeish tromped through the mudroom and into the kitchen.

"Your geese are loud."

"Yes," Jacob said. "Twice a year, spring and fall, they wake me up every morning with their infernal hwonking."

MacNeish took a few deep breaths, calming himself, and then joined him at the window.

"You could go fishing today, if you've a mind," Jacob said. "The Pumqua runs down there behind those trees." He pointed toward the forest that bordered the edge of the stubbly field beyond the pond.

"Ye really think I could enjoy me'self fishing when Rebekah's not safe?" He gave Jacob a steely look.

"No, I didn't think you could enjoy yourself. It was just an idea to help you pass the time. It's hard to sit and wait. Coffee?"

"Could use some brew strong eno' to stand on its own." MacNeish followed him to the coffee maker.

"I didn't think you Scots liked strong coffee." Jacob reached for mugs.

"I did'na, but then I went to work in the part of the world where their brew lends meaning to the words *strong coffee*. A powerful cup makes up for a hell of a lot of lost sleep."

"What *are* you going to do today?" Jacob handed him a filled cup.

"I'm going to worry, and then worry some more. In between, and during worrying, I'll probably go out and see some of your magnificent brown and yellow leafed trees, and then . . . . Oh bloody hell, I don't know." He dumped in sugar and cream and then walked over to the fireplace, sat down in a rocking chair, and stared off into space.

Jacob remained where he was, finishing his coffee. He had to leave in two minutes. Had to. He'd delayed enough, and he'd known all along he wouldn't call in sick as much as he wanted to. He hadn't eaten, but he'd grab something at a drive through and then spend the morning regretting that he hadn't bothered to fix breakfast.

"There are eggs and bacon in the refrigerator," he said, turning to leave. "And scrapple. Help yourself."

"Scrapple?" MacNeish jerked his gaze from whatever far away place he'd fixated on.

"It's a Pennsylvania Dutch breakfast meat. Laskey likes it so I keep it for when he shows up."

"I din'na quite understand this relationship you have with the detective."

"The detective is my godfather. We've been close ever since my dad died. Laskey and Dad were best friends."

"Sorry about your dad."

Jacob shrugged. "It's been a long time."

His two minutes were up, but still he delayed. "MacNeish . . . ," he said, going over and standing behind the other rocking chair, ". . . did you ever . . ."

"Call me Jamie."

"Jamie, did you ever overhear Rebekah telling her colleagues about her family's art collection?"

"I heard Annemarie Leitner telling people after she visited the Herschmanns."

"What did Annemarie say exactly?"

"Just that . . ." he tilted his chin up as though trying to remember. "Annemarie was just

going on about the things hanging on the Herschmanns' walls. I can't remember exactly what she said. Except, being from Austria, she recognized a number of the pieces by Viennese artists and knew their worth."

"Someone knows a lot about the Herschmanns, including Rebekah's exact time of arrival at the airport, what paintings they own, and that Fritz had a heart attack."

"It's a bitch, isn't it?" MacNeish leaned his forearms on his thighs, put his palms together, and hung his head. "It's a bitch."

Chapter Thirty-Nine

Z uela marched across the Temple University parking lot toward Ritter Hall. An inhospitable gust of wind lashed at her, and she drew her jacket closer. It was that time of year when the two greater forces of winter and summer played tug of war with the weather, summer hanging on for dear life, but winter hinting that he was about to get the upper hand. Or maybe winter was a *she*. Regardless, that's pretty much what spring and fall were, a battleground for the other two seasons.

She slipped in through the side door, barely avoiding colliding with two students. She went toward the stairs, heels clicking on the marble floor of the long corridor, tat-tat-tatting to the softer swoosh and slide of soft soled student shoes. It was too early for voices to echo up and down the hall since the students arriving for early classes were, at best, half asleep. She opened the door to the stairwell and started up.

The legendary Dr. Fenhouse, dinstinguished professor of linguistics, occupied an office on the second floor. Dr. Fenhouse had neither missed a day of work in forty-five years, nor had he been late in all that time. Or so the legend went. Knowing him, she believed it. He'd also never missed a faculty meeting. Three feet of snow, and he managed to get there. Attack on the Twin Towers, he managed to get there. Neither the plague nor the Martians landing would stand in the way of his performing his academic duty. So this had better not be the day he changed his habits. She'd hate to have to rouse him from his death bed or the arms of a lover.

She swung open the door at the top of the stairwell and barged into the long, dark hall. His office was at the end. She passed a couple of professors chatting outside a door, a few students lined up outside another – undoubtedly because there was about to be an exam, or there'd just been one. You could always tell who didn't do well on an exam by the line outside the professor's office the next day.

She let out a relieved sigh when she saw that Dr. Fenhouse's door was open.

"Well, good morning, Dr. Hay," he said looking up when she entered and emphasizing the *Dr.* He ran a forefinger over his mustache.

"Oh, get over it already," she said, and went in and sat down. The man was never going to let her forget. When he finished doing this favor for her, she was going to have to take care of that issue once and for all. She stuck her phone on his desk. "The recording is on the app."

He raised his white, bristly eyebrows which matched the longish hair fringing his bald pate. "How about a *please?*"

"I'll give you as many *pleases* as you want later. Just listen to it. It's important."

He looked at his watch. "I have a class in forty minutes and still need to do a little prep. I'll listen to it after lunch."

"You've been giving the same lectures for the past forty-five years, Fenny. We need to have you do this now."

"Who is *we*, and what's this all about?" He tapped his fingers on the desk. "You refused to tell me last evening."

"It's about a kidnapping." She fluttered her hand at the phone. "Would you just listen, please."

"A kidnapping?" He stared at her.

"Come on, Fenny. Listen to it. I'm not allowed to tell you the details, but I'll fill you in when the case is solved. This may be a long shot, but they don't have much to go on and time is running out."

"Alright," he said, pulling the phone closer. "What am I supposed to be listening for?" His forefinger hovered over the icon for *Voice Memos*.

"The man on the tape speaks English with an accent. I want to know where he's from."

"Who recorded this?"

"I did."

"I didn't realize you'd joined the legions of the technology-enlightened."

"I haven't. Someone else set it up. All I did was put the phone in front of the person and push the button."

"And the person on the recording didn't see you doing it?"

"Oh good lord, no one pays any attention to someone fiddling with their phone any more than they notice a person breathing."

"Well, then." He pushed "play," rotated his chair to face away from her, and sat back to listen.

The voices on the tape droned on. His and hers. She'd tried to get him to do most of the talking and had mostly succeeded, only having to throw in the occasional question. Fenny had his elbows propped on the chair arms, his hands templed, and an ear inclined toward the phone. A couple times, he hit "stop" and backed up the recording to listen a second time..

She tried to reign in her impatience by looking around his office at his collection of academic memorabilia. The framed diplomas and certificates. The stacks of tomes. The programs from conferences collecting dust on a shelf. Fenny was Temple's most renowned linguist, specializing in anthropological linguistics. He was author of too many articles to count and a guest speaker at innumerable conferences. He'd earned enough in honorariums to stuff an elephant and to buy a new shirt occasionally had he been so inclined. He'd even been allowed to have a go at the Voynich manuscript at Yale, but like other linguists who tried, he hadn't been able to decode it.

Her attention went to Fenny when he leaned closer to the phone and wrinkled his brow in concentration. He wasn't the most appealing man to look at with his bristly white hairs, thin lips, and flat cheeks. Fenny had come courting when her lovely husband decided he preferred a coed with big tits and tight pussy. Feeling rather murderous toward the male sex at that point, she wanted nothing to do with any man. Especially Fenny. In spite of not having one ounce of religiosity in his bones, he was as staid as a church pew and as dense as a concrete block in matters having to do with the fairer sex. He asked her out repeatedly, thinking she really was busy all those times she claimed to be busy. She finally put an end to his hound-doggedness by telling him she'd have to measure his equipment to see if it met her expectations. Beet red? Fenny's face had given new meaning to the term.

The recording ended and Fenny hit the replay button. Impatient, she let out a whoosh which he didn't acknowledge. He sat back with hands folded over stomach, nodding and smiling. Finally, he stopped the recording and handed the phone back to her. He leaned back again, clasped his hands behind his head, and smiled at the wall.

"Well?" She couldn't bridle her impatience.

"This speaker has something going on with vowel sounds and very definitely has an aversion to the elision of sounds. There's also the occasional hint of a glottal stop."

"Fenny, I neither understand your jargon nor do I want to . Just tell me where he's from."

He rotated his chair around to face her. "The man on the tape is a native Arabic speaker."

"Shit. Oh, bloody hell. Shit."

He raised his eyebrows.

"Fenny. I owe you big time." She shot out the chair, grabbed her phone, and headed for the doorway. "Thanks," she said over her shoulder. "I owe you, and the family owes you even more. Assuming we've discovered this in time."

She hit Jacob's number as she rushed toward the stairwell. "Answer, answer," she said, swinging open the heavy metal door and then clattering down the stirs. "Come on, Jacob." By the time she reached the bottom, she remembered he had an early meeting. His phone would be off. "Crap."

She burst out of the building and headed toward her office in Anderson Hall on the other side of Montgomery. Laskey's number wasn't in her list of contacts — she'd been too superstitious to put it there, afraid he'd cut and run if she took that liberty — but his number was in her purse, written on the back of a shopping list. She'd left her purse in her office. She was all but running as she detoured through a grassy triangle, nearly stumbling over a limb and barely catching herself in time. She shoved open the door to her building and made for her office halfway down the hall.

"Good morning, Dr. Hay, I was wondering if . . ."

"Not this morning, Larry," she said to the student waiting beside her office door. Larry, a curly-haired red-head had been trying for the past two weeks to wrangle an interview with her. She'd advertised for a new TA, and he was dead set on getting the job. "Next week," she said over her shoulder as she inserted her key in the lock.

She closed the door behind her. Before rummaging through her purse for Laskey's number, she tried calling Jacob again, tapping a foot on the floor waiting in vain for him to pickup.

Nor did Laskey answer.

She had a class in thirty minutes. Weighing her choices, she realized there was only one thing to do. If she drove fast, and if there were no red lights, accidents, or traffic cops, and if the gods were with her, she could be back in Goose Bend in an hour. If she couldn't get Laskey on the phone by then, she'd track him down. She sent Jacob a text message in the event he sneaked a look at his messages during the meeting.

When she exited her office, Larry was still standing in the hall, looking lost. Or maybe put out because of her off-putting.

"Larry?"

He perked up. "Yes, Dr. Hay?"

"I have a class in thirty minutes, but I have an emergency. Can you go over and wing it for me? Spend fifteen minutes comparing Shakespeare's villains in the various plays and then let the class go. Tell them I got called away for a family matter."

His eyes brightened. "Sure thing, Dr. Hay. Glad to help out."

Five minutes later, while stopped at a red light on Broad Street, she picked up her phone and . . . . Shit. It was dead. Shit. Shit. Shit. She'd forgotten to recharge it last night.

FINALLY, Jacob's meeting ended. He slipped out of the room before the others, and checked his phone as he strode down the corridor toward his office. The message jumped out at him, bringing him to a stop. In disbelief, he read it again: *You were right. He isn't who he says he is.*

"Are you okay, buddy?" Dodson, another newcomer to the organization, had almost run into him.

"I'm okay." Salt flooded his mouth and his stomach turned. "Just have to check on something." He ducked into an empty office and called Aunt Zuela. She didn't answer. Nor did Laskey when he tried him.

Three minutes later, he was on his way to Goose Bend. For once in his life, he'd wanted to be wrong. Now he understood Rebekah's reference to the wind. So easy, yet no one had thought of it.

Chapter Forty

They waited in the living room — Fritz in his chair, Laskey standing by the window, Carlos on the sofa trying to pass time by reading the paper. Leah had gone upstairs to get a sweater. The phone call could come any time now. Finally, it blared, vibrating against the table top.

"Speaker on, speaker on," Laskey whispered as Fritz reached for the phone. Laskey whipped the note pad and pen from his pocket.

His hand shaking, Fritz tapped the "speaker" button. "Hello," he croaked and then swallowed and repeated, "Hello."

"You have the goods packed and ready to deliver?" The gritty voice again.

"Yes. In a hard-sided suitcase like you said."

Laskey leaned closer, prepared to catch the phone should Fritz drop it. His friend's hands were shaking so badly he was afraid he couldn't hold on. He motioned for Fritz to set the phone down on the table.

"Bring them to Jupiter Mall. . . ."

"Let me speak to Rebek . . ."

"Business first, old man. Put the suitcase in the backseat of your car and make sure the doors are unlocked. You'd better double check that: *unlocked* doors. Drive around when you get to the mall. We'll find you."

"You'll let Rebekah go then?"

"Don't be stupid. We have to authenticate the works first. That'll take twenty-four hours. Maybe. Or not. We want to make sure you're giving us what we want."

Carlos rose from where he'd been perched on the edge of his seat and started toward the phone. Laskey held out a hand to stop him.

"You already know I'm giving you what you want," Fritz said. "What else would I give you?"

"Just need to make certain."

"I want to speak to Rebekah."

There was the sound of shuffling, a whisper, and then a voice saying, presumably to Rebekah, "Ten seconds."

"Dad?" Her voice sounded choked.

"Rebekah, darling. Are you okay?" Fritz asked, his voice breaking.

"Yes, Dad. I love you. Mom?"

"She's upstairs."

"Tell her I love her."

"I will. But you can tell her yourself soon."

Rebekah blew then. Not sighs, Laskey noted, but two long, intentional whooshes. She was trying to tell them something about wind.

"That's enough," Grit-voice said. "I think, old man, you shouldn't be the one to deliver the prize. Your heart might not last long enough to carry out the job."

In the background, Rebekah let out a wail.

Carlos, in spite of Laskey's upheld palm, had moved quietly to Fritz's side. "I'll do it," he said, bending toward the receiver. "I'll bring the pictures."

"Who the fuck?" The voice snapped.

"I'm Carlos Vientos, Rebekah's fiancé. I will bring the paintings."

Laskey was about to protest, but Fritz touched him on the arm and shook his head.

"Ahhhh, the fiancé. You're the BMW in front of the Herschmann place?"

"Yes, I'm the BMW."

"Who is the other guy?" Grit voice asked.

Laskey flinched. Someone had been watching the house.

"Friend of the family," Carlos replied. "He's standing by with the Herschmanns while I bring the paintings."

"Then you bring them, Mr. Fiance. Alone. The old man can give you directions, and I imagine you heard the instructions; I can tell when a phone is on speaker. No one in the car but you. Suitcase in the back seat. Doors unlocked. Jupiter Mall. Thirty minutes."

"That doesn't give me much time."

"You'll make it."

"Dad, I love you," Rebekah screamed from the background. "Tell Mom I love her."

Laskey's heart dropped. Rebekah knew that delivering six pieces of art might not be enough to save her.

Chapter Forty-One

L askey watched Carlos walk out the front door with the suitcase. As soon as the door closed behind Carlos, a few long strides brought Laskey back to the living room window in time to see Carlos stop for a few seconds at the bottom of the front doorsteps and look up and down the street. Then he walked over to the BMW and climbed in. Laskey watched him back into the street and then head in the direction of the mall. Grabbing his phone, Laskey punched in Bump's number.

"Get me," he said and strode toward the front door.

Fritz was close on his heels. "What are you doing? You're not going to follow . . ."

Laskey swung around to face him. "I'm doing what I have to do." He put his hand on Fritz's arm and squeezed. "Trust me, old friend."

Laskey switched off the *mute* button as he hurried out. He'd had it on *mute* all morning in the event someone tried to call him while Fritz was on the phone with the kidnappers. He looked at the call log as he strode toward Bump who was pulling around the corner in an unmarked police car, and saw he'd received calls from Zuela,

Jacob, and Annemarie Leitner. He crammed the phone back in his pocket. He didn't have time to talk.

A screech of wheels behind him stopped Laskey as he trotted over to where Bump was about to land at the curb. He looked around and saw Zuela's yellow beetle roar into the driveway and skid to a stop.

She jumped out and waved madly. "Wait, wait."

"Can't talk now," he said, lengthening his stride toward Bump. He heard the clatter of high heels on the sidewalk chasing after him.

"Wait." The clatter sped up. "It's important."

Bump had the window down and was motioning him to hurry.

"*Los Vientos*," she shouted.

Laskey, already crossing behind the Bump's vehicle to get to the passenger side, stopped and turned around. "What?"

"*Los Vientos*." Out of breath, she paused for a few seconds. "It means *wind* in Spanish."

"Wind?" he repeated dumbly.

"Carlos isn't who he says he is. Jacob had me do a recording. I took it to a language expert. Carlos is a native Arabic speaker."

It hit him them. What he should have noticed before. It was what Rebekah *hadn't* said, that should have clued him in. *I love you, Mom; I love you, Dad.* No mention of her fiancé even though she knew he was there. He felt the blood drain from his face. "Thanks," he said. He motioned toward the house. "Go stay with them." He climbed into Bump's Ford. "Let's go," he said.

"I heard," Bump said as he threw the vehicle into gear and shot off. "Do you think he's a Palestinian?"

"A Palestinian. An Iraqi. A Syrain. Just the fact that he went to great efforts to fool Rebekah is . . . ." He'd been about to say *bad*, but *bad* didn't nearly describe what Carlos had done. Whoever or whatever he actually was, Carlos was smart. He had to give him that. He'd found someone to impersonate whom he looked similar to and that had a verifiable background. Only problem was, they hadn't verified it.

As the Ford roared around the intersection where the BMW had turned a few seconds previous, Laskey's phone bleeped with an incoming message. He looked down and read the text from Annemarie Leitner: *MacNeish threatened to do something stupid. He may have.*

Good god. First Carlos, and now MacNeish. Just as he'd reached a different conclusion about the Scotsman. How could he have been so wrong?

JACOB SWUNG around the corner onto the Herschmann's street, jammed on the breaks, and stared after the car that had almost hit him because it was careening down the wrong side of the road. The Prius screeched to a stop, backed up, and MacNeish stuck his head through the window.

"Hurry; get in with me. Carlos is headed somewhere with the paintings."

Jacob rammed his car to the curb, jumped out, and climbed into the Prius which began moving before he finished closing the door.

"Bloody bassa," MacNeish said, gunning the motor and heading toward the intersection where the BMW had turned right. "And I'm a bloody doaty asshole."

"Move over to the right side of the road," Jacob said, belting himself in.

"I keep forgetting you Americans drive on the wrong side of the street. Keep your eyes on the bastard so I can pay attention to the road and keep from colliding with someone." MacNeish made a hard right at the intersection, again almost hitting a car.

"Take it easy." Jacob held up his palm. "If you're reckless, he'll see us, or we'll wind up beside the road waiting for the wrecker. How do you know he has the paintings?"

"Totsy."

"Totsy?"

MacNeish pulled around a van that had shot out of a side street in front of them. "I had her camping out in the shrubbery across the street. She saw Carlos come out with the suitcase." He sped up. "Din'na ask me about Totsy now. I've no time for that."

Jacob decided to let it go. He needed to let Laskey know about Carlos. He tried calling again but got a busy signal. Maybe Aunt Zuela had gotten through and was talking to him right now.

A picture of Rebekah at the bottom of a silo, neck broken, head smashed, and legs at an odd angle, kept going through his mind. Anyone evil enough to pull off this elaborate charade wouldn't care what happened to her.

"WHAT ARE the chances of Carlos actually going to the mall?" Bump asked, his eyes squinting into the sun as he tried to keep track of the BMW.

"Very little." Laskey suspected there wasn't a chance in the world Carlos would either go to the mall or lead them to Rebekah. Carlos' goal was to deliver the paintings, after which he'd collect a handsome stipend and then disappear in some foreign country. "But not to worry; I have this convenient little tool." He held up the device Thunder had given him. "I planted trackers in both Carlos' car and Fritz's. I'm guessing he plans to board an airplane real soon. He's headed in the direction of Allentown-Bethlehem-Easton Airport, but he could turn and go back to the Philadelphia airport. He could also hand off the paintings to someone along the way."

"To hell with the paintings," Bump said. "We need to find Rebekah. I have three unmarked cars sitting out at the city limits. I can send them to the mall." He shot Laskey a look. "Don't worry, the officers haven't a clue why I've put them in unmarked cars."

"Your department has three unmarked police cars in addition to the one we're in?"

"Hell, no. I borrowed the other three from the Lansdale department. Made up a story about a potential drug bust."

"Sounds good."

Laskey's heart thumped, and he could barely stay seated; he wanted to fly out the window and over the stream of traffic separating them from the BMW. Bump had sped up, aggressively passing several cars, so that Carlos was just a few cars ahead. Laskey gave a little sniff. Carlos, smart in choosing his alias, hadn't made an intelligent decision when selecting an easily spotted top of the line luxury car. But he could have another vehicle waiting somewhere. The thought of losing Carlos made him swear under his breath.

"We're getting close to the mall," Bump said a few minutes later as he craned his neck to the left to see around the increased traffic. "But Carlos isn't pulling into the left lane to turn." He frowned. "Can you see him on your side?" He veered toward the right shoulder.

Laskey leaned closer to the window. "He doesn't look like he has any intention of getting out of the right lane."

Laskey knew he had to make a decision. The three unmarked cars could run Carlos off the road, and he could try to force information from him, but Laskey's intuition told him that Carlos neither knew nor cared where Rebekah was. Stopping him could be dangerous if another party was standing by to receive the paintings. If Carlos didn't show up, that person would sound the alarm.

"I don't think he's going to the mall," Bump said. "He'd be getting in the left lane by now."

Laskey saw the rooflines of Macy's and Penneys rising above the strip of other stores on the left. He pressed his shoulder into the car door as he leaned hard to his right, watching for the BMW. When they passed Cheddars at the first mall entrance, Carlos still hadn't made a move to pull into the left lane. Laskey swallowed. Every fiber in his body urged him to stop Carlos and try to force information from him, but he knew it wasn't the right thing to do.

JACOB HAD both hands pressed to the dashboard to brace himself should MacNeish rear end a car which he threatened to do at any moment. Thanks to the Scotsman's erratically wild driving, there was only one vehicle separating them from the BMW as they passed the mall.

"I thought she was smarter than that," MacNeish said.

"You mean Rebekah?"

"Of course, I mean Rebekah. Who else would I be talking about? She fell for that ass of a lying . . . . whatever he is. She's smart; she's dedicated. She was the best epidemiologist we had, you know?" He flitted his eyes at Jacob.

"Watch the road." Jacob removed one hand from the dash long enough to motion to the road in front of them. "No, I didn't know she was the best, but I'm not surprised.

"How could she have been so . . ., so thick? Pish! . . ." MacNeish jammed on the brakes, barely avoiding the car in front.

As the Prius swerved toward the shoulder, Jacob got a good view of the BMW speeding up.

LASKEY KEPT his eyes on the tracking device, watching the green dot that was Carlos' vehicle. Once past the mall, the BMW had picked up speed. Carlos was now about a quarter mile ahead.

"Shall I have my men tail him?" Bump asked. "They can catch up, if I tell them now."

"Yes. But don't have them do anything other than follow."

While Bump gave orders to his waiting officers, Laskey recognized the steeple of Good Shepherd Baptist Church coming up on the right. He glanced at his tracking device and saw that Carlos was slowing. "I think he's going to turn," he said. There was a semi in front of them so he could only see him on the tracker. "Pull toward the right."

Bump steered the car toward the shoulder, and Laskey saw a sliver of the BMW. "He's turning into the church."

Laskey had passed the church numerous times and knew the parking lot was in the back. The entrance to the lot stood on the right side of the church, and the exit to the left. A dense row of sturdy Boxwoods lined both entry and exit, so there was no veering off the lane. They had come within a couple hundred feet of the entry when Laskey saw the BMW career around to the back of the church. As the BMW disappeared around the corner of the building, a Prius turned into the lane.

"Someone else followed him in," Laskey said.

"You don't have a gun, do you?" Bump asked.

"You know I don't."

JACOB dug his heels into the floorboard as MacNeish swung into the church lane. His heart was in his throat. Carlos was probably meeting someone behind the church and, while MacNeish might be crazy, *he* wasn't. He'd jumped into the car with the Scotsman without thinking. Almost as a lark, but now he *was* thinking. What they were doing could be dangerous.

MacNeish jammed on the breaks. An old Ford Explorer, mud-splattered, paint-nicked, and pulling a wagon with lawn equipment was exiting from the entry and had almost crashed into them.

MacNeish leaped out of the car. "Bampot, bloody bampot. Yer headin' off the arse wrong way. Back up." Moving toward the Explorer, he flipped the back of his hand at the man sitting motionless behind the steering wheel. "Back up."

Jacob jumped out. "Get back in the car, MacNeish." All they needed was a fight between an out-of-control Scotsman and a local who manicured church lawns. It wasn't hard to guess which man would wind up in jail, nor was a kerfuffle going to help them save Rebekah.

The driver of the Explorer scratched his head, looked back over his shoulder, and appeared to be about to back up when Jacob heard another vehicle screech to a halt behind them. He turned around to see Laskey bolt out of the car and take off toward the back of the church. Bump jumped out and followed.

Jacob and MacNeish exchanged glaces. In a flash they both raced toward the rear of the church. Jacob caught up with Laskey just as he reached the empty BMW. Bump and MacNeish came panting up a few seconds behind them. Carlos had disappeared. The door of the BMW was open, and the empty suitcase lay on the ground a few feet away, its two sides yawning open like the mouth of a crocodile.

Laskey shouted at Bump. "Grab the man in the Explorer." Then he ran toward the far corner of the church where the departure lane took vehicles back to the main road.

Jacob ran with him. He knew Laskey was trying to see what kind of vehicle Carlos had jumped into. When they came to the corner of the church, the vehicle had disappeared. Laskey whipped around and set off running back toward the Explorer in the entry lane. This time Jacob beat him.

Bump had pulled the driver, a fiftyish, brown-haired man with hard muscles, from the Explorer and handcuffed him. "I called one of the cars to come pick him up," Bump said. "What he refuses to tell us here, they can get out of him at the station."

Laskey walked over to the man, positioning himself so close, that the man drew back. "What kind of car did he get into?"

"Don't know." The man looked dazed.

"You'd better know real fast." Laskey leaned in closer.

The man's dazed look changed to scared. "Might have been a Corolla. Or something like that. A silver one. I didn't do nothing wrong. I was about to start work and they told me to leave and to drive out the entrance."

One of the unmarked police cars pulled into the lane. The officer got out.

"Take him to the station," Bump said to the officer. He nodded at the lawn man. "Call the church and find out if he was supposed to be here, which I doubt. Then find out who he's working for. He might be willing to give you more details if he knows he could be charged with abetting murder."

"No." The man shook his head. "No. No. They said it was just about a little crack. That's all. Just a minor exchange."

"You can give the officer the details," Bump said.

"Wait," Laskey said as the officer was about to lead him away. He narrowed his eyes at the lawn man. "Was it a man or a woman that arranged this?"

The lawn man, now shaking with fear, swallowed and said, "A man. But he talked to a woman on the phone while he was telling me what to do. I heard her voice, so I know it was a woman."

"Describe the man."

"Thirty maybe. A little skinny. Gritty voice."

"What do we do now?" Jacob asked when the man had been taken away.

"Sit and wait," Laskey said. "I have a phone call to make. Actually two calls." He walked away.

Jacob realized his shoulders were drooping. Crap, his whole body sagged like the kid who had no presents under the Christmas tree. MacNeish appeared from behind the church where he'd remained when the others went running off to apprehend the lawn man. He walked slowly toward them, looking like he, too, had missed the holiday express.

"Carlos had another car waiting," MacNeish said, stating the obvious as he came up to them. "There's a dirt lane back there that leads from the parking lot into the woods."

MacNeish slumped against the wall of the church, and Bump sat down on the concrete steps leading up to a side door while they waited for Laskey to make his calls, but Jacob edged a little closer to Laskey. He heard the low rumble of his voice, but not his words, as he spoke one quick sentence into the phone and then hung up. During the second call, Laskey mainly listened, nodding several times. Once, he let out a sniff of a smile. Then, realizing that Jacob was watching him, he turned his back. Finally, he finished, put the phone back in his pocket, and came back over to where they were. Narrowing one eye, he stared at MacNeish.

The Scotsman didn't seem to notice.

JACOB DIDN'T KNOW what they were waiting for as they sat in the parking lot at the back of the church, he and MacNeish in the Prius per Laskey's orders, Laskey and Bump in Bump's unmarked police car. He guessed it had something to do with the phone calls. The Explorer and trailer still blocked the entry lane, but Bump and MacNeish had backed their cars into the main road, driven two hundred feet to the exit lane, and then pulled around to the back.

Jacob felt contrite. This was another incidence of his jumping into something without thinking. How was it that in his job he was able to act with precision, forethought, and humility, but otherwise was ready to jump into an adventure without due consideration? They shouldn't have been here, and Laskey had let him know that in no uncertain terms.

"I came with MacNeish." Jacob had offered. The excuse earned him a glare from his godfather who chose to ignore the fact that MacNeish was present and also responsible. Jacob still chafed at Laskey's anger.

MacNeish stared off into space. Jacob, never comfortable sitting still, squirmed, rearranged his body, huffed. Mostly, he worried. Carlos must have seen them. What did that mean for Rebekah?

A few minutes later, Jacob had let his gaze meander down the dirt road that led into the woods, and didn't see Laskey get out of the Ford. His head snapped around when Laskey tapped on the driver's side window.

MacNeish rolled down the window.

"You need to go home now," Laskey said. He turned, took the few steps back toward Bump's vehicle where the passenger side door was still open, but stopped. Turning back around, he narrowed his eyes at MacNeish, then walked back over, and bent to look at them through the window. "I've changed my mind," he said. Get in with us. We're going to the airport."

Chapter Forty-Two

Fritz's eyes were on Grandfather Clock. Its hands barely moved, the passage of each minute encompassing a century. Dr. Donalson had come and gone, admonishing him to take it easy and leaving a few pills after exacting a promise from Leah to call at the slightest hint of anything not being right.

Leah and Zuela had gone to the kitchen, leaving Fritz to keep his vigil in quiet. The wine stained corner of a pastel drawing hovered in his mind, slapped him in the face, punched him in the ribs. The stain grew bigger and then smaller; it changed shape, got darker, lighter. Then it disappeared altogether just to reappear a few seconds later as a purple stain. Until yesterday, the only time he'd seen the stain was when his father unframed the drawing to have a copy made, and he remembered neither the shape nor size of the stain. Would Fuchs remember?

He heard the snuffle of voices in the kitchen. Leah's clipped words. Zuela's deep alto. He couldn't even begin to guess what they talked about at a time like this. Leah came to the living room every few minutes, squeezed his shoulder, and then left again. Or she'd sit on the sofa until she could no longer sit, and then she'd wander back into the kitchen.

Fifteen or twenty minutes ago, she and Zuela had gone upstairs. "Checking on Rebekah's room," Leah said. Like she hadn't already scrubbed it to death. Arranged everything in exact order. Spaced every item just right. Parted curtains evenly. Opened blinds to let in a little sunshine.

Zuela had run over to the grocery store and bought fresh flowers for Rebekah's bedroom. Leah arranged them in a vase and then rearranged them in another before placing them on the bureau. She'd checked the food in the refrigerator at least five times to make sure they had everything Rebekah might want. Maple syrup. McIntosh apples from Fluck's Orchard along with one of their caramel apples. Sweet gherkins. Fresh eggs. Rebekah hated the eggs in the Middle East. "They taste like old paper," she claimed. Leah had stocked up on bacon, unavailable in Jordan. They shouldn't have bacon, Fritz knew. Not because they were Jews, but because of the additives. They had no qualms about eating pork, Hadassah and additives aside. All was in readiness for Rebekah's homecoming.

He felt dead. Every muscle, every organ, every drop of blood – it was as though his body functions had shut down. As though a light had turned off. And that was good; he didn't want to feel. He wanted to go over to the factory and help Bay mix sugar into 'Bekah Bars; debate with Eli over which machines to replace, which to repair; he wanted to pick up bottles of water that had rolled into the aisles between stations; hand a birthday card to an employee. Normality.

A cabinet door in the kitchen banged shut, and then he heard the sounds of dishes being set on the counter. Cups and saucers? Were they making coffee? He rested his head on the back of the chair and closed his eyes. Making coffee – that was something to do; something to keep busy with for two minutes.

Chapter Forty-Three

Totsy flung open the front door, banging it against the wall. A mug with yesterday's left-over coffee sat on the coffee table and rattled at the impact.

"What the fuck!" Delores, still holding a shard of blue-green pottery in one hand and the glue bottle in the other, stared up from her work table.

"Did you have something to do with it?" Totsy's shout reverberated.

"Why are you yelling at me, and what are you talking about, *something to do with it?* With what?"

"With Rebekah's kidnapping. Don't be dense."

Delores stared. At length, she set down the shard and the glue. "Is this another one of your invented dramas?"

"Yes, mother," Totsy said. "This is one of my invented dramas. I made it all up. Little ol' Goose Bend just doesn't have enough going on to keep me entertained, so I invented the kidnapping of *little Miss Perfect* as you call her." She lurched over and grabbed her mother by the shoulders and shook her. "What do you know about it?" she screamed.

Delores shoved her away, causing Totsy to land on the floor.

Totsy hissed at her mother and then pushed herself to a sitting position. "I heard you talking to Uncle James the other day on the phone. You said something about getting even, and then you said you'd take care of stocking the place with food so they wouldn't starve while they were hidden away waiting for the big payout. I had no idea what you were talking about, but now I think I do."

"Don't you dare accuse me. We were talking about his new job."

"His new job involves being hidden away?"

"You don't hear very well, do you? I said *paycheck*, not *payout*. And now I have to put more groceries in Mom's cupboard because James is staying with her until he gets his *paycheck*, and you know how her cupboard usually is. Bare. Like Old Mother Hubbard's. Why do you think I never have any money? You can't bother to notice that I have to keep putting food on her table, too, and now James is mooching off her. All this play acting is getting to you, Totsy." She walked past Totsy and went into the living room. She nudged a blind slat open and peered out into the front yard. "I don't see that detective out there, but I wonder. Did he put you up to this?"

"No, he didn't put me up to this." Totsy got up off the floor and brushed off her slacks.

"Rebekah missed her plane so you think she's been kidnapped?" Delores asked with a sneer. "Well, aren't you the smart one."

"It's been five days. She didn't miss her plane. I had lunch with a friend who told me she was on it."

"You have a friend who knows she didn't miss her plance? What friend is that? And why were you having lunch when you were supposed to be at work? Your whole life has turned into one big stage play, I think."

"I do get lunch breaks, you know. And right now I have a terrible stomach ache." Totsy bent over, clasped her stomach in a false show of agony, and let out an extended moan. "What could they do but send me home from work?" she said, straightening.

Delores' nostrils flared. "Must be nice to afford lunches out while I'm having to feed your grandmother and uncle. Who did you *dine* with?"

"Jamie MacNeish. He's one of those doctors from Jordan where Rebekah works."

"I know where Rebekah works; I'm not stupid." Delores went to the sofa, removed one of the throw cushions, and sat down. Holding the cushion against her chest, she glared at her daughter. "What I *don't* know is, why you're accusing me of having anything to do with whatever's happened. That sure says a lot for how you feel about your mother."

"I'll tell you why. Because you're so goddamned jealous of Rebekah and the Herschmanns, and you're always giving me these speeches about how I don't appreciate what you've done for me, and how I should be thankful for what I have instead of wanting what Rebekah has, and how you'd like to teach her a thing or two. Rebekah has never been anything other than nice to you, and the Herschmann's . . ."

"Ah, yes, the Herschmanns who embarrassed me to death by paying my . . . ."

"Oh, shut up. Would you rather have lost the house?"

Totsy sat down opposite her mother, closed her eyes, and then took a deep breath. "I'm sorry, Mom," she said opening her eyes. "I'm just worried, and you kept talking about how you'd like to show *Little Miss Perfect* up. She was, is, my friend, and if I'm willing to accept the fact that she's a lot smarter and a lot richer than I am, why can't you? I don't know what it is, but there's *something* about me that Rebekah likes. Why can't you believe that?"

"I just wanted a lot more for you." She sighed. "Why on earth would you think I could possibly know anything about her being kidnapped?"

Totsy shrugged. Sometimes she imagined horrible things about her mother. For instance that she was mixed up with the losers that frequented the shithole bar where she worked. "I worry about those scumbags that keep flirting with you." She looked off sideways. "And that you flirt back with. I've been there a couple times. I saw what was going on."

"Any flirting I do has to do with tips." She threw the cushion to the other end of the sofa. "Beyond that, I don't give a damn about those scumbags, as you call them. If they're up to no good, I manage to not hear it."

Exhausted, Totsy slumped back in her seat. The Herschmanns probably wondered why she hadn't been over, but how could she tell them she couldn't face Carlos. Should she tell Rebekah when she was safe at home again? Should she *not* tell Rebekah?

"He made a pass at me," she said finally. "Carlos made a fucking pass at me when I visited Rebekah in Jordan. She had to work one evening so Carlos took me to dinner. He acted so interested in everything. My family. The Herschmanns. Goose Bend. He even asked about you and what you did, the name of the place where you worked. He kept giving me drinks and, like an idiot, I kept drinking. Then . . . . Oh, god." She covered her face with her hands. "I should have told Rebekah. But I couldn't bear to hurt her."

Chapter Forty-Four

Bump rocketed into a parking place reserved for police at Allentown-Bethlehem-Easton Airport. The car had barely come to a stop, when Laskey jumped out and raced for the terminal, thankful that he had Thunder to twist the arms of the TSA to stop Carlos. All he wanted now was to find Rebekah.

The others were right behind him as he burst into the terminal, where a TSA agent was waiting for them.

"We have him upstairs, but there's no suitcase," the agent said.

They bolted up the escalator steps to the second floor and hurried down a long corridor, until they came to a closed door. The agent opened the door and led them inside. Three agents stood guard around Carlos, and a large man in plain clothes stood in the corner. Laskey motioned for the agents to stand aside.

Laskey stood for a few seconds, trying to imagine his gaze burning streaks in Carlos' flesh. Rebekah's *fiance* was seated in a chair in the middle of the room, bent over with forearms on thighs and head hanging. His head dipped further when Laskey stepped closer and glared down at him. Laskey's stomach turned. Here, before him, was one of the biggest creeps he'd ever met. And there had been plenty.

"Thanks, Thunder," Laskey said without looking at the big man with hairy hands standing in the corner.

"My pleasure." Thunder said. "Always glad to assist in the downfall of a jerk."

"So, you've met my old FBI buddy, Thunder Ferguson," Laskey said to the top of Carlos' head. "It's wonderful how the FBI can disperse pictures of criminals to airports, and as Thunder said, the agency takes great pleasure in the downfall of jerks."

The agents in the room stood quietly except for one who shuffled his feet, but then became still again. Jacob had eased over to stand beside Thunder, but MacNeish remained a few feet behind Laskey, breathing like a bull about to charge.

Laskey clenched his fists. "Where is she?"

Carlos kept his head lowered.

"Damn it. I asked you where she is." Laskey kicked the leg of Carlos' chair.

Carlos looked up with a sneer.

Then Laskey felt himself being pushed aside. MacNeish grabbed Carlos by the collar, jerked him to his feet, and, with a cracking sound, hit him squarely in the jaw. The guards lunged toward MacNeish, but Laskey held up his hand and they backed off. Jacob had plunged forward to grab MacNeish's arm, but he, too, backed away. Thunder, rocking back and forth on his feet, watched from the corner, a smile twitching at his lips.

MacNeish had taken a step back after the first swing, but he stepped in again, his arms positioned for another punch.

"Don't," Laskey said, but his words were without urgency, and he made no move to stop him.

"You bloody arsehole of a bastard." MacNeish hit Carlos again, this time spinning him around. Carlos fell to the floor, and MacNeish kicked him in the balls. Carlos let out a scream and curled up into a ball. "Where is she, you scum of a beast?" he kicked him in the knees. "Where?"

Laskey still held up his hand to the guards. "You shouldn't be doing that," he said to MacNeish. He said it the same way he reprimanded his cats for chasing birds, understanding that it was the nature of cats to chase birds, and that it was the nature of jealous men to kick the hell out of a competitor when the competitor set out to destroy the loved one. He flitted his eyes at Thunder who gave him a thumbs up, and then at Jacob, who stared open-mouthed at MacNeish.

"Tell me where the bloody hell she is." MacNeish kicked Carlos in the ribs. "If anything happens to her, I'll kill you."

Laskey grabbed MacNeish's arm then. "That's enough." He nodded to Thunder and the two of them pulled MacNeish away.

"You're in deep shit," Laskey said to Carlos who had tears flooding down his cheeks. "Kidnapping. Theft. Murder charges? Besides, we're having a hard time holding MacNeish back. He's likely to break loose at any moment and get at you again. Where's Rebekah?"

"I don't know." Hands cupped over crotch, Carlos shook with pain.

"When we find her, and we will, you have no objection to spending the rest of your life in an American jail?"

"Totsy's mother," he gasped. "She knows."

Chapter Forty-Five

L askey held his breath. When Bump drove fast, he drove *fast*. They were racing toward Goose Bend, siren blaring, light flashing.

The car phone buzzed, and Bump hit the "on" button. "Delores Love isn't home," the officer said, his voice crackling over the speaker. "The rest of the force is scouring the neighborhood."

"Thanks," Bump said. "Stay there in case she shows up." He hit the "end" button and threw Laskey a quick glance. "Any other ideas?"

Laskey shook his head. The force had been given strict instructions not to alarm Delores, but to bring her in quietly. Most importantly, she was not allowed to communicate with anyone.

A groan drew Laskey's eyes away from the trees and buildings flying past, and he glanced into the back seat. MacNeish wore a look of agony as his left hand caressed his right. Judging by the blow he'd struck Carlos, Laskey wouldn't be too surprised if MacNeish's hand was broken. *Medezin sans Frontiere* in Jordan might have to do without their chief surgeon for a couple months.

Laskey twisted his head to glimpse at Jacob who sat behind him. Jacob had barely spoken either at the airport or since they'd begun their race back to Goose Bend. Something was eating at him, but right now Laskey didn't have time to worry about that.

"We'll be there in thirty minutes, or less," Bump said, turning off highway 22 onto 309.

"Hopefully they'll have found Delores by then."

Laskey was terrrified that finding Delores didn't guarantee saving Rebekah. James might not have told Delores where they were holding her in the event someone figured out the connection. Even with MacNeish hovering nearby, posing a further threat to his balls and ribs, Carlos had denied knowing where Rebekah was. He'd admitted to handing over the suitcase to someone in the airport parking lot. He gave them the name, but hadn't been able to tell them if that person had boarded a plane with the paintings or had driven away to some other destination. Thunder was alerting airports in the hopes of stopping him, but Laskey didn't hold out much hope. But the paintings weren't the issue now.

He owed Thunder big time. Thunder had stuck his neck out, making it look like he was acting for the FBI. If Thunder's superiors found out, both he and Thunder would be in trouble. He wasn't concerned about himself; he'd retire if he had to, and spend the rest of his days fishing for trout. But he'd hate to have caused a forced ending to his friend's career.

MacNeish let out a loud groan.

"You're late for your conference in Atlanta," Laskey said without looking back.

"Obviously, I'm no longer going to a conference."

"Why not?"

"You bloody well know why not."

"Did she spurn you, or were you too busy sewing up people to pursue romance?" Laskey looked back at MacNeish.

MacNeish pretended to look out the window. "I was too busy sewing up people."

"Hopefully, you'll get a second chance."

"And be second choice?"

"Since you said nothing, you'll never know whether you'd have been first choice or second."

"MacNeish is definitely the better choice," Jacob said, finally speaking up.

"You kept your relationship with Rebekah purely professional?" Laskey asked MacNeish, ignoring Jacaob. "You never even dipped your toe in?"

"Relationship? Carlos bloody Vientos had a relationship with her. Not me. She fell for an arrogant, smooth-talking, schmoozing, Latino."

"He isn't Latino." Jacob said, dryly.

"Well, then South-American, whatever."

"He isn't South-American either," Laskey said. Then he looked at Jacob. "Tell him."

"He's a native Arabic speaker," Jacob said. "We don't know from where. Aunt Zuela recorded him last night and took the recording to a language expert this morning."

MacNeish gave a short laugh – a coughed out *hah* – followed by another groan. He brought his injured hand up to his mouth and blew on it. "I told Annemarie that Carlos was a lying bastard of some sort." He lowered his hand to his lap. "I thought it was jealousy that made me think that. Why didn't I act on my suspicions?"

"Like you said, you were jealous." Double affliction, Laskey thought, noting the misery on MacNeish's face. Physical pain. Rejected lover's pain. Only he hadn't been rejected; he'd just never given it a shot. He felt a little sorry for the Scotsman, by reputation an excellent surgeon, but not so good with women. "At any rate, I talked to Annemarie. You have some explaining to do."

MacNeish closed his eyes. "I'm a bloody walloper."

Chapter Forty-Six

Delores followed the shortcut Totsy and Rebekah used to lessen the distance between their houses. After what Fritz had done to her brother, Mr. Rich Man deserved a few days of nervousness, but something was bothering her, and she was sure a quick visit to the Herschmann's would clear that up.

She walked fast, wanting to get the confrontation over with. It was only for a few days —this thing she'd helped with — then his precious Rebekah would come home. No skin off his nose. Just the loss of a few ugly paintings he'd stolen in the first place. Carlos had told her the shameful story when he tracked her down at the Bronco. Oh boy, did those Herschmanns have everybody in town fooled. When they found out Mr. Fritz's true colors, they'd think twice.

Carlos had showed up at the Bronco late one night three weeks ago, seated himself at a table in a corner, and rubbed a forefinger over his lips while giving her a look she couldn't quite figure out. There were other customers waiting for service but she ignored them and sauntered over to Carlos. It wasn't often that someone so good-looking showed up at the Bronco.

"I think you must be Delores," he said when she got to his table. "I've met your daughter, Totsy."

Before she could question him, he explained he was from out of town, had a bit of business to take care of, and that he needed a local consultant. If she'd meet him after work or the following morning for breakfast, he'd explain what he needed and, he added, the pay would be good.

She arranged to meet him after work. Good thing the Bronco was in Warminster. Had the bar been in Goose Bend, someone might have noticed and recognized him later.

She brushed aside a branch as she marched on in the silence of a deserted alley. Carlos had explained he planned to meet Rebekah at the airport and lure her away for a couple days for a "pre-honeymoon." He needed for Delores to set him up with someone to contact the Herschmanns and demand the paintings, plus do a few other little *odds and ends*. "If the Herschmanns want to think Rebekah has been kidnapped, then let them," he'd sneered. "There's nothing illegal about taking back what was stolen in the first place and nothing illegal about shacking up with your fiancé for a couple days."

Delores bit her lips. If nothing they were doing was illegal, then why were they hiding in an old farm house? Why had she been asked to leave groceries in the pantry as though they planned to stay awhile?

James had made it clear she wasn't to contract him. Frowning, she skirted a pile of dog poo and then kicked aside a torn soccer ball which lay in the middle of the alley. A dog ran toward her from a backyard, gave a few barks, and then came up to sniff at her crotch. "Get away you friggin' cur." She kneed him away and kept going.

She'd believed everything Carlos told her, but she didn't really know him, did she? Sometimes she thought she didn't even know her own brother so well. Had they pulled one over on her? Fritz Herschmann had accused James of stealing when he fired him, but James claimed there was more to the story. Problem was, James got so angry every time the subject came up, he couldn't explain to her what happened except to say he'd been framed and old man Herschmann was out to get him. Even after a couple years, James still wanted revenge. Maybe Carlos had been lying, and maybe James had been lying. Well, she'd see what Mr. High and Mighty had to say on the subject.

She came to the end of the alley. About to cross over Elm, she saw the police car creeping up the street. The officer inside sat forward, swiveling his head back and forth as though looking for someone. She drew back into the alley and hid behind an oak growing along the side. When the vehicle passed, she rushed across Elm into another alley.

"Get a grip, Delores," she hissed between clenched teeth. "It was only a police car. Goose Bend has police cars. They drive up and down the streets. Duh." She wouldn't get her knickers in a knot. There was no way anyone could know her part in this. Which wasn't much, actually. Just putting Carlos in touch with her brother. Buying a few groceries. There was no crime in that.

THREE FACES STARED down at her when the door opened. It was like they'd all raced over to see who got there first. Fritz and Leah gaped, clearly surprised to see her. And that woman with the funny first name who taught down in one of those schools in Philadelphia. Temple? Or the University of Pennsylvania? Drexel? Shit, what did it matter?

"Delores," Leah said after a pause. "Come in."

Head held high, Delores entered. She saw how reluctant they were to invite her in, their eyes flashing back and forth at each other, their mouths opening and shutting while they tried to figure out what to say. Well, she was tired of feeling ashamed and inferior, especially since Fritz Herschmann's father turned out to be a thief. That made Fritz a thief, too, since he kept the goods. People with lots of money usually had something shameful in their past. Otherwise, how did they get rich?

Fritz closed the door. Leah, still looking hesitant, bit her lips and turned to lead her into the living room. The other woman followed. What *was* her name? Ella? Zelda? Sometimes she saw her at the grocery store or the dry cleaners. But she was pretty sure the woman never saw her. Delores Love was invisible to people like that.

"You know Zuela Hay?" Leah said when they were all in the living room.

"I've seen her around." Delores stared at the spaces where pictures were missing. She couldn't remember what the paintings looked like, only that they were crazy. She turned to Fritz. "I want to speak to you." He looked gray around the gills. Good. She liked seeing him that way. His mouth drooped, his shoulders drooped; in fact, he drooped all over. Maybe now he could understand how people who weren't so fortunate might feel sometimes.

Leah and Zuela made no show of leaving. What the hell, let them stay.

Fritz held out his palm, indicating a chair. "Would you like to sit down?"

"I'll talk standing up. You fired my brother. That was some time ago, but I'm sure you remember. It's not like you fire people every day."

"Who is your brother?" Fritz frowned.

"I think you know. But in case you've chosen to forget, my brother is James Eakins."

"James is your brother?"

"Gee, you look surprised. Don't tell me you didn't know?"

"I didn't know."

Delores narrowed one eye at him. His voice had gone quiet and the gray of his face a shade darker. He really hadn't known James was Totsy's uncle? She glanced at Leah and Zuela, both of whom had hardened into statues. God, she loved this.

"You wanted to speak to me about your brother?" Fritz asked at length.

"You claimed he stole from you."

"Why are you bringing it up now?"

"You're guilty of that sin yourself, aren't you?" She meandered over to one of the blank spots on the wall, touched the picture hanger, and twisted her head around giving him what she hoped was a sly look. Ahhhh, the wheels were turning inside his head, but the great man had nothing to say. Grinning, she leaned against the wall, crossed her arms, and studied the three. She couldn't read the expression on Fritz's face, but Zuela Hay stared at her like she was a piece of trash. Leah gave her a searing look and then marched out of the room. The truth hurt the fine lady.

"I know that your father stole those paintings and sneaked them into this country. You kept them, even though you knew they were stolen property and worth something."

She waited for a response from Fritz but his face had turned to stone and, apparently, his tongue, too. What was wrong with him? He was supposed to be outraged. He was supposed to jump up and down claiming what she said wasn't true. Yet he just stood there. He'd get his Rebekah back, but first she was going to have the satisfaction of putting him in his place. She walked around the room, fingering objects, running her hand over paintings. She reared back and made a face at one of the paintings. "Well ain't that just grand. What idiot decided this was art?" Why wasn't Frtiz Herschmann getting angry?

Zuela Hay made a snorting sound then. "I gather you're a friend of Carlos."

Delores froze. She'd said too much. "I don't know . . . ."

"Of course, you know Carlos." Zuela held her palm toward the bare spots on the wall. "Where else would you have come up with a story about Fritz stealing what used to hang here? But don't waste your breath explaining it to me. Save it for the police. Hmmmmm, let's see . . . ." she crossed one arm over her stomach, propped the other elbow on that arm and ran a finger across her mouth. "I think there's going to be a list of charges. Kidnapping. Theft." She lowered her arms and widened her eyes. "Murder?"

Delores' stomach lurched. Carlos had said there was nothing to worry about when he offered her $5000 to set him up with someone who knew the area and who could round up a couple other people to help carry out his plan. "The part with Rebekah is just a prank," he said. "Something to give Fritz Herschmann a good scare for what he did to my friend. No harm done. Just a scare."

She braced herself, trying to regain her composure, and then turned to Fritz. "Your friend is nuts." She jerked her head at Zuela. "You've kept stolen goods, yet you had the nerve to accuse my brother of stealing and fired him. Do you know what that did to him?"

"And this is what I'm going to do to you." Leah's voice came from the archway.

Delores whipped around. Fuck! Leah had a gun pointed at her.

"Put it down, Leah. Put it down." Fritz took a step toward her, holding both palms out.

"No, I'm not going to put it down." Leah held the pistol at arm's length, pointed at Delores head. "I called Eli. She can hear what *he* has to say on the subject of James' firing. She's going to wait here until he comes, or I *will* use it. You left it in the kitchen drawer, Fritz. I assume you meant for it to be used, so I'm going to use it."

Delores broke out in a sweat.

"Leah, please."

Petrified, Delores realized it was the other woman speaking. Then she heard a door slam in the back of the house and steps running toward them.

"I fired James." Eli appeared, panting and red-faced as though he'd run the entire distance from factory to house. He took a step toward Delores. "You have a question about your brother?"

She didn't like his tone of voice. Ignoring the gun which Leah still pointed at her, she squared her shoulders, crossed her arms, and lifted her chin, daring him to speak.

"Your brother was caught red-handed taking the money employees donated for the Christmas Angel Drive," Eli said. "I found the funds in his pockets, still in the envelopes people used for their donation. I fired him on the spot. I was about to call the police, but Fritz stopped me. Against my advice, he gave your brother the chance to pay back the money and keep his job. Do you know what your brother did then?" Eli took a step closer, and she took one back. "Your brother spit in Fritz's face. He *spit* at him. You can thank Mr. Herschmann that your brother didn't go to jail. I was all for it. In the event you doubt me, there were a couple witnesses. Shall I call them?"

It was like something had just knocked her off her feet. Yet, she still stood. She shook her head and started toward the door. She had to get out of here. Lightning bolts were shooting through her head. Something wasn't right. She couldn't think, she . . .

She was almost to the front door when it burst open. The detective that had visited her earlier and the police chief rushed in.

"Where is Rebekah?" Laskey shouted as Bump yanked her arms behind her back.

She felt her knees buckle. What had she done?

Chapter Forty-Seven

Jacob strode past the emergency room registration desk and the payment cubicle. He continued down a corridor which smelled of alcohol, latex, and antiseptics. One of Bump's officers had dropped MacNeish off at the emergency room, driven Jacob to the church to rescue the Prius, and then Jacob had rushed back to the hospital. Dodging doctors, nurses, aides, wheelchairs, carts stacked with paraphernalia, someone mopping up a spill, he searched rooms on both sides of the corridor for MacNeish. Machines beeped, and the reverberations from a dropped metallic object echoed down the hall.

"Sorry," he said, almost bumping into an orderly carrying a tray of instruments. The orderly glared at him but kept going. Jacob hated hospitals. Even after twenty-one years, the memory of an emergency room and his father arriving too late punched holes in his gut every time he went inside one.

He found MacNeish in a room near the end of the corridor. His arm was propped on a table as a round-faced doctor put the finishing touches on a cast. *Dr. McVickers*, the name tag said.

"Broken?" Jacob asked, entering the room.

MacNeish, his face glum, nodded.

"Fortunately, a non-displaced fracture," Dr. McVickers said. "So far, your friend's refused to tell me what happened." He lifted his eyebrows at Jacob. "Did he wallop an elephant? It's still a little early in the day for a barroom brawl."

Jacob ignored the doctor's attempt at humor. Judging by MacNeish's tight-set face, he guessed the Scotsman hadn't bothered to explain to McVickers that he was treating another doctor, one whose career had just come to a screeching halt because of a broken hand.

"Well, that should do it," McVickers said and gave the cast a pat.

In a flash, MacNeish was out of the chair. Jacob led the way as they bolted from the room, ignoring the doctor who was calling out advice about elevating and icing.

"What have I missed?" MacNeish asked when they'd escaped the hospital and were hurrying toward the Prius.

"Haven't heard a thing." Jacob slowed to a walk. Why were they running? He had no idea what Laskey and Bump were doing, but whatever it was, his and MacNeish's presence wasn't welcome.

"Why are you slowing down?" MacNeish shot Jacob a desperate look. "We need to hurry."

"Why?" Jacob continued his slow amble toward the car. "We don't know what's going on, or where Laskey and Bump are, nor do we have a clue how to help. All we can do is go somewhere and sit and wait." And worry about Laskey not being armed, he thought.

SOMEWHERE TURNED out to be Aunt Zuela's front porch. She wasn't home, and her doors were locked. MacNeish sat in the swing staring at his cast, while Jacob huddled in a rocking chair, burdened by the same fear that had haunted him so many times before when he knew his godfather was involved in an operation. Laskey's SIG Sauer P227 was locked in the safe of his office. Jacob appreciated the Quakers' viewpoint about not taking human life, but if his godfather was going to be a law enforcement officer he needed to protect himself. Yet, he refused. How many times could

Laskey be caught in a showdown without a gun and not get hurt? Or worse?

"What did Laskey mean when he said you had some explaining to do?" Jacob asked finally.

"I said some things. I was a right bawheid." MacNeish looked out at the street instead of at Jacob. "As busy as we are over there . . ." He motioned with his good hand, indicating Jordan. ". . . we manage a little fellowship. We're like a family. You told me you lived abroad, so ye know how that is."

Jacob had lived abroad for five years, mostly in Africa, so he knew. Without their families around, ex-pats formed their own family. They celebrated holidays together, shared meals, and consoled each other when someone was sick or homesick.

"We knew all about each other's families," MacNeish said. "Including Rebekah's. *Especially* Rebekah's. Dinna know anyone with a story as interesting as hers – her grandfather's escape from Austria, the art collection, the Nazi villain." He swallowed. "What no one expected was that Annemarie would actually run into the villain.

"Annemarie's father teaches pharmacology at the Medizinische Universität Wien. You may no' ken, but that institution has earned a big name for itself in brain research. Her father also consults with Seltzer on laboratory tests for their pharmaceuticals. About a year ago, when Annemarie was home on leave, her parents took her to a reception sponsored by Seltzer, and she met Karl Fuchs and his father, Gustav. She realized right away that the bodach, the old man, had been the partner of Rebekah's grandfather. Annemarie talked to the bastart for a long while, she said. The arsehole pretended interest in Rebekah, going so far as to invite her to see him the next time she visited Annemarie in Vienna."

MacNeish crossed his legs, propped his broken hand on the thigh of one, and pushed the swing back and forth with the other leg. The swing squeaked like the ticking of a clock. CREAK, creak . . . CREAK, creak.

"When Annemarie returned from leave she told Rebekah about meeting Fuchs," MacNeish continued, "This all happened B.C.

Before Carlos. And that's when I turned into a complete bampot. I thought if I did something heroic, Rebekah might show interest in me. I packed up, flew to Vienna, and arranged a meeting with Gustav Fuchs, intending to bugger him into giving a bunch of free antibiotics in Rebekah's name. Because of the reparations laws. And as long as I was sticking me' neck out, I decided to negotiate on Rebekah's behalf for reparations payments for her grandfather's business. I know . . ." He held up his hand to block comments from Jacob. "I was a dunderhead. There's a button factory in Prague where the descendants of the owners are still battling to get what should be theirs, so I din'na know why I thought I could do what a battalion of lawyers could'na do. Arrogance, I guess. But I thought, surely, I'd get a few antibiotics from the swicker."

"And that would make her happy enough to throw herself into your arms?"

MacNeish looked down at his feet. "I was a right warmer."

"Warmer?" Jacob held up a hand in puzzlement.

"An idjit. I was stupid."

"Yep, it was stupid. Was there something wrong with using your charm and charisma to win a woman?"

"Woudna' been if I had any."

"Oh, buckle up and stop feeling sorry for yourself. If you can't figure out what your assets are, then how do you expect a woman to?" Jacob realized he sounded like Aunt Zuela. How many times had she said something like that to him?

MacNeish flinched. "I din'na feel sorry for myself. I ken I'm not the smoothest operator around." He stopped moving the swing back and forth. "Fuchs told me, in so many words, to piss up my kilt. So I flew back to Amman, tail tucked between legs."

Jacob narrowed his eyes. "And that's all? The story of your interference ends there?"

"Not quite." MacNeish shifted positions, uncrossing his legs and then recrossing them the opposite way. "Carlos showed up a couple weeks after I got back from Vienna. He told me he was making a documentary for the World Health Organization and wanted to follow one doctor around for a more intimate story. He chose

Rebekah. I thought it was almost like the arsehole knew before he came that he'd pick Rebekah, and I turned out to be right." His face reddened. "You know what happened after that. The bastard spent as much effort wooing Rebekah as he did making the bloody documentary. I said things I did'na mean when I saw what was happening." He shrugged. "To be honest, I did mean them, I just did'na have any way to carry out my threats."

"What threats?"

MacNeish gave Jacob a wry smile. "That I was going to kidnap Rebekah to stop her marrying the arsehole."

Chapter Forty-Eight

James Eakins opened the refrigerator, took out a Coors, and after popping the tab, leaned against the counter and watched his partner. Freddie Haynes was seated at the trestle table, engaged in another of his endless games of Solitaire. Each time Freddie added another card to the tricks in front him he smacked the table instead of just laying the card down, and then he thumbed the corner of the remaining deck in his hand, swishing the cards. Freddie was starting to get on his nerves. Nah, Freddie wasn't *starting* to get on his nerves; Freddie had been getting on his nerves since day one, which was to say since last Thursday when the operation commenced.

Freddie slapped a black queen down on top of a red jack, pulled another card from the stack in his hand, and swiveled his head back and forth, looking to see if the card fit somewhere. Suddenly, his head jerked up.

"What was that?" Freddie asked. He cocked his ear toward the window.

"A pig, a chicken, a plane, your heart beating. Would you calm down? You're hearing things."

Freddie hesitated, then he pushed his glasses back up the bridge of his nose, pulled an ace from the stack in his hand, and set it down beside the other ace. "You're getting a little cocky," he said without looking at James.

"And you're turning into an old lady." James took a long drink of the Coors.

"Better an old lady than a caught-off-guard one." Freddie turned over a red three and placed it on top of a black four.

James fought the urge to smack him one. Freddie moaned about having to hide in an old farmhouse with no access to the outside world. He bitched about the sloping floors, ratty furniture, and torn formica in the kitchen. As if he lived in anything better himself. He complained about having to keep the shades down and the curtains drawn. He griped about the food Delores had stashed in the cupboard and, especially, the lack of vodka. Freddie liked vodka a little too much. Herschmann wasn't the first boss who'd canned Freddie for stumbling around work, drunk off his ass, so they definitely didn't need vodka around when several thousand dollars were at stake.

Freddie cocked his ear toward the window again. "You're sure you didn't hear anything?"

"It was the pigs."

Freddie pushed back his chair with a scraping sound, got up, and headed for the window.

"Don't." James moved to block his way. Short, but beefy, James could wrestle men a foot taller and fifty pounds heavier to the ground in ten seconds, and he sure as hell could handle a skinny wimp like Freddie in five. Or less.

"If you're so damn sure no one will find us in this god-forsaken place why can't I look out the window?"

"The same reason you buy life insurance."

"What the hell does life insurance have to do with it?"

James shrugged. "I'll let you figure that out yourself. Sit down. I'll make sure no one is out there."

Resigned, James went to the window. Standing to the side, he stuck a forefinger beneath the shade, lifted it about an inch away from the pane, and looked out. He saw the side yard, if you could call a patch of weeds a yard, and a sliver of the front yard and the road running past.

"Nothing going on out there," he said.

"You sure?" Freddie hadn't sat down, but stood in a half-crouch, looking like he was about to jump in a swimming hole.

"I'm sure. I'll check the back windows." He set down his beer. "Don't you go looking out while I'm checking." Instead of pulling window covers back a smidgen, Freddie tended to yank them far enough open to stick his face in between shade and window, or between curtain and window. "Sit down and play cards." James pointed at the table.

The living room window gave a clearer view of the front as well as of the side opposite the kitchen. James saw nothing he hadn't seen during the past several days: the road, the field across on the other side, bunches of trees on both sides of the weedy lawn. He moved on to the back bedroom windows where it was the same story. Nothing different. A barn on the verge of caving in, a silo behind it, chicken house off to the left, a rusty tractor next to the pigpen, and woods creeping up to the silo. The pigs were another thing Freddie complained about. Slopping the hogs was part of the deal he'd worked out with the owner of the farm. Thanks to James' *special* coin, it had fallen to Freddie to feed them, and he had to do it after dark when no one would see him. James grinned. Freddie had slipped in the muck the first day and come in stinking to high heaven.

The woods came almost up to the barn making a getaway possible should they need it. In the beginning he'd been dead sure everything would go as planned, but after that detective had shown up at Delores' front door he had to admit he was a little edgy. He didn't think his half-sister would crack, but just in case she did, he'd taken out a little insurance in the form of a coffee can full of gasoline. He was certain things wouldn't come to that. In a few more hours, they'd be out of here and collecting their money. His cousin, gritty-voiced Eddie, had called two hours ago, saying he dropped Carlos at the airport and everything was going as planned.

The nearest farm was two miles away. There were very few

areas in Bucks County where farmhouses were this far apart, and it had taken him a while to find this one but not long to convince the biker who owned it to go to Florida for a week, all expenses paid thanks to Mr. Deep Pockets, aka Carlos. He threw in a packet of skunk as a bonus. Maybe he should of taken to this business years ago and hired himself out as a crime-location specialist. All those puff-headed guys who ran businesses weren't honest, including Fritz Herschmann, so why should he be honest?

You never knew, maybe Carlos might have another job for him even though Carlos came from some other country. And for sure he had deep pockets. Thanks to Totsy's big mouth, Carlos had flown in a few weeks ago to track down Delores and set things up. Then he'd flown back to wherever he came from until Rebekah's arrival. James gave a little laugh. Some fiancé Carlos had turned out to be. Anyway, after Carlos grabbed Rebekah at the airport and saw her safely locked up in the farmhouse, he'd flown to South America so he could fly back when the Herschmann's expected him. Just in case someone checked. All that flying around; all the money he was paying out to various people — yep, Carlos had very deep pockets.

He heard whimpering from the second floor as he passed the stairs on the way back to the kitchen. Bloody bitch. Chained to the bed as she was, she couldn't go anywhere but was a fucking pain in the ass anyway. Every two hours she had to pee. Either he or Freddie had to go up, unlock the chain, and then stand guard at the bathroom door while she did her business. Half the time Freddie forgot the combination on the lock when it was his turn. *James, James, I forgot.* Then James had to go traipsing up the stairs to unlock the thing. The first time, he'd been about to call the combination up to Freddie but caught himself just in time when he remembered Rebekah would also hear it. An old pair of handcuffs and a bicycle chain had seemed sufficient, but now he wished he'd given more thought to the lock. They'd pretty much stopped giving her water so she wouldn't have to pee so much.

Freddie, engrossed in his game of solitaire, didn't look up when James walked in. "Coast clear?" Freddie asked.

"No one's out there." James picked up the beer and looked over at the Folger's coffee can next to the microwave. It was their emergency plan in the off chance Delores let out where Rebekah was. She wouldn't. But just in case, it was there, filled with gasoline. They'd turn on the gas and open the oven door. Then they'd stick the can in the microwave, set the cook time for five minutes, and run like hell into the woods behind the house. The lawmen would come inside. They'd probably find Rebekah a couple seconds before the house blew. Any evidence would be destroyed in a massive explosion. Eventually, they'd figure out who the bitch

was with all that DNA stuff they talked about now, but they'd never know it was him and Freddie who did it. The only ones who knew that were Carlos, Delores, gritty-voiced Eddy, and the man in one of those countries across the pond. He couldn't remember which country.

He went in the living room and sat down in one of the ratty chairs. They were the same kind of chairs he had in his apartment. When this was over, and he'd collected for his services, he'd find a better place to live, get some decent furniture, a new car, call up the cute guy he'd met at the gym a couple weeks ago.

He heard a clunk. Shit. . . . He sprang out of his chair. It hadn't come from upstairs. Or had it? His ears trained toward the second floor, his hand on the gun stuck in the waistband of his pants, he listened for a few seconds but heard nothing other than the squeak of a mattress and a long, drawn-out sigh. He let out his breath. It was just the bitch. One of the damn magazines they'd given her had fallen to the floor, he guessed. Jeez, he was getting as edgy as Freddie.

REBEKAH LAY on top of the rumpled covers. Except for the occasional trip to the bathroom, the only break from lying on the bed had been to sit on the bed since the chain wasn't long enough to move more than a couple feet. They'd given her a stack of magazines. To help pass time and to keep fear at bay, she'd pretty much memorized every word in every magazine. An entire copy of *The Mennonite* had been devoted to sisterhood in action. There were several issues of *Modern Farmer*, each with a picture of an animal on the front: a goose, a sheep, a donkey. She now knew more about the feeding and breeding of animals than she'd ever wanted to know. In *Progressive Farmer* she'd read the article on "Land Values at a Crossroad" several times, and from *Mother Earth News* she'd learned to knead bread. Theoretically, at least. The question that clouded every breath of air, that stalked her from all sides, that sent her into spasms of grief was: Would she live long enough to knead bread?

She'd tried to work out a way to escape. All she could think of was to learn the lock combination. She had asked to go to the bathroom more than she needed to go so she could discover the sequence of numbers, but mostly they kept their hands cupped around the device so she couldn't see. She'd tried random combinations, but knew the possibilities lay in the millions.

She was hungry; she had to go to the bathroom again; and her cheek ached where the stocky one had hit her. *James, the Bully*. She'd named the other one *Dirty Freddy* because of his oily, dish-water colored hair and his soiled T-shirt. She got a degree of satisfaction at calling them names – one degree out of ten thousand, leaving nine thousand, nine hundred, and ninety-nine degrees heavy with fear, anger, and longing.

She lay her palm over her cheek. Raw and swollen, the cheek burned, but feeling the warmth from her own hand gave her a bit of comfort. The slap had been the only time they'd hurt her physically. When she got in the car at the airport, someone in the back seat had grabbed her, put the damp rag over her face, and she was out so fast she'd barely felt a thing. She'd been looking at Carlos when it happened. He was standing outside the car door, bent over to look at her with a sneer. *I tied up my business and got here two days early*, he'd said on the phone. *Couldn't wait until Saturday to see you. My car is right outside the baggage claim.* He'd greeted her with a smile and kiss, opened the door for her and, still smiling, gestured for her to get in. That was the last thing she remembered: Carlos bent over smiling at her as he stood outside the car.

Her next conscious moment had been when they carried her inside the house. They tried to make her walk on her own, but she kept collapsing, so they pulled her up the stairs, each holding an arm, laughing as her thighs bumped on the steps. In the bedroom, they jerked her to her feet and shoved her onto the bed where they chained her and then poured a pitcher of water on her face. "Can't have you dying on us," James the Bully said. They'd gone away, leaving her to lie in the wet spot.

Fear and fury had shaken her by turns. As hope of escape slid away, she began to feel like she was floating near the ceiling and looking down on her own body, on the woman and the girl they called Rebekah – the reddish-blonde, pig-tailed girl smiling from the wrappers of 'Bekah Bars; the child spoiled by her grandfather; the student who . . . . She sobbed. None of these were the real Rebekah Herschmann. The real Rebekah Herschmann was the broken hearted child who wanted to go home to Mom and Dad. But she'd heard them talking – the bully and the dirty one. Her destiny resided, not in going home, but in a Folger's coffee can filled with gasoline.

JAMES PICKED up the remote and aimed it at the TV. They'd agreed as long as they kept the volume down, there was nothing wrong with catching a little football here and there. About to click the power button, he heard what sounded like the clunk of brakes needing service. He froze, his uplifted hand still aimed at the TV. Then he set down the remote and tiptoed to the window, inched the curtains apart, and looked out. Shit! A police car had pulled behind a growth of bushes. He saw the car's turret light. Three officers emerged from behind the bushes, bullet-proof vests on and their guns drawn. He edged the curtain a little wider apart, swiveled his eyes in the opposite direction, and saw a tall, dark-haired man coming toward the house with two armed officers following. He opened his mouth to warn Freddie, but the words stuck in his throat.

Freddie stuck his head through the doorway. "Is something . . . ."

"The oven," he said, finding his voice. "Turn it on. I'll do the gasoline."

He raced for the kitchen, nearly knocking Freddie over. "Do it," he yelled. "Turn on the gas!"

"Let's get out of here," he hissed when they finished. He dashed for the back door, Freddie at his heels. They both had guns, but he'd watched enough TV to know who usually won in a shoot-out with the police.

Chapter Forty-Nine

L askey followed the two officers who crept toward the front door. Four others had disappeared around the house to position themselves near the back door, and another two stood behind a squad car parked along the road, their rifles pointed toward the house.

Doing this in broad daylight was a risk, Laskey knew Waiting for nightfall was also a risk. The paintings were on the way to Gustav Fuchs; he had succeeded in getting what he'd set out to get which put Laskey's thoughts back at square one. If all Fuchs wanted were the paintings, then why not just arrange to have someone steal them? The man was evil or crazed, probably both. Laskey was afraid the stolen works weren't enough to satisfy Fuch's lust for revenge.

They were about fifty feet from the front door when he heard shouts from the back of the house. James and Freddie had fled right into the arms of the waiting officers, he guessed. They might have been smart enough to forego a shootout with the police, but not smart enough to figure out if their hiding place had been found, it had also been surrounded. He and the two men preceding him stopped to watch the corner of the house. The two officers assigned to the back door appeared, forcing two handcuffed men along with them.

"They claim there were only two of them," one officer called out, but McMillan and Creasey are still back there just in case.

Laskey, barely aware of what the officer said, had his eyes fixed on the two handcuffed men. Instead of looking down at their feet or glaring at the lawmen, their eyes were glued to the house which they seemed to shrink away from. He took a step backwards just as the explosion blew the house apart.

Chapter Fifty

F ritz and Leah sat on the sofa, side by side, shoulders touching. He held her hand, occasionally squeezing it. Time had stopped. Compared to a lifetime, the hours of one afternoon were barely the flit of a milli-second, yet this afternoon comprised an eternity.

Zuela had gone to the den, mumbling an excuse. Fritz knew the excuse was a pretext for leaving them alone. Zuela would be there when they needed her. Next week, when this was over, they'd fete her, along with Laskey and Bump. Jacob, too. Even MacNeish, if he hung around. There was no way to ever repay them for their efforts and their kindness, but he and Leah would try. Once they got over their emotional exhaustion.

Maybe even right now things were drawing to a conclusion. If Rebekah weren't too far away, Laskey and Bump would be there already. They'd rescue her and be on their way back. It could be as little as thirty minutes before she was home.

Chapter Fifty-One

Laskey picked himself up off the ground. He opened and shut his eyes several times, trying to regain his vision. Sulphuric fumes burned his nostrils, and he smelled the sewage-like odor of the mercaptan. What was left of the house was in flames. Burning debris floated to the ground. Bits and pieces of clapboard lay scattered for fifty or so feet around, along with shards from window panes, roof shingles. What looked to be the leg of a table lay at his feet.

Those knocked to the ground by the concussion wave were pulling themselves up, dusting away plaster dust, rubbing eyes and ears. One officer was throwing up.

"Are you all okay?" Bump, far enough away that he hadn't been knocked over, had run over, followed by the two officers stationed behind the car.

Laskey was aware of Bump's question; he was aware of people dusting away plaster dust and rubbing eyes and ears; he was aware of Bump grabbing the handcuffed man with the bald head by the collar and screaming, "Where was she?" He was aware of all this, but he'd died on the inside.

"Where was she?" Bump yelled again.

James Eakins nodded toward where the house had stood.

Laskey moaned. He didn't have enough tears in him for this, not in his life time would he have enough tears for what had just happened.

"MacMillan and Creasey are still back there," one of the officers said and started in that direction. "I'd better check on them."

"Look . . ." an officer who'd been stationed behind the car pointed.

Rounding the corner of the house, MacMillan and Creasey trudged toward them, shouldering something between them. At first, Laskey wouldn't let himself believe what he saw. But it was. . . It really was . . . It was Rebekah.

Barely able to walk, hair falling in face, clothes and skin blackened with soot, she stumbled toward them with the help of the two officers. A pair of handcuffs hung from one wrist; a chain attached to the handcuffs trailed behind.

"Uncle Bill," she cried when he went to meet her. She threw herself in his arms.

Chapter Fifty-Two

"It's Laskey," Jacob said, pressing the phone closer to his ear.

MacNeish sat bolt upright.

"What?" Jacob said into the phone. "I can't understand you." Laskey was stumbling over his words, barely able to speak. "Just tell me if everything is okay," Jacob said. "Say *yes* or *no*."

"Yes."

Jacob heard Laskey take several deep breaths before he found his voice. "Can you drive Fritz and Leah to the emergency room?" Laskey asked.

"Of course. You have Rebekah? Is she hurt?"

"She's been handcuffed to a bed for five days. Other than that . . . They're checking her out. Tell Fritz and Leah it's common procedure, and that she's fine."

JACOB SAT next to Laskey in the emergency room reception area, their shoulders touching. He felt the heat of Laskey's body and, for a few moments, he thought he felt Laskey's pulse until he realized it was his own. Bump's account of the explosion had sent his blood pressure soaring. He guessed Laskey's was in the stratosphere.

He knew Laskey wasn't ready to talk yet. Jacob had seen his godfather tired, frustrated, annoyed, puzzled, peeved, and a list of other emotions, but never looking like he'd escaped hell. He knew Laskey liked to tie up lose ends himself, but this time he seemed relieved to leave it all to Bump. Bump had left the hospital to file charges against Carlos, the two men at the farm house, and the pretend lawn man at the church. Officers were looking for James' cousin who made the calls and met Carlos behind the church with a change of cars.

"It was too close," Laskey said, breaking his silence.

Jacob nodded. He guessed Laskey would have nightmares about explosions and Rebekah stumbling out of a burning farmhouse for a long time.

Fritz and Leah were with Rebekah in one of the rooms down the hall. The smells and sounds and frenetic activity that permeated the emergency room area when he picked up MacNeish were still here, but they barely registered. He turned and looked out the window behind him and saw MacNeish walking relays between a Ford pick-up and a silver Corolla parked fifty feet away. A few minutes earlier, MacNeish had been pacing the reception area, occasionally wandering down the hall to stand against the door of the room where they had Rebekah.

Laskey stirred.

"Would you like some water?" Jacob asked.

Laskey shook his head.

"How did she get out of the house?"

"They used a combination lock and a bicycle chain to fasten her to the bedpost. She watched when they unlocked it for her to go to the bathroom. She'd picked up on the first number and the last, but not the numbers in the middle. Then, somehow, at the last minute, she hit on the right combination. She made it out a few seconds before the explosion."

"You look pretty shaken up."

"I *am* shaken up. There were a few minutes there . . ." He swallowed. "For a few minutes I thought she was gone." He leaned over, elbows on thighs, and propped his head in his hands. "Never, do I want to go through something like this again."

"I hope you never have to."

"For a little while, I thought I was the cause of her dying." Laskey sounded hoarse. "I kept thinking to myself, if only I had just let things go and waited for them to return her after the paintings were delivered then maybe . . ."

"Were they going to keep their end of the bargain?"

"Not if they found out . . ." He wiped his eyes with the back of his hands and looked up at the ceiling.

"Found out what?"

"The Kokoschka drawings were copies. Fritz's father sold the originals to fund the enlargement of the factory. If we hadn't found her, and if Fuchs realized they were forgeries . . ."

A shiver ran down Jacob's back. "You did the right thing, Lask."

Someone dropped a metal object in the corridor and the sound reverberated into the waiting room.

"I hope that wasn't a bedpan," Laskey said, twitching one side of his mouth in a wry half-smile.

Jacob narrowed his eyes. "How did you get the TSA to stop Carlos at the airport? I'm not an expert on law enforcement, but *this* I do know: an off-duty official can't, on a whim, have the TSA stop people at airports without some kind of warrant or something."

"Friends in the right places."

"That wouldn't be Thunder, would it? Your former FBI partner? The bird-watcher with big, hairy hands?"

"Confidential information. I took pictures of Carlos with my Iphone, and the photos somehow wound up in the hands of the TSA. If the TSA chose to think Carlos was a possible terrorist based on my friend's ability to make things sound like what they aren't, then . . . ." He shrugged his shoulders.

Jacob stood up. He'd seen Fritz coming down the corridor toward the reception area.

"She's going to be all right," Fritz said when he came within a few feet. His eyes glittered with relief and happiness, but at the same time they were shadowed with a deep sadness. "At least . . ." His voice broke and he rubbed his hand over his forehead as he sought to gain control. "Carlos did a lot more than break her heart. I doubt she'll ever trust a man again." He blinked a couple times. "She wants to see Uncle Bill." Then Fritz looked at Jacob. "You and Zuela are the ones who figured out Carlos wasn't who he said he was. Other than my eternal gratitude, there's no way I can ever repay you."

Jacob clutched Fritz's hand. "Friendship is reward enough."

LASKEY FOLLOWED Fritz into a room halfway down the corridor. Rebekah sat on an examination table, wearing a hospital gown. Leah stood beside her holding her hand. The nurses had washed the soot from Rebekah's face and limbs except for a smudge beneath one ear. Her hair had been combed, but hung limply around her drawn face .

"Uncle Bill," she said feebly.

Laskey went over and grabbed the hand Leah had dropped when he came in. He squeezed it, and then kissed Rebekah on the forehead. "We had quite a scare."

"I'm so sorry I did this to all of you."

"It wasn't your doing." He was shocked she would even think that.

She shrugged. "In a way it was. I was stupid." She sobbed once, and then swallowed, regaining control. "I should have known something wasn't right." She picked up a towel that lay on the table beside her and wiped her eyes. "I was so blown-away when a handsome . . ." She closed her eyes. "I will never marry; I will never . . ."

Laskey touched her arm. "Stop."

He turned to Fritz and Leah. "Could I have a few moments alone with her?"

Fritz nodded, took Leah by the hand, and led her out of the room.

How to begin? He'd never told anyone the story. Like Rebekah, he'd been guilty of succumbing to *Love is Blind*. Thunder knew because he'd been there, but Thunder also knew it was a forbidden subject, never to be mentioned between them and never to be told to anyone else. In his head, Laskey knew he had no reason to feel ashamed or embarrassed, but in his heart he felt differently.

"Rebekah you're a beautiful girl," he began. "You're brilliant. You're . . . . Well, when I have more time, I'll try and remember to remind you of all your good qualities. But right now, I want to tell you a story about myself." He took a deep breath and began. "It was a long time ago. Another life and . . ."

When he finished, she reached for his hand and held it between both of hers. "I'm so sorry, Uncle Bill. I didn't know."

"Can this be just between the two of us?"

She nodded. "I won't tell anyone. Jacob doesn't know?"

"No, he doesn't."

"Well, it isn't too late." She almost smiled. "You could still . . ."

He shook his head. "I'm a frumpy old bachelor; Too set in my ways."

"I don't believe that."

"I'm afraid it's true. But you have to make me a promise."

A look of doubt crossed her face.

"You're not going to forget Carlos, and it's going to hurt for a long time, but the day will come when you'll move on and find someone worthy of you.

"*Hurt for awhile?* Like maybe two-hundred years?" Her face hardened. "I'll have nothing to do with another man as long as I live."

"Ahhh, but you're wrong about that, Rebekah."

"No, Uncle Bill, I'm not wrong about that."

"Well, I'm afraid you have to be because there's a man standing outside your door right now who wants to see you in the worst way."

He strode to the door where he'd caught a glimpse of MacNeish's cast. He reached around the door frame, grabbed MacNeish by his good arm, and pulled him into the room.

"Jamie?" Rebekah's eyes went wide. "Jamie?" She shook her head as though trying to shake away visions of a ghost. "You're here?"

"Aye," he said weakly.

"Ask him why he has a broken hand," Laskey said.

Her eyes landed on his cast, then rose to meet MacNeish's. She held up her palm in a question.

Laskey slipped out the door, leaving MacNeish to explain. Or to not explain. He could do only so much to promote young love; they had to do the rest themselves.

Vienna, Austria

Tuesday Evening

"You're happy," Karl said to his father, looking at him over the vase of yellow roses that stood in the middle of the dining table. "You must have enjoyed the outing to Pöchlarn."

Gustav nodded and reached for his wineglass. He took a sip. "Good wine."

"You said that last Tuesday."

"So I did." Tuesday was their evening to have dinner together. He was written into his son's schedule: Tuesday evening – dinner with father. Instead of having to make conversation with Karl, he would have preferred to have the evening alone to gloat.

"Tell me about Pöchlarn," Karl said.

"What's to tell? It was a good day to be out."

Karl, always intuitive, was studying him, but his son would never guess what ran through his mind, or that he'd invented an errand to keep his secretary/nurse/jailer away for most of tomorrow morning. Karl would be occupied in a board meeting, so the coast was clear for the paintings to arrive.

"There's a special exhibit next month in the museum," Gustav said. "Kokoschka: a Retrospective. They've borrowed several dozen paintings from around around the world for the occasion."

"Do you want to go?" Karl took another helping of peas.

"Yes. Can you could arrange for the driver again?"

"Of course."

Eventually, he'd have to tell Karl that he, too, would be loaning works for the exhibit. He'd tell his son something like: "I tracked down Fritz Herschmann and had an agent approach him and make an offer." Then he'd explain that Herschmann needed the money for his daughter's college tuition. Karl wouldn't know that Herschmann had only one daughter, and that she was well past college age.

"I think it's going to rain tomorrow," Karl said.

Gustav grunted an affirmation. The weather was a reliable topic. His son tired him. *It's going to rain tomorrow. Tell me about Pöchlarn. Pass the peas.* His father had refused to make him a partner in the business, and then his own son had shoved him aside and would only talk to him only about wine, weather, and driving out to Pöchlarn.

"Cook made Sachertorte," Karl said. "She enjoys making you your favorite dessert."

Gustav smiled. Not because of the Sachertorte, although Karl would believe that was the reason. It would never occur to his son – his always politically correct son – that his father still had a bit of power, if not in the business, at least in other places. The last of his pawns would deliver the paintings tomorrow morning and then fade back into the woodwork. Carlos would get shipped back to Iraq because his refugee status had been revoked. Carlos, of course, had no idea what was about to happen to him. Stupid man.

Thursday

October 25

Chapter Fifty-Three

"Ahhhh, the wonderful smell of sawdust." Laskey tilted his chair back to rest on its two hind legs. They were in Zuela's kitchen. The kitchen lights, along with every other light in the house were on even though the sun had only begun to fade. The fear and gloom of the past week made them both long for brightness.

"If you break my chair, you'd better have a few skills other than detecting. Like carpentry." Zuela set a gin and tonic in front of him. "And don't knock sawdust, because fixing a broken chair is going to involve sawing."

"Believe me, after the smell of sulfur and sewer, sawdust is perfume." He clunked the chair legs down. "Is that a word? Detecting?"

"If it isn't, it should be." Zuela sat down across from him and nodded at the gin and tonic. "You won't be in any condition to drive if you do what I think you want to do right now."

"You're right. I won't be." He gulped down half the drink. "If I pass out, call Jacob to rescue me." He drained the remainder of the drink. "Another?"

"I'll get you another, but you're not getting behind the wheel."

She went over, opened the freezer, and jiggled the ice to loosen it. "You still look pretty beat," she said. "That was a movie-worthy finale, so I guess two days recuperation doesn't quite do it."

"Two months maybe." The rapidity with which he'd consumed the drink had set the kitchen swirling, and he thought he detected the sound of electricity buzzing in the walls. Once he'd heard someone claim he could hear electricity pulsing through the walls. He hadn't believed him, but maybe it was true; he definitely heard something. He also felt his inhibitions crumbling. He knew he'd regret it later, but he said it anyway: "I like you, Zuela."

"Really?" Raising her eyebrows, she clunked ice into his glass.

"Don't you believe me?"

"I think you're like Jacob. You enjoy coming to my kitchen to eat, drink, and get a pep talk."

"I definitely like eating and drinking in your kitchen."

"Well, then, you're welcome anytime." She poured half a jigger of Tangueray in the glass, filled the rest with tonic water, and plunked in a slice of lime.

He fished out the lime when she handed him the drink, squeezed it, and then dropped it back in. In spite of the swirling room, he'd seen her shortchange him on the gin.

The front door slammed followed by the sound of footsteps coming toward them.

"Let me guess," Zuela said. "Hmmmmm. Let's see. It's coming up on supper time, so who would possibly drop by this time of day? Aha, Jacob Gillis."

Jacob stopped in the doorway. He held a grocery bag in each arm.

Zuela feigned a look of shock. "What a surprise. Don't tell me you brought food?"

"Am I interrupting something?" Jacob looked from Zuela to Laskey.

Laskey guessed Jacob didn't much care if he'd interrupted anything or not. His godson had that *I-need-some-company* look.

"What's that?" Zuela motioned to the bags.

"Goodies." Jacob walked over to the counter and set the bags down. He took two gallons of cider from one, and then began extracting various items from the other. Oreos. Pretzels. Chips. "Why are you indoors?" He fished out a bottle of ketchup. "The evening is perfect, and it's probably going to be one of the last good days before next spring. I thought we could fire up the grill and have hot mulled cider and hotdogs." He pulled out hotdogs and buns and held them up for inspection. "MacNeish will be along later. He's at the Herschmann's right now."

"That's enough hotdogs for an army," Zeula said.

"And . . . just in case your spice cabinet is missing certain essentials, I have cinnamon and cloves." He reached into the bottom of the bag and then clunked spice bottles onto the counter.

A few minutes later, the grill was lit, the cider mulled, and hot dog fixings on the picnic table ready and waiting. Jacob was standing over the grill, fanning the flames, while Laskey and Zuela sat in lawn chairs a few feet away. Laskey had thrown on his jacket, and Zuela sat wrapped in an afghan. The warm liquid running down Laskey's throat slowed the spinning in his head generated by two rapidly consumed gin and tonics. He might not have to depend on Jacob to drive him home after all, especially after a couple hotdogs. He would have preferred something heartier − a T-bone, hamburgers. Someone down the street had the same idea. He caught a whiff of steaks on a grill. But hot dogs were fine. Everything was fine.

"What made you suspect Carlos?" Jacob asked. "You must have arranged to have him stopped at the airport before Aunt Zuela's professor friend listened to the tape."

Laskey held his mug up to his nose, inhaled the sweet smell of cidar, the pungent smells of cinnamon and cloves, and let the question float off into the void.

Zuela nudged him. "Are you going to answer Jacob?"

Laskey took a few sips, stared into the flames, and felt his face relax. He looked up at Jacob. "You mean you don't know?"

"No, I don't know."

Laskey rose, sauntered over to the large thermos on the picnic table, and refilled his cup. He held the thermos out to Zuela and Jacob, both of whom shook their heads.

"Oh, good lord," Zuela sniped. "Stop playing prima donna, and put us out of our misery. When did you suspect Carlos was up to no good?"

Laskey went back over and sat down. "Jacob's attitude when he met Carlos planted a tiny seed of doubt. My godson might have been incorrigible growing up, but there's one thing he's always been skilled at, and that's reading people. As soon as he professed a dislike for Carlos, my antenna went up."

"And you pissed me off by ridiculing me about being jealous?" Jacob came over and gave him a playful punch on the arm. "If I didn't otherwise like you, I'd call you a shithead."

"May we join you?"

Laskey twisted around to look behind him. MacNeish was standing in the kitchen door, a tall, slim woman beside him. She had wide cheekbones and light-colored hair cut bluntly at chin level. She looked a bit rumpled and had dark circles under her eyes as though she hadn't slept.

"Didn't mean to startle you," MacNeish said. He pushed open the screen door, waited for the woman to descend the back steps, and then followed. "Let me introduce Dr. Annemarie Leitner."

So now it's turned into an international gathering, Laskey thought while introductions were being made and Annemarie's surprise arrival earlier in the afternoon explained.

"You're the one who woke me up at midnight." Annemarie said to Laskey.

"Sorry about that."

"Not to worry. I'm just glad things turned out okay. On Tuesday I wasn't sure what was going to happen, so I booked a ticket. I had to come."

"How's Rebekah?" Zuela asked.

"Happy and thankful to be home, except she keeps breaking into tears," MacNeish said. His cockiness was gone. "Yer all invited to dinner tomorrow night. A *family dinner*. Fritz and Leah said they've kenned there's more to *family* than DNA. Yer family."

"Sit down, sit down." Zuela motioned toward the chairs. "Jacob, go grab a couple mugs from the kitchen and give them some cider."

"What are you going to do about Gustav Fuchs?" MacNeish asked Laskey. "How does that work with international law?"

Laskey shook his head. "We'll have to wait and see." As much as he'd like to fly straight to Vienna and string up Gustav Fuchs, he had to wait for the wheels of international law to turn. He looked at MacNeish's cast. "How's your hand?"

Tightening his lips, MacNeish looked at his cast. He tried to wiggle his fingers but managed only a small motion.

"I don't think you're going to be amputating limbs and closing guts for a while," Annemarie said.

"Was it worth it?" Laskey asked MacNeish.

"It was worth it." MacNeish narrowed his eyes. "Why did you na' stop me?"

"You were too fast." Laskey tried to keep from smiling. MacNeish had done exactly what he'd wanted to do, but couldn't without losing his job.

Jacob reappeared with the extra cups. He grabbed the thermos. "What will happen to Carlos?" he asked.

Annemarie jumped in. "I know you meant that question for Laskey, but if you don't mind . . . There are two bad choices lined up for Carlos. Although I guess *choice* is the wrong word. I'm sure you'll send him to jail." She looked at Laskey for confirmation. He gave her two thumbs up. Annemarie continued, "If, for some reason, he's sent back to Austria, he'll be exiled to Iraq."

"Iraq?" Laskey straightened. "Carlos most definitely isn't going to be shipped back to Austria, but explain."

"My imagination went into overdrive after your call on Tuesday. I realized I shouldn't have said what I did about MacNeish. Sorry Jamie." She gave him an apologetic look. He shrugged. "He's a big talker," she said to the others, "but not much of a man of action."

MacNeish raised his eyebrows.

"That isn't quite true." Annemarie smiled. "He's the best

surgeon I've ever seen and keeps the unit running efficiently in spite of a long list of problems."

"You mentioned Iraq," Zuela interjected.

Laskey suppressed a smile at Zuela's curiosity.

"I went to see Karl Fuchs," Annemarie continued. "He was about to go to a board meeting. I practically had to hold onto his coattails to keep him from rushing off. It took me a few minutes to make him understand what was going on. When he finally did, he took me to his father's apartment. The old man wasn't happy to see us, to say the least. He said he wanted to take a hot bath and a nap, and we should go. While he was trying to get rid of us, someone knocked. Karl opened the door, and a tall, skinny man dressed in sweats was standing there with a yellow hard-sided suitcase. The man backed away as if to run, but Karl grabbed him by the arm and forced him inside. Then he made him open the suitcase." Annemarie pressed her fingers to her forehead and shook her head.

"And then?" Jacob was still holding the thermos.

Annemarie dropped her hand into her lap. "Gustav Fuchs' mind went. Just like that." She snapped her fingers. "He started jabbering. Between his babbling and the suitcase man's unwillingness to talk, it took a while to piece together what Gustav had done." She held her hand toward Jacob. "Are you going to give us some cider, or just stand there like the Statue of Liberty?" There was a twinkle in her eyes.

"Oh, sorry." Jacob filled the two mugs and handed them to MacNeish and Annemarie.

"There's more to the story?" Laskey found himself sharing Zuela's impatience.

"It turns out that Carlos had been employed by Seltzer," Annemarie said. "He worked in the publicity department, translating ads and sales materials into Arabic. His parents were Iraqi refugees so he knew both Arabic and German. His other talent was seducing women. Seltzer fired him for sexual harassment."

"Ahhh," Zuela said. "So he'd previously practiced what he did to Rebekah."

"For sure." Annemarie took a sip of cider. "Es schmeckt," she said, holding up the cup. "It's good. Anyway, Karl explained that his father had been pretty much confined to his apartment by Parkinson's for years, and that he entertained himself by keeping track of gossip and rumors that went on in the company. He also had time to bristle over grievances, and to plot."

"I never could understand why people with smarts would choose to use their brains in devious schemes.," Zuela said. "Carlos was no dummy. He found a real person to impersonate, studied what he had to do, and fooled all of us. Any clue how he discovered the name *Carlos Vientos?*" she asked Annemarie.

"Gustav Fuchs had a translation of Vientos' novel in his apartment. He must have been the one who came up with the disguise."

"There's one thing that hasn't been explained," Laskey said. "Rebekah's phone."

"Carlos stole her phone in Jordan while she was at work one day," MacNeish said. ". . . and replaced it with an identical one with all her contacts entered."

"She told you that?"

He nodded. "When James Eakins was going through her purse he laughed at her stupidity for not noticing."

They sat in silence then, twilight enveloping them. Venus was visible, the moon full, and the air had taken on a noticeable chill. Laskey looked around at the group. Like him, they were drained. There was still a loose end, but as the thought entered his head, he glanced at the corner of the house and saw Totsy. The others turned to see what he was looking at. Totsy seemed to be struggling over whether to join them.

Zuela went to meet her. "Come join us," she said, and taking Totsy by the hand, urged her forward.

Laskey rose. Totsy's gaze flitted here and there, her eyes not meeting anyone's.

"Take my chair," Jacob said. He dragged another one from the picnic table for himself.

Totsy seemed reluctant to sit. Her stage presence was gone. The actress had disappeared. There was just Totsy. Finally, she sank into the chair, perching on its edge. "What's going to happen to my mom?" She asked Laskey.

"I don't know, Totsy."

"Will she go to jail?" Totsy had a plaintive, but resigned look.

"We'll have to wait and see," he said. It was a cut and dried case of abetting. He knew she'd be tried and spend time in jail.

LASKEY AND ZUELA sat side by side at the picnic table, he, clutching his jacket close around him, and Zuela cuddled in her afghan. The night had turned cold, the fire in the pit had gone out, and the hot cider consumed. A couple extra hotdog buns lay on the table, along with a puddle of ketchup from an overturned bottle. Jacob and MacNeish had gone home, dropping Totsy off on the way. Annemarie was in Zuela's spare bedroom, sound asleep Laskey guessed.

"How can I say this . . .?" he began. There'd been a breach in the wall he'd built around himself. The thing inside him that kept that wall in good repair was struggling to repair the breach before he blurted out too much. If what he said came out wrong, he'd be in too deep to crawl out gracefully. Maybe she wouldn't understand anyway, even if he said it right.

"I'm sixty-five years old," he said.

She gave him a quizzical look. "That's an interesting fact. If the question ever comes up in Trivia, I'll know the answer. You're sixty-five. So am I."

He wasn't off to a good start. *Just say it plain and simple, you old fart. Forget trying to wrap it up in a nice speech.* "I like you, Zuela, for more than your culinary offerings, but I'm a crusty old bachelor. I'm ornery. I'm hard to please. I have a barrel full of eccentricities. Or so says Jacob. Despite all that, I enjoy the occasional company of an intelligent and witty woman."

"Hmmmm. Am I an intelligent and witty woman?"

"The best. I was wondering if I could see you from time to time, without . . . I'd like to see you without your thinking . . ."

"You can rest assured, Mr. Detective, that I'm not ready to hitch myself to another man. Can we agree to see each other whenever we feel like it and let the rest take care of itself?"

Laskey smiled, straightened his shoulders, and they raised their empty cups in a toast.

Friday Afternoon

The man made his way toward the Herschmann's front door. Dressed in a business suit, his gray hair meticulously combed, and shoes shiny from a recent buffing, he carried a large suitcase. He didn't appear to be in a hurry. He stopped every few feet to look around at the neighborhood — at the brick or shingled Colonials that stood in contrast to the Herschmann's modern glass and concrete house; at the trees shedding the last of their leaves; at a jet trail chalked across a blue sky. He nodded at a jogger. The runner nodded back and then slowed to ogle the limosine parked at the curb. The runner's dog strained at his leash in an effort to trot over and welcome the man to the neighborhood.

From the way the man shifted from foot to foot when he stopped to loiter, or paid undue attention to an ordinary site like a pile of yellow and brown leaves or a patch of dandelions, one might draw the conclusion his dawdlings weren't due to an interest in studying the surroundings, but arose from a desire to either procrastinate or compose himself. Eventually the sidewalk ended and, composed or not, he found himself at the front doorsteps. Inhaling deeply, he mounted them, set the suitcase down on the top step, and rang the bell.

While he waited, the man let his arms hang slack in front of him, one hand folded over the other, his head bowed. An observer might think he was praying, but what that observer wouldn't know was how tired the man was, not because of the slightly more than 4000 miles he'd traveled, but because the distance spoke of more than miles.

The door opened, and the man raised his head. "Fritz Herschmann?"

Fritz nodded. "Can I help you?"

The man picked up the yellow suitcase and held it out to Fritz. "I have something that belongs to you." Then he extended his other hand. "I'm Karl Fuchs. Our grandfathers were friends."

THE END

Acknowledgments

It is impossible to write a book alone, and I am very lucky that I have extraordinary people to help and cheer me on. I owe a huge debt of gratitude to my readers Mary Allen and Julia Pezzi. I am also much indebted to the members of my two writing groups. Jesse Siskin, Joy Welch, Mary Morton, and Jeannette Lucas of my bimonthly group have been with me from beginning to end in the writing of *Unringing the Bell*. Anne Peschke, Jane McCord, Sharon Thelin, and Mary Allen of Bluegrass Wordsmiths have all given me wonderful advice on the chapters they read. I couldn't have done it without all of you!

The cover artist was the inimitable Nat Jones who does the best covers ever!

Kim Stewart, Administrative Assistant of the Wilmore, Kentucky Police Department helped me with background information, as did William E. Craig, Chief of Police in Wilmore. Officer Chris Taylor of the Lexington, Kentucky Police Department spent an afternoon with me answering questions. Robert King of the Lexington Fire Department instructed me on how to blow up a house after I assured him that I didn't really mean to blow one up.

My family has been 100% behind me in my writing endeavors. I want to especially thank my three oldest grandchildren, Kyle, Jon, and Karina Pezzi, who always show an interest in my progress and have helped me in various ways. Kyle, a financial analyst specializing in health care, helped me with background on the pharmaceutical industry. Jon is my go-to person on anything related to sports. I've often left messages interrupting him while he was sitting in classes at Washington and Lee asking him to contact me asap with the answer to various sports questions. Karina gamely dressed up in a tutu and toe shoes and let me pour fake blood over her for the pictures on my website. She also posed as the Lady for my *Lady* website.

Also by Judy Higgins

Book One of Bucks County Mysteries

Unringing the Bell

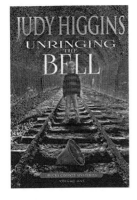

"Fabulous all the way to the startling conclusion!"

In the small town of Goose Bend, Pennsyvania, people don't forget — especially something as sensational as 12-year-old Jacob Gillis burning down the town. Nineteen years after the accident Jacob returns, hoping for redemption, but instead finds himself entangled in a murder investigation and in danger of losing his reputation forever as well as his career.

The Lady

"This isn't a good book; This is a GREAT book!" ABNA Expert Reviewer.

The Lady was a semi-finalist in the 2012 Breakout Novel Contest.

South Georgia, 1956: When Quincy Bruce's beloved Aunt Addy is accused of being the inspiration for Nathan Waterstone's infamous novel, *The Lady*, Quincy sets out to learn the truth and prove her aunt's accusers wrong. Instead, she discovers other secrets which place her own future in jeopardy.

Call Me Mara

The Story of Ruth and Naomi

The Hills of Moab, oil painting by Julia Pezzi

Book cover not available

The beloved three-thousand-year-old story of the love between a mother and her bride-daughter comes to life in the novel, *Call Me Mara*. Set in Bethlehem and Moab, the story follows Naomi as she leaves her home in Bethlehem to travel with her husband and sons to the land of their enemies and then, after a series of misfortunes and disasters, returns to Bethlehem, bringing Ruth, a Moabitess despised by the Jews.

Available November 2018. Sign up for publication announcement at http://www.callmemara.com

GOSSART
PUBLICATIONS

About the Author

Judy was born in South Georgia where she grew up playing basevball, reading, and taking piano lessons. To pay for her lessons, she raised chickens and sold eggs to neighbors. She attended Mercer University for two years, and then Baylor University from which she graduated with a BA in German. She received her MA in German literature from The University of Michigan. After teaching German for several years, Judy decided to become a librarian and earned a MA in Library Science at Kutztown University in Pennsylvania. Judy's life took an exciting turn when she left her teaching job in Pennsylvania to be Head of Library at the Learning Center School of Qatar Foundation. She lived in Qatar for eight years, traveling widely during every vacation, and enjoying the experience of living in a different culture. She now lives in Lexington, KY. Judy has two children, Julia and Stephen, two children-in-law, Jim and Erin, and four grandchildren: Kyle, Jon, Karina, and Addy.

For more information or to sign up for Judy's publication email list:
www.judyhigginsbooks.com
judyhigginsauthor@gmail.com

facebook.com/judyhigginsauthor
twitter.com/JudyHBooks

Made in the USA
Columbia, SC
16 May 2018